D1492516

GALE FORCE

NOVELS BY
ELLESTON TREVOR

Chorus of Echoes
Tiger Street
Redfern's Miracle
A Blaze of Roses
The Passion and the Pity
The Big Pick-Up
Squadron Airborne
The Killing-Ground
Gale Force
The Pillars of Midnight
The V.I.P.
The Billboard Madonna
The Burning Shore
The Flight of the Phoenix
The Shoot
The Freebooters
A Place for the Wicked
Bury Him Among Kings

GALE FORCE

Elleston Trevor

HEINEMANN : LONDON

William Heinemann Ltd
15 Queen Street, Mayfair, London W1X 8BE

LONDON   MELBOURNE   TORONTO
JOHANNESBURG   AUCKLAND

First published 1956
This edition 1972
Reprinted 1976
434 79302 7

Printed in Great Britain by
REDWOOD BURN LIMITED
Trowbridge & Esher

TO
ROSA AND VERNON

AT midnight the *Atlantic Whipper* was two hundred-odd miles from Land's End, steaming north-east and homeward through a quiet sea. She was a deep-water merchantman on voyage from Buenos Aires, with four thousand tons of grain and ten passengers. She was bound for Avonmouth. Above her to the north there was a sick half moon; beneath her the sea was black. The only sounds were her wash and the low drone of the rigging, tuned by the wind of her own passage. There were few lights burning in this, the graveyard, watch; the ship was as dark almost as her element, and as quiet. Her size, shrunk to a pin-point by the vastness of sea and sky, allowed of no surprise that a mass of six thousand tons with forty men in the crew could make so little disturbance in the night. For all her great dead weight of thick cold steel and the tonnage of cargo in her holds, she was her true size here between the far horizons, a drifting mote.

On the bridge the watch was quiet, part of a slow hypnotic rhythm that seemed motionless. The second mate took two more paces to his left, and stopped, and balanced on his heels, and turned, and paced again slowly to his right, and stopped again, and came back, his tread monotonous and measured as if he were waiting for something. Ten paces to the left, ten to the right, and then back again, and back again. He had walked miles here, and got nowhere.

He stopped and stood at the binnacle, looking at the compass card. He said in a casual grunt:

"Where the bloody hell are you going?"

"Ay, ay, sir," said the helmsman, and put the wheel down a spoke, watching the indicator and the card. The

I

officer paced off again. They were both glad of the sound their voices had made in the quiet wheelhouse; the spell of the night had been broken for a while by the unnecessary question and the ready answer. Tug Wilson was a good enough helmsman to steer through a needle's eye, and Beggs a good enough officer to let him alone at the wheel; but the respite from silence in the graveyard watch was a little relief.

Beggs went out to the port wing of the bridge. The lookout was as still as a stanchion.

"See anything, Mounsey?"

The white of his face turned in the gloom. "No, sir." They listened to the bow-wave and the rigging's drone. "I'd say she's freshening, sir."

Beggs sniffed the wind. The glass had fallen, hours ago, and before midnight there had been gale warnings on the radio. He said, "She'll freshen all right, don't you worry." But ahead of the *Whipper* the sea looked flat, a flinty black waste with not a chip of white in it anywhere. When he turned and looked astern he could see where the breeze was coming from, up from the South Atlantic. It would follow the *Whipper* home.

From the wheel Tug Wilson glanced up and had a glimpse of the second mate's back through the door of the wheelhouse; he looked down again at the compass card, thinking of Mr. Beggs, and the bit of a scrap there'd been in Buenos Aires the night before the *Atlantic Whipper* had sailed for home.

Wilson hadn't been in Mickey Green's when the scrap had started, but Mounsey had told him about it, grinning like a long monkey with his white teeth fanning out in the delight of it—"It was a couple o' cowsons o' drunken Scowegians, first go off. They come bargin' into Mickey Green's lookin' for trouble, an' by God they got it, see, 'cause the place was stuffed to the ceilin' with dagos, Yankees, Scots, Irish, Liverpool-Irish, Geordies, Lascars

2

an' bloody Chinks. Not to mention a mob o' Canadians."

"Oh gor bli'," Wilson said.

"These Scowegians have a pint, see, an' then turn their mugs upside-down on the bar—you know. They didn't have time to see who was goin' to 'ave a go—they was down on the floor before you could look round, hollerin' out for daylight."

"What were you doing?" asked Tug Wilson.

Mounsey's grin cracked his face. "Me? What the 'ell d'you think I was doing'? I was tryin' to find the door, quick. Then some clot smashed the lamps, so I got under a table for the duration. After a bit, in comes Jimmy Beggs."

"How did you know it was him?" asked Wilson. He knew Mounsey never embroidered his stories, keen though he was on telling them in all their detail; Wilson just wanted to know how he'd recognised Jim Beggs from underneath a table in the dark.

"I knew by 'is voice, mate. The door come open an' there 'e was, hollerin' out, 'Who's from the *Whipper*? Who's from the *Whipper*?' One or two blokes answered 'im from above the din, an' went outside, but I stayed where I was."

"Why?" asked Tug Wilson. You had to keep asking Mounsey questions, to keep his steam up, when he was telling a story. He liked to know you were listening.

"Well, there was some bastard got 'is teeth sunk into my ankle, an' I was tryin' to get a grip on a bottle to 'it 'is 'ead with an' make 'im stop. In the end I had to break it over 'im before he'd give over." He dragged his sock down and showed Wilson. "You can see I'm tellin' you gospel, mate."

Tug looked at the three red marks on Mounsey's ankle.

"Gor bli'," he said, "it looks like a rat."

" 'E was a rat, all right." He pulled his sock up and

3

grinned again as his memory delighted him anew. "An'
then someone gets a lamp goin' again, see, an' Jimmy
Beggs starts in. From where I was I could see the bosun,
stood on top o' the bar with a chair-leg in 'is fist, waitin'
for customers, an' there was poor little Tich Copley bein'
torn apart by one o' the Irish——"

"Poor little Tich," said Tug Wilson.

"I know." He lit a cigarette. "Where was I, mate?"

"Under the table."

"I mean what was I sayin'?"

"About Jimmy Beggs——"

"Christ yes, old Jimmy. Well, 'e got started in, soon as
the lamp was goin' again. You should'a *seen* 'im! It was
bloody murder, honest to God it was!"

"Well, what did he do?" asked Wilson.

"Well, 'e weighs sixteen stone, don't 'e, an' 'e come in at
a run for the Irishman who was tryin' to stuff poor little
Tich Copley's face with one o' the walls——"

"Why wasn't you helping him, then?"

"Who, Tich? Christ, by the time I'd'a got across to 'im
from where I was, 'e'd've been dead, mate, an' so would
I." He spread his hands out, worried by Tug's reproach.
"A shortarse like Tich ought to keep out o' places like
Mickey Green's on a Saturday night. Christ, any sixteen-
year-old sawn-off pixie ought to keep clear o' places like
Mickey Green's on a Saturday——"

"Go on, then," said Tug Wilson. "What did Jimmy do
to the Irishman?"

"I couldn't've 'elped poor little Tich, honest, not from
where I was, mate." He spread his hands wider. "It
would've been——"

" 'Course you couldn't," said Tug Wilson. "I can see
that. Now what did Jimmy do?"

The sun of Mounsey's grin came out again and he said,
"What did 'e do? It was a treat. A treat, mate. There
was nothin' rough, see—that ain't Jimmy's way. 'E just

4

bent down an' picked up the Irish's feet. He come down with a wallop on 'is face, hollerin' out something cruel an' tryin' to kick Jimmy through the roof, but o' course Jimmy wasn't 'avin' any, so 'e goes on holdin' the Irish with 'is head down until Tich gets out. Then, when the Irish gets a grip on someone an' swings 'is arm round at Jimmy, Jimmy just kicks 'im in the face till 'e stops." His grin exploded into a chuckle, and he blew out smoke from the cigarette in a luxury of delight.

"I see," nodded Tug Wilson, "nothing rough."

Mounsey spread his hands again in defence of the second mate. "Well, 'e had to look after himself, didn't 'e?"

" 'Course he did," said Wilson. "What happened after that?"

"He drops the Irish, who's out cold, an' starts on a couple o' gits that are tryin' to get the bosun off the bar. I found a bit o' space, just then, so I got out an' dived through the door, see, just as some bastard lobs a bottle. It catches the door, right by my 'ead, just as I'm divin' through." He turned his head and leaned towards Wilson, to show him the scars. They were just healing, but still looked messy. "You can see I'm tellin' you gospel, mate."

"You were lucky," said Wilson.

"I'll say I was lucky. I stopped outside to have a look, an' there's Jimmy Beggs still in there, hollerin' for the rest o' the *Whipper* boys to get out. I seen him pick up a Lascar an' throw 'im through that door so fast that 'e fetched up in the dock!"

"From Mickey's?" Wilson frowned. Mounsey tapped him solemnly on the knee.

"From Mickey's, into the dock."

"Ber-*li*'," said Wilson.

"Then I found poor little Tich Copley, bent down double over 'imself, winded——"

5

"Poor little Tich," said Wilson.

"I know. I picked 'im up an' carried 'im to where it was quiet. The coppers'd come up by then, an' someone was tryin' to get the Lascar out o' the dock, an' there was a Yankee hollerin' out that he was dyin', every time they went to pick 'im up. It'd come on to rain a bit, too, so I got hold of poor little Tich and carried 'im on board."

"Before he got wet," nodded Wilson.

"Eh?" Mounsey dropped his cigarette and stubbed it out. "But you should just've seen Jimmy Beggs, mate."

Standing at the wheel, Tug Wilson looked now at the second mate, catching a glimpse of his back before he looked down again at the compass card. Beggs was all of sixteen stone, with a head like a boulder on which thin hair grew like seaweed, and a face like an ageless rock that the storms have weathered to a stony crag; yet he was a quiet man, with a small high voice that piped from the button-mouth that was lost somewhere between the hook of the nose and the butt of the chin. He was a slow-moving man with gentle eyes—alert enough and alive enough, but gentle—and his big hands, clasped behind him as he paced his ten paces to the left and ten to the right, had seemed to have come together for a prayer. Watching him with a brief glance at long intervals, Wilson found shelter in the man. If he were in bad trouble, he would like to be somewhere near Beggs.

As for Mounsey's story, it had made him shudder to the heart of him. He had seen dockside fights himself, one of them fatal and with no more cause than a laugh from a coloured whore; and they had always scared him. He was strong, and not much under six feet tall, and didn't mind heights or depths, or snakes, or dentists, but a big fight among drunk seamen would frighten him, perhaps because they usually sprang from nothing, and achieved nothing. He'd seen half a bottle of liquor make a monster of a quiet Scot and send him at the nearest throat with a

6

will to murder, and for nothing; he'd seen a kid of a Greek dragging one broken leg along behind him, out of a Marseilles bar, too sick to scream with his pain, for the sake of an argument about a girl—you could say, for nothing. He had seen men behave worse than beasts, with less dignity and far less cause than beasts—men who were his own shipmates with a mother somewhere and clean collars at home. A fight had to be about something important, and then Tug Wilson could be counted in; but these senseless brawls made him sick to think about.

Beggs stopped by the binnacle and slapped it gently with a big hand.

Wilson brought the wheel up a spoke. "Ay, ay, sir."

The *Whipper* ran on through forty-seven north, seven west, north-east to England with her grain and passengers in the quiet of the middle watch. The lookout on the fo'c'sle thought he could smell the Channel, and thought of his home. Soon, when smoke began drawing down across the bows thickly as if the *Whipper's* hair were tangled over her eyes, he turned for a quick look at the sea in the south. The smoke was billowing down from the funnel, and on each side of it he could see the white chips in the black flint sea. He remembered what the bosun had said last evening, when the sea had been glass-calm and the sky clear as a girl's eyes. "There's a breeze o' wind down south'ards," Art Starley had said. And here it was, true enough, coming up astern and chopping the water, touching the ship and darting away, to swoop back and tug the smoke from the stack and pull it down across her bows; it sang in the rigging, the soft song rising and falling, lifting to a thin high drone and dying away as if far distant suddenly; it came back and banged a door, and slapped the Red Duster at the mainmast; it fled up, the wind, and dived in little gusts at the sea, cuffing and curling it. A breeze o' wind down south'ards, and now it was here. The bosun knew his weather and that was a fact.

7

The lookout stood with his back to the wind and watched the shift of smoke going away in the dark ahead of the *Whipper*. It made his work more difficult. A ship's light could come up through that veil of smoke and not be seen until the last few minutes when the two masses in their thousands of tons drew together in the night at thirty knots or maybe forty, and the shouts would go up and the bells ring and the wheels spin hard to break a collision-course.

Then the smoke thinned as the coal brightened in the furnaces, and his mind was eased. Towards the end of the graveyard watch a man on the fo'c'sle was prey to all the fancies of the night, and stood there jostled by the crowd of his superstitions until his very reason was sore at the elbows, pushing them away. In less than an hour the light would come and the day break, and he would go off watch. Roll on, the bells.

TWO

A QUARTERMASTER woke the first mate at ten minutes to four. Turnbull was alert within seconds.

"What's that sea doing?"

"Gettin' up, sir."

The first mate got out of his bunk and looked through the scuttle. It was still dark, but no longer night. In the darkness there were the fragile tints of the coming day, a small cloud very high, touched with first light, and a softness to the east horizon too feeble to define; but they were there. At this time, when a day was born, he often felt that it was touch and go with so delicate a birth: you could smudge out the small high cloud and draw the dark of your hand across the horizon and the day would die in the womb. It would not matter to Turnbull.

He washed in cold water and shaved deftly, watching his face afterwards in the oblong glass with his mouth tight and eyes unfriendly, for he was a vain man and over-critical of himself at this time of the day. Towards evening with a drink or two in him he could relax and admit to himself that here was a rare man, well-knit and superior to most in many things. He would turn in at night, satisfied; but each new day was a challenge to his faith in himself, and he knew it, and was ready with a quick temper if anyone tried to cross him.

He went on deck, and was hit by the morning's hand, by the gusty wind and the light sharpening against his eyes, the clip of the waves as the *Whipper* met them and broke them along her sides. He could hear crying, under the sky, and looked up. There were sea-gulls, out from England. He went into the wheelhouse.

"Good morning, Mr. Beggs." A tight mouth, formal.

" 'Morning, sir."

"Where's the relief quartermaster?"

Able-seaman Robins was behind him. "Sir?"

"Very good." He stood at the binnacle. "Course?"

Beggs said, "North forty-one east, sir." He stood with his back to the windows, waiting for the chief officer to get his eyes. He was not worried by Turnbull's brusque formality. He was rather fond of Turnbull, because he was a man with a worse weakness than most, and it must be hard to bear with, alone. Turnbull had a master's certificate and had skippered the *Sea Lord II* for Watson and Blount three years ago in the Pacific; but these days there were more masters than ships, because a sailor was born quicker than a ship was built, and only one master for each.

"Take over."

"Sir."

The wheel changed hands. Wilson looked neither at Beggs nor Turnbull as he went below. It was dead funny to see the two of them in the wheelhouse together, Jimmy and Old Bull, with all that parade-ground blarney flying about as if the owners themselves were there to watch the business. Mounsey had said, two days after the chief officer had got this berth, "We're goin' to have trouble with that one, you see if we don't." But there hadn't been much trouble from Turnbull. He'd go barking about the place with his eyes everywhere and pull you up for nothing, but when you stood your ground and stared him out he'd suddenly go under, and you'd know it. All he wanted was a lot of quick seamanlike ay-ay-sirs to show him you knew your place, and he was satisfied.

There was something inside the first mate that was as soft as a rotten apple, cowardice maybe, or kindness gone bad. Some said he was scared of something, but he wasn't scared of the sea, and that was enough for Tug Wilson. He'd been through a fog collision with Chief Officer

Turnbull, off the Dogger, and he was all right. Whatever it was that had gone soft inside him, or had been born inside him, it wasn't the fear of the sea or of anything the sea could do to a ship or a man. To Wilson, who had crawled about in the scuppers in his nappies on board his father's trawler more than twenty years ago, Turnbull was a reckonable sailor, and he was satisfied. But it was dead funny to see him in the wheelhouse with a man like Jimmy Beggs, twice his size and twice as quiet.

At the wheel, Able-seaman Robins checked the course at north forty-one degrees east and put the midships spoke down a bit, feeling the slight beam-sea. The first mate said to Beggs:

"Have we had more warnings?"

"Yes. Southerly gales. She's force four now, near enough." A minute passed, and Turnbull said:

"All right, I've got my eyes."

For the benefit of the helmsman, Beggs said cheerfully, "All's well, lights a-bright!" He went below to turn in. Robins waited for the nonsense to start. They had told him, shipping out of Buenos Aires, "You'll be in the mate's watch," and he had cursed his luck. There was nothing much wrong with Old Bull except that he couldn't keep his mouth shut. Looking as thin and as tight as that mouth did, you'd never think it'd ever come open, but you were wrong.

The relief lookout on the wing sang out in the same moment as the telephone buzzed from the fo'c'sle—"Steamer lights two points on the starb'd bow!"

The first mate went out to the starboard wing. In the faint light of the dawn he could see the outline of the other ship as well as her red port lamp. She was long and low in the water, her midships freeboard lost in a smother of foam. She'd be down from the Irish Sea. Mr. Turnbull watched her, fine on the bow, and judged her distance and her speed and the speed of the *Whipper*, the run of the tide and the lie of the wind. He came back into the wheel-house.

"Steer five degrees to starb'd."

Robins moved his hands. "Steer five degrees to starb'd, sir!" The sea came round from her quarter and followed astern.

You'd never hit that tanker, thought Robins, if you kept your course and drove at her full ahead. You could go five points west, at this speed, and still miss her by a mile. But the Old Bull was on the bridge, so he had to talk, and chuck the ship about, or things wouldn't be right. The nonsense had started. Not that Robins minded. He'd as soon put the *Whipper* in circles as leave her be, for she was a well-found ship and fine to handle. Turn her round on a dinner plate if you had to. He'd taken her through the Needles, once, when the Skip had been on the spree; and two or three times up the Thames, in ballast and with a force ten wind and half the North Sea shipping coming in for shelter. She was all of a ship, all of a woman, and nothing she wouldn't do for you, if you loved her. But you had to do that.

"Steer five degrees to port."

"Steer five degrees to port, sir!"

The tanker went slipping through the dawn, clearing their course. She was flashing her Aldis lamp, and Turnbull stood on the port wing of the bridge, reading.

Penny for the guy?

Turnbull said to the lookout, "What the hell does he mean?"

"Fifth o' November today, sir."

"Fifth of November, is it?" He went back into the fug of the wheelhouse and took out the lamp. He sent:

Will you dive for it?

The tanker dropped away to port under the lightening sky. Up there, mares' tails were beginning to fly from the south-west. He was not worried. Already there were a few big Cornish gulls escorting the *Whipper* home.

Just after seven o'clock he went and stood in the door-way of the wireless-room, where Mr. Bond was tuned in to London. *There are gale warnings in operation sea areas Rockall, Hebrides, Irish Sea, Fastnet, Biscay, Bristol Channel, Plymouth and Dover.*

"Well, the next watch can have it," said Turnbull.

Bond glanced up. He had a round pink face and the eyes of a man who normally wears spectacles, though his sight was perfect. He gave a quick nervous grin.

"It'll get it."

"There's no need to look so bloody cheerful."

"I always look bloody cheerful, sir. It conceals a sad heart."

There was Morse coming through on the trawler band. He corrected the signal. Turnbull stood there for another half minute, listening.

"All they can think about is stinking fish," said Bond. He looked up, but the first mate had gone back into the wheelhouse. Alone again, Bond relaxed in his swing chair, listening to the trawlers and thinking of his wife. Alone, he didn't look cheerful; there was no need for the quick nervous grin. He found himself staring at the photograph on the bulkhead, as often he found himself doing through the long hours on watch. She was young-looking and pretty, the sort of stranger a man would want to meet in the flesh, if this were a good likeness. It was a good likeness, but she wasn't a stranger to him, and he would meet her again only because he had to. A ship must make landfall, and a man must come home; it was the order of things.

She might, of course, not be there. The last letter had said she was all right, and that she was sorry about 'all that'. But that was three weeks ago and in three weeks a lot could happen to change Thelma's mind. It could change overnight, and she could wake up feeling 'different'. She would tell him she had been thinking about 'things', and that she had decided there must be an end to 'all this'. She had a label for everything that was past. The long mounting crisis between them was 'this business', but it was not yet past. What, in plain words, did he call this crisis himself? He could never give it a name; it was not a positive thing but negative, and all the clues to it went springing away whenever he tried to slam his hands down on them and hold them still for inspection; all the complicated moral structure of it collapsed and rebuilt itself unrecognisably as soon as he cleared his mind to view it objectively. Nothing positive, but negative; they were breaking up because they couldn't get on; she wasn't ill, but she was unwell; he had sympathy, but couldn't understand. There was, when he thought about it, nothing wrong . . . but there was nothing right.

The photograph smiled down. *Love, Thelma.* Love from Thelma, her love to him. The love of the young-looking pretty girl to him, her husband. This photograph, here, to remind him of her when the long voyages blurred her image and name and form, dissolving the memories. And now, at last, no love.

He felt the movement of the ship about him. The sea was short and she was lively. He longed, perhaps without fully realising it, for the *Whipper* to turn about, and steer from home, and go on steaming to anywhere else in the world or to nowhere, just go on steaming. He had felt like this at school, at the end of the term in the summer when his mother had died. They had sent him home for two days, because she had not died there but in Wales, two hundred miles away. His father had talked to him at home, trying to ease the shock to the young schoolboy mind, to explain that everything had been done to prevent this terrible thing and that nothing more could be done now, nor tears help. But of course tears helped and his pillow was soaked by morning, and came springing hot again as the hateful day began. He went back to his school, where he would be busy among his friends and not idle in a saddened house; and slowly through the rest of the term the first throat-filling ache diminished, and whole minutes came when he had no time to think of his dead mother, and then one whole hour when there was a vital match with a visiting team. And there were treats planned and promised in his father's letters, and even the terrible relief that the funeral was over without him there —"she'll know that it's not out of any disrespect, Anthony, and you must believe me when I say that she'd rather you stayed with your friends and just remembered her as she was, pottering about the garden with her flower-scissors and calling for help when she came across a worm, and then laughing at herself afterwards when she'd brought us all running, remember?"

It had been wrong, writing that. It had brought it all back, and the pillow was blotchy again because he would never hear that comical little scream from among the rose-trees, and never say again, "Hello, Mummy's found a worm!" But there were other wrong things inhis father's letters, all of them meant for kindness, and he learned to cry less about them and one day was shocked by his first unselfish startling thought that his father must feel this, too. There were, towards the end of that term, the dreadful moments when he caught himself enjoying the drama that surrounded him; when he walked by himself along the trees by the pavilion, playing the part of the boy who'd lost his mother. 'What's up with Bond, d'you know? Haven't you heard? Is that why they sent him home?' He walked in his short-lived grief, hero of his dreadful situation, and then hated himself for it, and then forgot about her again for another hour; and finally he reached the end of a term that should have been impossible for him to live through, unthinkable, a nightmare that would never let him go. He reached the holidays, and got into the train; and then, minute by minute, he dropped out of the noisy chatter and sat watching the trees go by, and suddenly began wishing the train would never stop, but go on through his station and go on and on to anywhere in the world or to nowhere, just keep on going.

This was the feeling that was on him now, so similar that he recognised it, and remembered the train and his school-friends and even the stained corner of his attaché-case where Smithy had spilled some acid, larking about in the chemy-lab. The house at the end of the journey was not the same as the one he had left; he didn't want to go back to it. Thelma wasn't dead, but her love was, and that was much the same.

Making in to Brixham . . . a poor catch . . . it's blowing hard. . . .

We passed Willow Girl . . . She's staying out. . . .

He switched wave-lengths and heard Niton. The distress metres were blank, and he picked up a coaster reporting a patch of timber south of Fastnet. It was ten minutes now to the end of his watch, and he could soon go below and take his time to think.

The movement about him developed a rhythm; the seas were growing longer as the wind built them up from the south, gathering small short waves into one green ridge and blowing the froth off. He could watch the sea from in here without even looking at it. He knew by the rhythm, because it was the same rhythm and the same sea that had rocked him through that part of his life from school until this day. A fortnight ago he had turned thirty-one.

He felt old, not because of his age but because he would have to begin again, any time now. There had been years wasted. Had he been forty he would probably have realised that he was still young and had plenty of time; but at thirty-one a man feels that half his life has gone.

The ship's movement calmed him as she ran into the

16

bright morning with the sea astern. When he went off watch at eight bells he paused on the wing of the bridge and drew the air in deeply. Oh God, how clean the sea was, with the soft wind sweeping it and building the blue-green water into serried trough and ridge, then frosting it with crisp white caps and touching spindrift off; how clean the gulls' wings overhead and astern above the wake, cutting the pale sky and wheeling, bearing a mournful cry aloft, sharp in the sad morning; and clean the astringent tang of the salt, the raw slap of it against the skin, the cold of it against the eyes as he stared across the curve of the world and was lost again, over the horizon where he should have stayed for ever.

"Hello, Cock."

He turned and saw Costain, up for the forenoon watch. Bond gave him a quick grin. "How's Little Audrey?"

Costain kept a tight face, only his eyes amused. He was very much alive, this thin dark boy, a third officer in his early twenties with a straight future mapped out for himself and a quick heart to get him through it.

"I wouldn't know," he said. He stood with his hands stuck into his jacket pockets, his eyes going to slits as the wind slapped, then widening as he watched the sea.

"I said she'd let you, didn't I?" said Bond. He was interested in other people's affairs, because they were less dreary than his own; and he envied Costain, who was young, and had no house to go to. Costain said, watching the sea:

"It's none of your bloody business."

"It certainly is. We've got a bet on." He studied the third mate's face. He had laid him five shillings that Ann Brown, the only unaccompanied woman passenger, would leave her door ajar in the middle watch. This was usually the time, within a day or two of landfall, when campaigns were concluded; though Costain, with his thin good looks, worked faster than most.

He moved his hands suddenly and found a half-crown and a florin among the coppers. "I'll have to owe you threepence."

Bond grinned again quickly and took the money. "Keep it for luck. Was she nice?"

Costain said slowly, "I think you're just a lecherous old pimp."

"I'll bet she was a honey."

"No more bets. I'm broke as it is."

Bond made a great show of licking a finger and wiping it down the windbreaker, marking another one up for Costain.

"*Vive le sport*," he said, and left him. Costain looked up at the sky. It had been a high dawn, with clouds on the horizon below the sun; and now the mares' tails had merged to form oily-looking banks, sharp-edged below a steel-blue sky. One or two gulls were dropping ahead of the ship and flying straight, leaving her for the land. There wouldn't be much of a muster for lunch today among the passengers. He turned and went into the wheelhouse, and looked in at the doorway of the wireless-room.

"What's on the met.?"

"Dirt."

He wandered across to the binnacle, checking the course and compass. The *Atlantic Whipper*'s E.T.A. at Avonmouth was two o'clock the next morning. The weather would get there first, at this rate.

Pacing along the windows, turning and pacing with his hands in his side-pockets, stopping and turning, pacing and coming back, he thought of Ann Brown. He still didn't know who she was. He knew she was a teacher in some kind of school, and knew her name and where she lived . . . "with a blank wall a yard from the window and a sooty windowsill, and that damned bus depot right opposite—that's why I can't keep away from this port-hole, because of all that glorious space out there . . ." but

18

he didn't really know who she was. Not married, he imagined. A teacher in a school of some odd kind (sitting on the bed, sharing her cigarette in the faint glow of the pilot-lights defining the port-holes, it hadn't been easy to listen to what she was telling him, as close to him as that, her promise already obvious or he wouldn't have been there at all), a school for the deaf, he remembered now—

"You mean deaf children?"

"Yes."

"All of them?"

"Yes." She took the cigarette and drew on it, and passed it back, touching his hand but not feeling it. "We try to teach them how to speak."

He didn't want to talk about deaf children, because that was a sad enough subject, God only knew, and this would be the last whole night at sea and it was nearly two o'clock. But he said, "It's very difficult?"

"Yes. They were all born deaf, and so they've never heard anyone speak."

He looked at her silhouette, a slight profile with the lips moving, a gleam of light reflecting in her eye on this side under short spiky lashes. In the silence, his wrist-watch ticked. He began smiling in the darkness at himself. Here he was, alone with her, sitting on her bed . . . talking about deaf children. Poor little wretches, granted, but it was no good letting yourself start worrying about things like that or you'd spend your whole life weeping for beggars and polio cases and the blind. At any moment, anyone in the world could become one of them, and then regret the selfishness that had gone before. Misery was a thing you had to help when you could, and forget for the rest of the time.

"Poor little devils," he said.

"They're wonderfully happy."

"They're what?"

She turned her face to him and he saw she was smiling.

"They don't know what they've missed—I mean things like music and birds—so they've nothing to long for, and I suppose we're kinder to them than in ordinary schools." He gave her the cigarette and she said, "It's burning rather short."

"I'll put it out." He leaned over to the ashtray, and in the silence the pull of his sleeve made a great deal of noise. He could hear her swallowing. She said:

"I'm a washout, you see."

He leaned back, not wanting to take her hand. He wanted to go. They had started this meeting on the wrong tack, and now they were well adrift.

"Are you?" He tried to get interest into his tone.

"At this kind of thing."

Feeling suddenly very annoyed he wanted to ask, 'What kind of thing, for God's sake?' If he were to get up and go, saying good-night, would she be hurt? Did she even realise there was a man in her cabin, in the dark? She was different, so absolutely different, from the person she had been when they'd danced together in the saloon after dinner. It must have been the wine. That had happened before. He had nearly been thrown off his ship once, when he'd shown up in a cabin during the middle watch, fully confident after a warm invitation, and had his face slapped and the door slammed in it. She had threatened to tell the captain in the morning. Now this was another one. A glass of wine and she'd melt in your arms, dancing, and whisper heaven and earth in your ear; an hour later she'd whinny for help if you picked up her handkerchief. The Canadians had a word for them.

She said quietly, "You're furious, Peter."

"Why?" If she wanted innuendoes she could have them. It was dead easy. All you had to do was ask a lot of silly questions that couldn't possibly be answered except with another silly question. Women were great conversationalists.

She touched his hand, and found it limp. "How old are you?" she asked.

"Twenty-three."

"That's young."

He thought bitterly, 'All right, call me Sonny.'

"But very experienced, I should imagine."

"I've had my ticket two years."

She was laughing suddenly and softly, startling him because for nearly half a minute she couldn't stop. He said, "I don't see it."

"I'm sorry." She got a handkerchief and sniffed into it, and he wondered why people always had to make a gesture of apology after a good laugh. "How many does your ticket entitle you to?" She put her handkerchief away. He felt thoroughly fed up, and sorry for those poor little bastards. But they were happy, she'd said, so he could forget them.

"Anyway, please try not to be furious, Peter." She waited, but he just said something about his not being anything of the sort. It was very difficult. She had stopped talking about her job, because she had realised it was wrong, but they couldn't sit in silence holding hands. Shouldn't he do something? She had read that it was the man who set the pace, but was that wrong?

He found his cigarette-case and opened it for her.

"No, thank you."

He took a cigarette and put it between his lips, but while he was getting a match she said, "I've told you I'm a washout. That really meant you don't have to stay, just out of politeness." She held his hand firmly, the one that had the box of matches in it. She was terrified now, but didn't know whether it was by the thought of his going or staying.

As kindly as he could he said, "I know when I'm being kicked out." He stood up and dropped the fresh cigarette into the ashtray. Bitterly he thought she might see it there when she woke in the morning, and be sorry. "Good-night, Ann."

Before he reached the door she was sobbing, loudly because she was trying to stifle it. He came back, bewildered.

"What have I done?" he asked, but she was too busy with her handkerchief to hear. He knelt by the bed, without thinking, and touched her. He was young, and tears from a stranger could move him. And it might be his fault, so he had to find out before he left her, and if necessary apologise.

She got a grip on herself and said almost without a tremor, "I'm not attractive enough."

"You're madly attractive." His tone made the cliché sound sincere. He really meant it. She was damned attractive and he wished to God he'd never met her.

"I thought you—you wanted me."

He said, "I did. I mean, I do." He was still sincere. "What the hell are you crying about, Ann?"

She brought her face down and kissed his brow, trembling. She said in a small voice, "I don't know what I've got to do."

"Oh, Ann . . ."

Pacing, turning, pacing back, hands in his pockets, past the binnacle and back again, he went on cursing his stupidity. Certainly he had slept with only five women since his unthinkably clumsy initiation at the age of nineteen, but that should have given him enough experience to steer him through last night with more pleasure and less humiliation for Ann. He had behaved like a callow adolescent awaiting the attack of a full-blown seductress, instead of realising her sensitivity and her unfamiliarity with the situation. The others, before, had all been the same sort, who made love between gins and forgot about it by breakfast-time.

Poor little Ann.

"Ship three points on the starb'd quarter!"

He wandered moodily to the wing and looked across the sea. A liner, Southampton-bound, yawing a lot in the hard swell. He answered the lookout and went back into the wheelhouse.

He'd make it up to her, if they ever met again. She couldn't be having much of a life, shut up first in that room with a blank wall a yard from the windows and the bus depot opposite, then in a schoolroom full of poor little deaf mutes. No husband: he was certain of that. Then what did she do for sex? She wasn't used to it, to judge from her constraint last night (hell, he could talk!), yet she'd enjoyed it enormously. When she was back in England, what then? The cramped room, the school, and the short journey between, and nothing else?

It was the first time he had felt sorry for a woman he had slept with, and it worried him. A gin, the bed, another gin and then thanks for the memory—the routine had changed, last night. Standing here by the binnacle, automatically checking the course, he was seized with an incredible thought: was there something more to making love than that?

He'd have to be careful, damned careful in future. This thing had the smell of dynamite.

"Mr. Costain."

"Yes?" The second wireless-operator was in the doorway.

"The owners are asking for confirmation of E.T.A. Any change?"

"No, but remind 'em we've had gale warnings and that we're still sixteen hours outside. What the hell are they worried about?"

"I don't think they're actually worried." He went back to send the signal, wondering what was up with Pete this morning. He sounded more like Turnbull.

Costain went out to the port wing, and caught a wind-gust; he clamped his cap on and looked at the sea. The water was a wicked green, topped with white crests. Half the south sky was clouded, and the clear blue that had been in the north was hazing over. The last gull had gone. The wind was alive in the rigging, and a halyard was crackling somewhere, quivering against timber. Ahead the sea was a flat of white spindrift, but when he looked astern he could see the true shape of it. There were waves racing in ranks with hundred-yard troughs between. The horizon was lost.

His feet swayed to the broken rhythm of the ship as she yawed to the following sea, plunging uneasily and lifting, sometimes bringing her screw clear and shaking it, sending the vibration through the deck beneath him. For'ard of the bridge the bosun had some men out along the hatch-coamings, checking on the covers. They had put oil-skins on. A wave broke and came over white, with the spindrift curling back in the wind. The bosun's team worked more quickly, tapping the wedges, testing them, moving along the coamings like bent black beetles as the long foredeck shuddered and was still, shuddered again as the next sea came and broke along the sides.

The owners, he thought, had better have another signal. It was a pity they didn't pay more attention to the met. reports themselves. They knew where the ship was and they knew what the weather was: why waste Sparks's time?

He clamped his cap down again and turned back into the wheelhouse.

"Good-morning, Mr. Costain."

The captain was up.

"Good-morning, sir."

"It looks like a nice fresh morning."

"Yes, sir."

24

★

THREE

★

RON MOUNSEY counted the rivets above his head. He lay flat in his bunk, staring up at them and making patterns: those three rusty ones where the paint had chipped off were almost equidistant, and made a fair triangle. There was a fly on one rivet, and every time it moved he was able to make a new pattern, with the rivet the fly was on and the three rusty ones. Sometimes the fly landed between them and he watched it sourly until it chose another rivet. It had been in no-man's-land for half a minute now, and didn't look like going on with the game.

"Get up, you bastard," said Mounsey, his face dark.

Across the cabin, Tug Wilson dropped his guitar tutor and picked it up, and began using the plectrum again with the confident emphasis of the true novice.

"Get up, sod you," growled Mounsey.

Wilson got his tongue in and rested his guitar. He looked across at Mounsey.

"What are you griping about?"

"That bloody fly."

"Is that who you're talkin' to?"

"Ay. He won't shift."

Tug watched him for a moment. "P'r'aps he's a Frenchie, and don't know your lingo."

Mounsey's sense of humour was simple. He grinned. "Don't give me that. I'll make the little cowson shift in a minute if he don't move 'isself."

Tug plucked again at the guitar. It was a beauty, with mother-of-pearl decorations and the maker's name inside the sound-box. He'd had to trade in quite a lump of ship's chandlery for this.

Ron's fly had gone off, out of sight. He cursed it and

turned his idle attention upon Tug. "You don't get any
better, y' know."

"I'm trying," said Tug mildly.

"What you want to play that thing for, then?"

"Can't you shut up?"

Mounsey hitched himself on to one elbow. "Well, look
who's talkin'!" He listened for a while to Tug's careful
search for the right note, and then his patience wore thin.
"Can't you go an' practise that in the wheel'ouse or
somewhere?"

Tug lowered his beautiful guitar and said casually:

"Teresa said she'll marry me when I can play it."

"Don't give me that, mate."

"She says a Spanish girl can't marry a man who can't
even serenade her with a guitar." He studied the tutor
again.

Ron Mounsey gave a laugh like a window breaking.
"She's not any Spanish girl, mate, she's a bloody Mexican-
Peruvian with a touch o' Chinese-Irish about 'er. Don't
you know Teresa yet?"

Tug did not answer. He plucked again, listening
enraptured to the twang of the strings. He was getting on
like a house on fire. He could hear himself improving
every day. He'd got a real talent for this, and no mistake.

"Teresa . . ." grinned Mounsey. "The las' time I was
in Buenos Aires she was callin' herself Lula. Ask me, I'd
say she was christened Fanny."

Tug struck a chord, in self-congratulation. "Stow it,
mate. She's a nice girl."

"Are you serious?" Mounsey's deep voice was pinched
into a squeak of disbelief.

" 'Course I'm serious."

"Then you're crackers, mate. Real crackers, you are.
I can tell you a thing or two about your little Teresa that'd
make your short-hairs curl. If she——"

"Then don't."

26

He played three slow notes, almost perfectly. Ron leaned towards him from his bunk.

"Are you honest-to-God *serious*, Tug?"

"Much as I'm fond of this expensive instrument," said Wilson slowly, "I'll crown you with it if you don't let up."

Mounsey fell silent, not because of the threat but out of respect for his shipmate's feelings. If poor old Tug was off his loaf about that half-breed little dockside judy, it was his business. But it made you laugh, all right.

He rolled a black shag cigarette and threw it across to Wilson. "There y'are, Don Juan, set your mustachios on fire wi' that." He began rolling another one for himself. The cabin gave a lurch, making him spill some leaf. "Jeese, she's pipin' up a bit, isn' she?"

Tug lit his cigarette. "We've got more to come. Didn't you hear what the bose said? Force-ten gales comin' up from the south."

"Garn, what's a force-ten gale to the *Whipper*? Now if we was on some lousy packet full o' cockers with a dead-beat skipper, that'd be diff'rent. Christ, where did they get this shag from, out of a brewer's dray 'orse?"

The ship took another sea on the quarter. Mounsey's locker door swung open and hit the bulkhead with a bang. Wilson just saved his guitar.

"Here it comes," he said.

"Well, let it come, we're 'omeward bound, mate."

Sea-boots crashed down a companionway and the bosun's mate poked his head in. "Put up the deadlights an' secure. Where's Stubbs?"

" 'Aven't seen 'im. What's this about deadlights?"

"Just get 'em up, an' look lively." He left them. A door banged, somewhere topsides. Mounsey swung himself out of his bunk with a grin.

"Be a bit o' caviar left over from lunch today, from what I know about passengers. Make a nice tuck-in for the likes of us."

Tug Wilson put his guitar away carefully, and then saw green water go sliding over a porthole. A tin mug clanged down from a locker; a book slid off a sea-bag and fell spread-eagled.

"Let's get them deadlights up," he said.

.   .   .   .

The bosun had his team and the chippies on the after-deck, working steadily along the battens of number three and four hatches. Above them the whine of the shrouds and aerial had become a constant song and they no longer heard it. Spray exploded across the bulwarks at intervals and white water drained through the wash-doors, banging them and making percussion for the high wind's drone.

"Stubbs! Where the hell've you been?"

The man leaned on the wind towards the bosun.

"I've not been feelin' so good, Bose."

They stood together for a moment while the seamen worked on.

"Listen to me, Stubbs. You've not been feelin' so good since we started out. You've had a loggin' from the skipper once, an' you're workin' up for another, quick. What the hell's up with you, man?"

"There's nothin' up wi' me." Their faces stared at each other, framed by the black oilskins and the green sea beyond. They were having to shout into the wind. "There's nothin' up wi' me that your good riddance won't cure."

Art Starley waited for a couple of seconds. He didn't want to say a wrong word. He wanted to tell Stubbs exactly where he stood, with no misunderstandings. "What's your complaint? I want to hear it. If it's justified we'll get somethin' done about it, double-quick. If not, you'd better pipe down about it, for good. Come on now?"

"I got no complaint—why should I have? I get all the

bloody jobs while Wilson an' Smithers an' Harris an' that lot take it nice an' easy on their bloody arses." Spray came over the side and slashed them; they turned against its white sting but did not look away from each other. "Some on us are expected to work like blacks," Stubbs shouted against the wind, "an' the rest can hang on the slack, for all you care." He stared into the dark round face of Art Starley and hated it and hated all bosuns and all officers and masters and owners, superior snotty-nosed bastards full of their bloody class-consciousness because they went about with a lot of brass crap on their sleeves and called each other Mister. The hate was in his voice. "You call yourself a bosun, do you? Eh? Call yourself a bloody ship's bosun?"

Starley didn't hit him. There was a big sea running and a lot of work to do. He shot out his hand and gripped the seaman's arm, and Stubbs jerked his muscles instinctively to ward off a blow and give it back. He didn't shake the bosun's grip from his arm but his hands were squeezed white at the knuckle. They stood together with their stance shifting for balance as the deck tilted, their heads turned away from the side where the sea broke and the wind rushed. They stood a degree below fighting-point.

"Listen, Stubbs. Wilson an' those other two are among the best men I've got on board an' they pull their weight. It's no good you thinkin' you can make 'em out to be bosun's favourites. It's men like them I can leave alone, an' they'll go on working. You? You're a bloody free passenger in this ship. Soon as we're through on this job, we'll see the skipper, you an' me. You've got ten minutes to think out what you're goin' to tell him."

He released Stubbs's arm and turned away to help two men who were stowing deck-rope before it fouled the wash-doors. Starley didn't like a following sea. A ship was designed to take her punishment on the nose, where she could see it coming, and meet it and deal with it, shaking

29

the last sea from her head before the next one came. This gale was southerly and it had come stalking up behind the *Whipper* and she couldn't turn, but had to run on where her course lay, chivvied and harassed by the stern seas where there were no sharp bow-plates to cut at them as they came.

"Watch it—here comes a dipper!"

The men heard him and dodged for what cover they could, or clutched at the nearest stanchion while the water hit them, the white salt spray bursting over them with tatters of green flying between the rails. They were working again within a moment, carrying on until the next wave came. The bosun watched the length of the swell and judged its height. If this wind strengthened according to forecast, the sea would start pooping.

Watching him from the port wing of the bridge, Captain Harkness stood with his hands buried in his coat. The bosun did a job handily; such men were good to watch. He turned to face for'ard, and a few minutes later went back into the wheelhouse and said to Costain:

"Get the lookout up from the fo'c'sle."

"Ay, ay, sir." The third mate unhooked the phone. The shipmaster stood at one of the windows, a short big-shouldered man whose strength was expressed more in his stillness than his movements. He listened to the tick of the echo-sounder by the chart-room door and watched the sea ahead, his thoughts faster than his ship but on the same exact course, to England. The *Atlantic Whipper* was due for a refit, and he was due for leave. He was not excited by the immediate future. He would spend the next few weeks in the perfect comfort of his home, where his slightest wish would be met by dear Margaret. He knew that she was living impatiently through this day, working without any trace of anxiety that their house would not please him in the smallest respect. The doorstep would be a glow of red tiles, the knocker shine, the windows glitter, admitting clear light to gleam on the polished wood and burnished ornaments. The fire would be bright and the scuttle filled. (Did she really dust the coals? He believed she did.) The place would be perfect.

He thought, standing with his feet balancing his short strong body as the ship moved in the swell, that in the long list of imperfections with which a man must live, perfection came somewhere about the middle.

The fo'c'sle lookout came up to the bridge with water still draining from his oilskins. He took up his station, shielded in part by the windbreakers. He watched with pleasure the ship's head dropping, bringing up water and shipping it across the rails and winches on the fo'c'sle head, where he had been standing before. Mr. Beggs, coming up the companionway, said to him cheerfully, "Getting soft, are you, Phillips?"

The man grinned with a wet face. "Orders, sir."

Beggs came into the wheelhouse and fetched the sextant.

"Taking sights, sir, before the sun's gone."

"Good, Mr. Beggs."

The sun was a hazed blob; in half an hour it would be lost above the cloud-packs, well before noon. He worked with the sextant and went into the chart-room to mark their position and course. While he was in there the bosun came up to the bridge and asked to see the captain.

Harkness went out to the wing. Starley said:

"I'm sorry to trouble you, sir. I want to report one of the hands." There was a mist of salt clinging to his heavy eyebrows, and a drip on his nose. The ship lurched and they both leaned to the movement.

"I'll see him in fifteen minutes, in my room."

"Thank you, sir."

"Is everything secured, Mr. Starley?"

"Yes sir."

"Very good."

Harkness returned to the wheelhouse. Beggs was out

of the chart-room. Costain was watching the compass card. Beggs had told him the drift, and he was worried by the skipper's presence. In a few months he would be sitting for first mate's ticket, and he wanted a good recommend.

"Starb'd ten," he said carefully.

"Starb'd ten, sir."

They could feel the sea coming stronger on the beam.

"Meet her."

"Ay, ay, sir, meet her."

Costain checked the new course and stood back from the binnacle. Harkness was gazing through the window. The sun was being absorbed by the clouds' fringe; it threw down a last ragged light and then the sea darkened, and took on the colour and heaviness of lead. The spindrift lost its ice-white sparkle as the wind-gusts whipped it from the crests; between the crests, the troughs were scooped out and ran in shadows. The last of the blue had gone from the sky, the last of the green from the sea. The ship rode in a world of monochrome greys with the tinting harsh and metallic. In the foreground of the captain's vision, out at the edge, the bright red of the fire-extinguisher glowed in contrast with the rest.

"Meet her."

"Meet her, sir."

The telegraph showed Full. With the seas quickening, the screw was losing thrust. Costain counted the minutes. At noon he could hand over to Jim Beggs and have a drink and thank the Lord. He had no liking for a rough passage, keeping watch with the Skip up here.

A few days ashore, Beggs was thinking, and he could fish the old Aston Martin out and run up to London, caning her all the way and drifting the bends, with a bit of a welcome from the boys at the Hub Club when he got there.

His clothes would be ready for him, thought Harkness,

perfectly pressed, his shoes perfectly polished; and there would be nothing out of its place; and Margaret's devotion would minister to him without fuss; and he would wait in patience for these comfortable weeks to pass, and feel the excitement rising in him on the last evening, when his thoughts would leave home ahead of him, and go to the ship and the sea and the demands they would make on him, and the happiness they could give him that Margaret never could.

Costain thought, 'The small cramped room, and the school, and the short journey between, and nothing more? Poor Ann.'

Eight bells were rung and their thoughts fled away in the clangour and the call to movement. Beggs took over the watch. Costain went below. The wheel changed hands. The captain moved away from the windows, and with the sight of the rising seas in his mind and the feel of the ship's uneasiness beneath his feet he said:

"I'll be in my cabin, if you want me."

FOUR

THE bosun had taken off his oilskins and stood with his cap tucked under his arm. Already the atmosphere of this sacred cabin was making him regret having reported Stubbs; but the threat had been made and it couldn't be withdrawn.

He should have hit the man and got it over with. Stubbs would have understood a thing like that, and it would have saved all this palaver within a few hours of the crew paying off at the end of the trip.

"Yes, Mr. Starley?"

The captain was sitting. Stubbs stood on the bosun's left. The cabin was warm, and quiet, and full of the smell of pipe-smoke. Starley said:

"This man is giving me constant——"

"This seaman, Mr. Starley." The captain's face was bland, his pale blue eyes almost sleepy. His voice was gentle.

The bosun swallowed bitterly, and began his rehearsed speech again. "This seaman, sir," and he made the tone of the word sound as much like 'bastard' as he could, "is giving me constant trouble on deck—when I can find him, which isn't often. He is a malingerer, and insubordinate."

It wasn't a bad speech, he thought. It was short, and couldn't be misunderstood.

Captain Harkness turned his bland face to Stubbs, the expression unchanged. It was an amiable stare that he might be giving two of his closest friends, or two cockroaches he was about to crush underfoot. An impartial man, he had an impartial face. He had corrected the bosun just now with no thought in mind of taking him down a peg in front of Stubbs. It was simply that Stubbs, on board as a member of the crew and with his book and rating all in order, was a seaman, and must be allowed the right of that title in a formal interview.

His quiet, ordinary question had all the force of a long silence behind it.

"Well, Stubbs?"

The seaman met the master's eyes with a directness that was out of character for an insubordinate malingerer.

"I'm not satisfied." It was said with firmness.

The captain's stare was bright and his voice still gentle. "You will address me as 'sir'."

Stubbs looked down. Starley gazed at the curtain over the scuttle. He began counting the seconds as they crept nervously by through this silence. It was the kind of silence that brought sweat out on you the longer it went on, until you began praying that you wouldn't have the ghastly misfortune to burp, or cough, or give any audible sign that you were still here in this unbearable, unbreakable trap of soundlessness that went on and on, until you were certain that when someone dropped a pin your feet would clear the floor with the shock.

Stubbs brought his head up, and looked at Harkness. Harkness was still gazing at him, bright of eye. Starley was sweating. Stubbs had brought his head up with the effort of a man dragging a rock to a mountain-top. A neck muscle creaked.

"Sir."

Starley collapsed inside himself. Where had the Skip learned to do things like that, for Christ's sake? It was murder.

Gently, "You're not satisfied——" a slight pause— "with what?"

"With this ship." Starley tensed again. The silence had begun. If it went on he was going to blow up or fall apart or—"Sir." He went slack with relief. He was a

35

good bosun. He could work. He knew the sea and ships and men. He could fight, and draw bad blood in a good cause if necessary. But he wasn't built to stand this kind of war, when a mere syllable went clipping through the air like a bullet. He should have just thrown Stubbs overboard. Hanging was better than this.

Captain Harkness was speaking. It was all right, thought the bosun, so long as people spoke. The devil's own voice would be sweet music compared with the kind of silence the Skip could conjure up.

"You are not satisfied with my ship. I am anxious to know in what particular respect we have failed you." He thought Stubbs was being absurd. Nearly two hundred miles out in the ocean, this ship was the world, and he was saying he wasn't satisfied with the world. Who was?

"The bosun picks on me, sir. Ever since that last time he's 'ad 'is hooks into me."

"What last time?"

Stubbs began talking more quickly, more easily. You couldn't make sense to anyone if you had to stare them out and refuse to address them properly. The thing was to put your case, and make it sound better than the other one. The Skip had got sense, you could see that. It was this cowson of a bosun he was up against.

"When you logged me, sir. I reckon I deserved it, that time. But this——" he jerked his right hand—"but the bosun won't forget it. He's been chasin' me ever since, while some o' the others can take it easy, go as they please. It's not good enough, is it, sir?"

Captain Harkness had listened attentively, had looked once at the bosun and then back to Stubbs. There was a lot of sincerity in the seaman's voice. Harkness believed him, in part. It was probably true that the bosun had been chasing him; it was probably untrue that some of the hands were allowed to take it easy. He said slowly:

36

"You said you weren't satisfied with the ship. Let us hear about that."

Stubbs moved a mouth muscle, shrugging. "I reckon I meant the bosun, sir."

Harkness sat farther back in his chair and stared for a while at the middle distance. Looking at him, you would not know whether his mind were a blank, or deeply occupied, whether he was calm or in a controlled rage. You didn't know where you were. "You 'reckon' you meant the bosun. Can we for the sake of saving our time be quite *sure* you meant the bosun, and not the ship?"

Stubbs said, reluctantly, as if he were making a late attempt not to appear unfair in actually accusing the bosun:

"Yes, sir."

Harkness looked at Starley. "Have you been chasing Stubbs, Mr. Starley?"

"Yes, sir."

"Why?"

"You've got to, sir. He won't work otherwise."

"Are some of the other hands allowed to go as they please, and take it easy?"

"You'd know it, sir, if the ship was bein' run like that."

"I'm not asking you what I know or don't know. Shall I repeat the exact question?"

Starley's head had begun aching. This wasn't the idea at all. He'd meant to shoot Stubbs into this cabin so the Skip could boot him out again with orders to pull his weight. This was a sight worse than the Old Bailey.

"No, sir. Every man in this ship's got a job and he does it. Except for Stubbs. I have to chase him, an' it makes my own job a deal harder. I don't do it just because I've got nothin' else to do."

There was silence; this was an impressive one, to the bosun, and it didn't worry him.

"You mentioned your last logging, Stubbs, just now. You say you reckon you deserved it. I remember at the

37

time you reckoned nothing of the kind. You left my cabin feeling very hard done by." He gazed bright-eyed at Stubbs, waiting.

"Well, it's natural, sir, isn' it? At the time, you always feel you're gettin' a bad break."

"It is very natural, yes. You are feeling it now. But later, are you going to 'reckon' you deserved it?"

"All I know is that I'm bein' chased about, an' I'm fed up, sir. Fed up."

"So is the bosun. This is very sad." He turned his stare upon Starley. "Have you anything you'd like to add to your accusations, Mr. Starley?"

"No, sir."

"Then you can go back on deck."

"Ay, ay, sir."

Starley shut the door firmly behind him. He didn't know what was going to happen about Stubbs, and he didn't give a curse. There was work to do, with a gale coming. All he knew was that the next time Stubbs gave him any trouble he'd knock him across the scuppers and call it a day.

In the quiet of the cabin, Harkness said gently:

"You hate his guts, don't you?"

Stubbs was surprised into a rueful grin. "I reckon we don't get on, sir."

"It may well be," said the captain sadly, "that he hates your guts too. It sometimes happens, in the close confinement of shipboard." He got up, and tucked his hands behind him, going to the scuttle and looking out at the sea. After a moment he said, with his back to Stubbs, "We have a gale forecast. We shall need to work well to run through it with the minimum possible discomfort to the passengers and ourselves, and the least possible damage to the cargo that is in our charge." He turned slowly to stare at Stubbs. "Your record is not the best. You must realise that, once off this ship, you'll not be signed on again, so long as Mr. Starley is bosun. You're prepared to accept that. There are many other ships. But at the moment you are serving in this one, and have certain obligations not only to me but to every other soul on board."

The deck gave a tilt, and Stubbs watched the gold-coloured curtain behind the captain hang away from the scuttle by a degree, two degrees, three, until it hung motionless. He waited for it to swing back, as it must. It hung without moving. The blurred white horizon did not appear. He felt the vibration of the engines under him, and heard timber creak as it lay strained to the angle. He must watch the curtain swing back. It hung where it was. Without knowing that he was going to speak, he said:

"She's listing, sir."

The curtain moved, a degree, two degrees, three, and swung back to lie against the edge of the scuttle. The vibration grew worse, then eased. The timber creaked again, then was silent.

Sweat pricked his scalp.

The captain said, gazing at Stubbs's cold face, "So that I am going to demand of you that until we reach port and you are paid off, you will work hard, as befits your responsibilities as a seaman on passage." Slowly Stubbs drew his eyes down from the curtain to the captain's face. "If you fail to carry out that order, I shall personally see to it that you are never given a berth again at sea as long as you live."

Stubbs had nothing in his mind to let him make an answer. He had been scared by the curtain. You always knew that when the ship rolled she'd go back; but you waited for it to happen, and sometimes waited for so long that it broke you down, slowly. On deck you could watch the sea and the ship, and sometimes see the crest that she was mounted on, and work out how many seconds it would be before she ran clear and righted. But here in the cabin, with the quiet stare of this shipmaster on him, his nerve had broken quickly, so that he had believed that it wasn't a roll but a list, and he had been forced by his nerves to tell someone, to shift some of his fear on to another man and make him share it.

Vaguely he was now aware that this man could share nothing he could give him, least of all fear.

"That is perfectly understood, Stubbs?"

"Yes, sir." He just wanted to go, get out of here. "Yes, sir."

"Then get on deck, and work."

When Stubbs had gone, Harkness lit a pipe, feeling the next uneasy roll of the ship and waiting for her to right. She was a good weatherly ship, neither stiff nor tender; she would be all right. But if the gale was a big one, a full force twelve, they would have to work hard into Avonmouth with all safe and the cargo sound.

When he had levelled the ash on his pipe and put the tobacco jar safely in the drawer he went on deck, meeting his boy in the alleyway and telling him to make things secure in his cabin. On the bridge the second mate was in his reefer, standing on the wing and watching the stern.

Harkness stood beside Beggs, shielding his pipe from the wind. The swell had drawn out farther, leaving fifty-yard troughs. The south sky was black. Above, there was dirty cloud-scum topping the milky haze that was brought up flying from the sea. Astern of the ship the waves rose twenty feet high, some of them broken by the stern before they were full-grown, others reaching their height and falling across the wake. When one of those waves timed it right, the *Whipper* would be pooped.

"What's our position, Jim?"

"Five minutes ago it was forty-nine north, fourteen twenty-one minutes west, sir. Course north seventy-two east." They watched the next sea coming. It looked taller than the rest, a big curler, maybe a seventh wave.

40

This one had timed it right. It swelled, lifting strongly until the wind tore at the crest and ripped white streamers from it; then it curled, and hung its great dark hook against the ship's taffrail; then it fell, exploding against the stern and blotting the poop-deck from sight until the welter went tiding across to the hatch-covers and leaping high against the side of the companionway, to fall again and join the main rush of water to the scuppers where the wash-doors banged. Number four hatch had taken it solid; the tarpaulins gleamed black as the last foam drained.

"She's pooped, sir!"

Harkness nodded. They felt the *Whipper* heaving bows to wind as the quartermaster held her back to the course. She yawed heavily and her mainmast shivered, the stays tautening on the one side and slackening on the other as the wind sang through. A knot of deck-hands were pressed round the port stanchion below the samson post; now they broke away and trotted round the coamings, making for the shelter aft of the bridge.

Harkness went into the wheelhouse and through into the chart-room to study the markings. When he came out he lit his pipe again and stood for a few minutes at one of the wheelhouse windows, to watch the sea and the sky. Turnbull came up and went into the wireless-room, then came and stood a few feet away from the captain, face to the window. He had put a reefer on. Harkness looked round.

"Mr. Beggs."

"Sir?" The big second mate came in from the wing.

"Find out our position."

"Ay, ay, sir."

Mr. Turnbull said, "The *Valenca*'s in trouble in Biscay, sir."

"*Valenca?* That's timber."

"Yes, sir. She's sent out a call, distress wavelength."

41

"Any reply?"

"*Abeille IV* is within an hour's steaming-distance. She's making there."

"Then she'll be all right." The *Abeille IV* was a deep-sea tug, the answer to a sailor's prayer.

"Yes, sir. This is pretty widespread. There's colliers making in along the west coast."

Beggs came out with his dead-reckoning. Harkness knocked the ash out of his pipe, bracing himself against the bulkhead as the ship gave a lurch. Vibration started as the screw came clear. There were shouts from below, and a distant tinkle of something breaking, crockery or glass. Ahead of the ship the sea was lost in haze that went flying above the troughs, veiling them. The open doors at each end of the wheelhouse were oblongs of black sky. The long-awaited gale was force eight or nine, and it was strengthening. A smaller ship, or a ship this size in ballast, would have turned about before now, to lie hove-to.

Beggs and Turnbull were waiting, already obeying in detail the order that must soon come. The helmsman worked steadily at the wheel, finding the seas and meeting them, waiting for the next and judging it and meeting it, keeping his stance on the grating as the *Whipper* rolled, yawing and planing as the sea crept to the quarter and sent the wheel alive.

"Mr. Turnbull, is all secure?"

The first mate answered almost before the question was out. "All secure, sir. I went round after the bosun."

"Very good." Harkness went over to the telephone and got through to the engine-room. "Chief? We're going to come about and heave-to for a bit. I shall want two or three minutes' full speed as soon as you're ready. Yes. Thank you, Chief." He hooked the telephone back and looked round for the third mate. Costain was here; he had not seen him come. Costain, he thought, was reliable for his age. He said to him, "Tell the chief steward to go

42

round the passengers. We are turning about in a few minutes, so that we can ride quiet until the gale passes. Absolutely no cause for alarm, but things will be a bit noisy."

"Ay, ay, sir." Costain left the bridge.

"Mr. Turnbull, we'd better shut all watertight doors. Chief won't be ready for a few minutes."

Turnbull went below. The captain stood by a window again, reaching there in time to see spindrift racing in a white cloud past the bridge and foremast from a shipped sea aft.

"Mr. Beggs, have a signal sent to the owners. We are heaving-to until the gale abates. Ship in good trim and all happy aboard."

"Ay, ay, sir."

A metal door clanged below the fo'c'sle head; the sound was whipped away. Timber was straining under his feet and behind him; it was a contenting sound, the easy give-and-take of flexible structure dealing with a stress that would break a more rigid design. There was very little welding in this ship; she was built with rivet and joint and would give the seas best as they came for her, but only to a degree, enough to weaken their force and leave her own strength untouched. He had all faith in her and in her crew.

A minute passed and she was pooped again, and he watched the rush of white past the starboard door. As it died away and merged with the haze ahead a telephone rang and he picked it up.

"Engine-room, sir. Ready when you are."

"Thank you, Chief." He hung up and crossed to the binnacle, watching the card and lifting his eyes to watch the sea. He said to the quartermaster, "Wilson, stand by to come about to starb'd."

"Stand by to come about to starb'd, sir!"

Harkness watched the waves and felt a seventh hit the

43

stern, a big one that lifted the screw out and sent a blizzard of spindrift past the bridge. When the wave was rolling ahead clear of the bows he reached his hand to the telegraph and gave a double ring Full Ahead.

They felt the rise of the engines in the deck, and the stern go slowly down to the screw's thrust. A minute passed, and he said to the helmsman:

"Hard a-starboard."

"Hard a-starb'd, sir!"

The *Whipper* began to turn. The sea came round to her starboard beam and slowed her, and she leaned to port, and shook herself. A wave took her and she leaned badly, then came back and began wallowing half-way through the turn with the sea full on the beam. Her speed had been drawn down as she began struggling to bring her bows into the face of the gale.

The helmsman worked hard, giving a spoke and taking it back. The captain watched the compass bowl, the glow of its light on his quiet face as his ship was made to fight from the worst position, beam-on and broached-to, with the seas coming hard.

"Ease her."

"Ease her, sir."

She leaned again as a sea came, pounding her plates; then she wallowed with the helm slack in her mouth until Harkness said, "Bring her back to starb'd."

"Bring her back to starb'd, sir!"

She found her shoulder against the seas and held it there until she took a big one on the flare of her bow. It struck at full height and was sent climbing in a hard white fountain across the fo'c'sle head before the wind took it and broke it away into haze. In the moment of the impact a sharp sound came from below for'ard, a cracking of timber that was loud even in the wheelhouse.

Captain Harkness looked up from the compass bowl and saw Turnbull staring at him.

FIVE

In the engine-room the chief engineer heard the crack and looked at the Third, who stared back at him. Their expressions were very different. Mr. Brewer was close on thirty but still a boy to look at, perhaps because he was below average height and brushed his putty-yellow hair straight across from the parting and had nothing of the sophistication of his age in his appearance. He was a chief engineer-officer of the new kind that was finding its way to ships and to the sea: educated boys, some of them from universities, their heads packed with theory and their hands inexperienced. Many went back to the land; those who stayed were among the best of them.

"Christ!" said Brewer. "What was that?" He had given a brief explosive laugh when the noise had sounded above the high sweet run of the Kincaird engines. It was the sort of laugh anyone would give when his best friend became merry and suddenly took his trousers off to amuse the company: a laugh of shocked amusement tempered by the thought that he must shortly get out of here, or his trouserless friend might claim him in front of everyone. Brewer, for a man who was certainly no prig, had a sense of the rightness of things. Sudden disorder shocked and amused him. He had given this familiar laugh of his a few weeks ago when a dockside crane had dropped a four-hundredweight crate of glassware into the dock. He had enjoyed the noise and been impressed by the comment of the boss stevedore who had been standing beside him; but his real shock derived from the disorderliness of this event.

His third engineer, Gyorgy János, was unable to understand this peculiar sense of humour. He stared at his chief with his thoughts almost visibly written in his eyes.

Brewer stood listening, his hands stuck into the belt of his white overalls. The sound might come again, and give a clue to its direction. He thought it was from for'ard somewhere. It had been a very disorderly sound, the kind to alarm a less confident man.

The Third said something in Hungarian. They both waited. János was watching a rag tied to a rail; one of the greasers had knotted it there, so that he would find it easily. It was hanging away from the vertical by ten or fifteen degrees. The ship was broached-to and still trying to go full round and finish up head-to-sea. János became slowly fascinated by the hang of the greaser's rag.

Mr. Brewer put his hand on the telephone, but decided against calling the bridge. They would be busy up there, trying to bring the ship round; he must not interrupt a manœuvre that in this sea was difficult. They would have heard the noise; he was certain of that.

János watched the rag with a child's serious interest. He was much bigger than the chief, with a massive head and fine features; he expressed much with his eyes. They sparked as the telephone rang and he watched Brewer pick it up.

It sounded like Peter.

"You all right down there, Chief?"

"I'm fine. How are you?"

"Did you hear that crack?"

"Not half. What was it?"

Costain said, "We don't know."

"Well, it wasn't the mainshaft. It came from well for'ard of here, I'd say."

"We'll find out. We're still turning."

"I know. We're standing on the bulkheads down here. Can we do anything to help?"

"Keep steam up."

"Naturally." He put the telephone back on to its hook. János was still watching him. Brewer shrugged. The bridge didn't know. They could feel the ship fighting to get her head round, with the helmsman giving her a bit and then taking it back; the rag moved a degree and moved out again from the vertical. They watched the gauges and listened to the beat of the pistons. The sinews of the ship were alive about them as she fought to complete her turn. János looked deeply unhappy, his quick imagination trying to riot and unnerve him. Brewer did not move away from the telegraph. He expected it to ring. They both looked now and then at the greaser's rag. It had hung out like that for a long time.

Above them and for'ard the chief steward was trying to push a tray-stack back on to its shelf, so that he could fix the movable ledge and lock it. He was poised on the balls of his feet, his arms out straight, his hands braced against the trays, so that when the roll of the ship corrected he could push them in and fix the ledge. He had stood like this for half a minute now, and had begun sweating. He had begun trying to push the ship back straight, as well as the trays. He didn't like this. They were playing a fine bloody game up there on the bridge.

An assistant steward looked in, his face a muddy white.

"Stack o' crocks gone, Jack."

"I heard. Give a hand with this lot."

The assistant steward lent his weight. Jack Persham could feel the aura of fear about the man. They both pushed at the heavy steel trays and shifted them back. Persham snapped the ledge up and flipped the end-bolts. He stood away and wiped his face, looking at Dodds, giving him a cigarette.

"Why aren't you in your bunk, mate?"

"I couldn't sleep, with this lot." They lit up, but Dodds wouldn't meet his eyes. "What was that noise, Jack?"

"God knows."

"It wasn't the crocks."

47

"Bose has been through, checkin' up." They had turned to look at the porthole, but they could see nothing outside except flying white spray. The deck under them was still on the tilt. It must be a full minute now. Persham smoked nervously, his anxiety deepened by the colour of Dodds's face. It had been an awful crack, and this was a nasty list. The ship was out of hand. He took another lungful of smoke and nipped the cigarette out, dropping it neatly into the top pocket of his jacket. "I better go an' calm the passengers."

The chief steward left him, limping down the alley-way as if one leg had become shorter than the other. It was a list, all right. She wasn't going back. They'd all be in a state, the passengers. He was in quite a state, himself.

He found Mr. and Mrs. Jocelyn standing in the main doorway to the promenade deck, on the lee side.

"I'll have to shut those doors I'm afraid, sir."

"All right." Jocelyn gave him a hand with the vertical bolts while his wife stood back and watched them. She lit a new cigarette from the butt of the last. She said when the steward straightened up:

"What's all the excitement?"

"No excitement, madam. We're jus' comin' about."

Jocelyn looked at Persham with a smooth bland face. "We got the message about that, but no one's told us what the noise was." He stood with his hands in the pockets of his uncreased gaberdine slacks, looking like a gentleman-beachcomber in his shirt and cotton scarf. "I mean that cracking noise."

Persham darted to the scuttle along the bulkhead, calling over his shoulder, "Noise, sir?" He slammed the scuttle and fixed the catch, hoping as he swung round to see something else that needed immediate securing, before they could question him more fully. He didn't know what the noise had been. He thought that if it was nothing worse than the foremast splitting in half they were all lucky.

Penny Jocelyn, a small pert woman with lovely eyes and a cat-like grip on life, said to her husband, "Are you really a good swimmer, Pooch?"

He watched Persham dodging round the tables in the saloon, checking on their chains. "M'm?"

"I mean, have you done life-saving and everything?"

He smiled suddenly, and his fresh round face went amiable again. "Balls. Let's go and get a little drinkie. Someone might know something." He thought for a moment that under his feet he could feel the ship righting herself, but he couldn't be sure. This was the first time he'd been on the sea, except for fishing-boats round the coast, and his inexperience gave him nothing to go on. Was this a bad angle for the ship to take? What had that breaking noise been? Someone had said it was crockery smashing, but he knew that wasn't right. Why were the stewards lying? He preferred going in aeroplanes. Next time he'd take a nice clean aeroplane; one good meal and you were there.

His wife took his hand and they edged along the port side of the saloon towards the bar. At the bar was little Papasian, sitting as upright as he could. They had never seen him at the bar before; he was usually glimpsed for a couple of seconds, darting into the toilets or across to the rail with short delicate steps and a green face, hurrying as unobtrusively as it was possible to any haven where he could privately deliver himself of his misery.

"Would you like to join me in a drink?" He managed a smile, hopping off the stool and waiting until Mrs. Jocelyn had sat down, then hopping up again, the gold tooth winking its welcome as he smiled, the yellow brief-case tucked beneath his arm. The only thing they knew about him was that he was an Armenian.

"On us," said Jocelyn, feeling for money. Tonio, behind the bar, was looking pleased with them. He liked passengers who made for the bar in time of uneasiness.

He hoped, when he grew old enough to be tired of keeping young, that he would be giving such passengers as these their last drink when the siren sounded abandon ship.

"Please no," said Dr. Papasian, and put down a note, nearly toppling from the stool because his left arm was permanently incapacitated by the yellow brief-case. Jocelyn steadied him.

"Well," he said politely, "thank you, sir." He looked at his wife. "We'd love a Scotch."

"For me," Dr. Papasian said as Tonio got a brandy glass, "cognac."

"Cognac, Doctor. Two Scotch."

Everything suddenly shook: the counter, the bottles, glasses, mirrors, artificial flowers, the stools under them. Then it was over.

Tonio had paused, so that he should not spill the brandy. He set the glass down so close to Dr. Papasian and so near the edge of the bar that he must pick it up at once. It would be safer in his hand.

"Cheers," said the Jocelyns when they had their drinks.

"Cheeri-ho," said the little man. His idiom was too studied, but this was almost the only imperfection in his English. Alan Jocelyn was trying to think how the man was able to come here and have a drink when the ship was roughing it; throughout the earlier smooth crossing he had been plagued by sickness. Or had he made up his mind to get quickly sloshed, and thus anæsthetise himself?

"For you," Dr. Papasian was saying. Tonio thanked him with pleased surprise, perfectly simulated, and reached for the bottle of Valdepeñas that he kept behind him in a corner. As a child he had gone up the hillside every autumn to help his family pluck at the vines, and had mastered the family *porrón* before he was ten, trickling the light young wine expertly into his throat with his eyes closed against the burning turquoise sky and his sister Maria's voice in his ears, for she was always singing and had sung until she died of the tubercle. Now he drank from the round plain glass, his head first inclined in thanks to the doctor, his feet braced to the angle of the deck, his eyes open to watch the flying horizon beyond the windows, but with these old memories on his tongue; for this was the same wine, perhaps even from the same hillside.

The vibration came again, and he thought of mentioning it, saying it was just the screw coming out of the sea and meant nothing at all bad; but the little doctor was perched with his nose buried in the fumy glass and the English couple were turned to watch the windows and the sea. They were not interested in the vibration, so Tonio did not mention it.

In her cabin, Miss Brown filled another blue-tinted page, still rather proud of the monogram in the top corner with the ship's name below it. For a few more precious hours her address would be this tiny moving island somewhere in the Atlantic. Miss A. K. Brown, on board the *Atlantic Whipper*, at sea. It should go on like this for always, always, with the bright veneered woodwork and rich curtains and the rose-shaded lamp, and outside the clean wide world of the sea and sky, enormous enough to be lost in and never found, never brought back, never called Brownie again nor requested not to water the window-box so carelessly that drips went down into the area, nor warned that the milkman had called three times this week for his money and would stop leaving her any on Saturday, nor asked to be firmer with Tommy Watson who was badly in need of discipline. . . . Poor Tommy, was he still there beyond the horizon with his red face and squint and steel-rimmed spectacles, kicking at the girls, at the teachers, at the table-legs if there were nothing better handy?

This breathless winging life could not go on for very long, even if she could afford to give up her work and to travel where she chose; because of Tommy. He needed her ankle to kick when his miniature rage sought the only relief within reach and his eyes were red with watching the laughter—the silent unhearable and unbearable laughter of small cruel mouths—when the others felt the need of an easy clown to make their fun with. She would go back tomorrow (tomorrow was as sad a word as yesterday), and be careful not to let the water drip, and not to forget the milkman's money; but she would not be firmer with Tommy. She must make a resolution for the small new year of her landfall; and it would be that.

She wrote again. *It has been utterly perfect, and if it is the last real holiday I ever take, I shall always remember it. It probably will be, too! I had no idea how much the little extras would come to—but I mustn't start regretting the expense. It has been worth it, every single penny.* She looked up from the paper. It would be her last chance of even mentioning his name. Once on the land again this heady champagne mood would go, and she would never tell a soul, even his name. This would be the last chance of leaking just a little of the miracle away, before she drowned in it. There was no need to say much. *By the way, I have been . . .* been what? Dancing . . . *dancing with an awfully nice young officer on board, and he's . . .* and he's what? Wonderful— can't put wonderful, shouldn't have started this at all. Tear up the page and begin again? Why should I be frightened, spinsterly and naïve and scared of even mentioning his name? He's magnificent, and kind, and in a way very boyish, though his eyes are like young eagles' eyes when he watches the sea—he must love the sea; no one could not love it, and he's so obviously at home with the sea and the ship . . . *been telling me all about the ship. His name is Peter.*

Peter Costain.

I expect I shall see you before this letter reaches you, so I suppose it's rather absurd.

Absurd to be going back, or absurd to have come away, half the world away? She wrote: *with love*, and signed the letter, uncrossing her legs and leaning back along the padded seat, to think about him and try to see his thin young face and the way his eyes changed when he looked at the sea, and changed again when he looked at her. Peter Costain. Would it be very long before she could hear that name spoken by chance, and not remember, not feel her heart go tight and her breath catch? How many years? When the year came, bringing so great a forgetfulness, she would be old, very old. There would not be another Peter, because . . . one knew these things, one felt them. There wouldn't be any more impulsive trips to South America, costing the last penny of her savings; and at home there was too much to do and think about, too little time to let herself become interested in—in anything like that, and besides . . . besides nothing—she didn't have to explain to herself why there wouldn't be another Peter. So, when she was old, and someone said his name, she wouldn't remember.

She wouldn't remember anyone called Peter Costain. After tomorrow she'd never see him again, and by this time next year would have forgotten what he looked like and the sound of his voice; another year and her memory would play tricks by sly degrees and change him little by little so that the fine dark hair would perhaps lighten, and the shape of his chin alter, his whole face change so that she would be thinking of a face that was not his nor anyone's, only a dream face with a dream voice masquerading in his name because she had to remember Peter (more and more desperately as the years went by) and what he looked like. But she would be looking at the ghost-face of someone who had never existed. The time would come when by chance she might catch a glimpse of the real face, Peter Costain's face, and not recognise it because the face in her mind, recomposed by a failing

53

memory, would be utterly different. In a few years. . . . She tried to think of fresh tortures for her mind to purge itself with. This bitterness must be got over before she reached home. There mustn't be any quiet shutting of the door, and the dusty embrace of the old familiar loneliness, and then the thoughts of Peter whom she would never see again. No sudden pangs, no tears and no self-pity, up in that small high room; because up there she would not be able to bear with it. She must get it over now.

These tears were not deliberate. She wanted to cry, to be rid of them; but she could not have manufactured this suddenly blinding misery that took hold of her now and left her crumpled on the padded seat with her slight body shaking and her breath fast as if she drowned.

The knock at the cabin door was quick and brusque; the door was opened before she could call out, and for an instant she was scandalised by the violation of her privacy as she flicked a hand to her face, brushing away tears and covering her mouth to still the tremulous breathing.

Peter was astonished, and closed the door, coming to her quickly. "Darling . . . it's all right." He was crouching in front of her, taking her wet cold hands; she knew he was watching her face and thinking how ugly the sobbing had made it; and this thought, together with his presence and immediate sympathy out of the blue, brought the tears freely again, and she tore her hands away from his so that she could cover her red ugly face.

He held her shoulders. "Darling, it's honestly all right, honestly. We're only turning about, because of the weather." He must make her understand; she mustn't be as frightened as this. He remembered the Skip's phrase, and used it to persuade her. "There's absolutely no cause for alarm. We're all perfectly safe, darling. Please, Ann . . . please."

She wriggled away from him, nearly falling as she crossed the cabin, forgetting the angle of the floor. She

54

found a handkerchief; to Costain it looked as though a whole white-laced cloud of them came blossoming out of the drawer. She snivelled and tried to pick some of them up, and he helped her. "Gosh, what a lot of handkerchiefs."

She blew her nose. "I seem to need them, don't I? A permanent waterworks." They both stood up, with most of the handkerchiefs back in their drawer. She was smiling.

He said gently, "It's perfectly all right, darling. I know it's noisy, and we're tilting over a bit, but it's honestly quite safe."

She smiled again, bravely, and let him hold her.

"Honestly, Peter?"

"Of course. But I know how you feel. As a matter of fact the Skip sent me down to let everyone know there's nothing to worry about."

"Then—then that's all right. That's fine." She gave a last snivel and tucked the hanky away. He could scarcely bear his pity for her, for this slender body that still trembled a little in his arms, for this small hot face with the tears wet on it. He had never been so sorry for anyone in his whole life, and this was an attractive girl who only last night had let him . . . it was almost unbearable. He stroked her soft brown hair.

"Poor darling little Ann, poor darling heart."

She began laughing. "I'm laughing at myself, Peter." The laughter made her body tremble again, and he held her closer. Oh God, if only the ship weren't in trouble, with the captain on the bridge and orders flying about . . . if only there were a few minutes, now. . . . "Darling, darling Ann."

She made him let her go. "Peter, you mustn't stay. You're on duty."

He had to make the effort; she was right. If anyone found him here—Turnbull, perhaps!—with a passenger in

55

his arms at a time like this when the ship was . . . Could say she'd broken down when he was reassuring her . . . only obeying orders, calming the passengers . . . this one was very frightened, and . . .

"You must go, Peter. Please. I'm all right now, honestly." She went to the door. "You mustn't get into trouble." He moved and stood with her for a moment, making her kiss him. The feel of her hot mouth and the salt of her tears sent him dizzy again with pity and with love. She pushed him away.

"I'll get into trouble too, for keeping you here." He nodded, not able to speak. When he put his hand on the door-catch she caught him again suddenly and rubbed the back of her hand against his mouth, laughing softly again. "Lip-stick . . . they'd murder you!"

"Oh, my Lord!"

"It's all right now."

He opened the door, touching her hand quickly. "Listen, darling. The ship's perfectly safe. If there's a lot of noise, or anything, just remember. There's absolutely no cause for alarm."

Quickly she said, "I'll remember. I'm not frightened now."

He left her, shutting the door and hurrying along the alleyway, padding one hand along the bulkhead to steady himself, listening to a sound that must be Ann laughing aloud in her cabin, alone there and laughing . . . giving in to relief, it must be, now that he had told her it was all right and there was no danger . . . always crying or laughing, sometimes both at once, until you didn't know where the hell you were or what you'd done or what she was going to do next . . . poor darling Ann. . . . His hand went padding along, hitting the bulkhead. Gosh, were they all like that, when you got to know them, or was it only the marvellous ones like Ann who could let themselves go and make you feel . . . oh gosh! The others hadn't been like that, before. This was dynamite, but he didn't want to be careful any more. He was ready for blasting.

"Dodds!" The steward was coming along from the pantry, with a sick-looking face. "Knock at number nine, and ask if Miss Brown would like a drink brought. Brandy, or something."

"Nine, sir?"

"She's worried. Ask her if she'd like anything."

He went on past the steward and shot up the companion-way, making back to the bridge. Thank God the Skip had sent him to reassure the passengers. She would have been so lost, crying alone in there. Poor darling Ann. It had made him feel very strong, suddenly. A man. In love. God, what a time to fall in love, with the ship broached-to in a heavy gale and a noise like the crack of doom down for'ard somewhere.

He climbed to the bridge, pushed aloft by the gusts of wind that were sending water along the decks in a stiff fluttering cloud that stung his neck as he clambered on to the bridge-end where the lookout stood huddled and alert.

He tugged the door open and slammed it behind him. The wheelhouse was quiet, the Skip and Beggs and the quartermaster all standing quietly, engrossed in their work. He wiped the spray from his neck and tried to compose himself and fit into this haven of calm.

"Ease her."

"Ease her, sir."

Timber creaked. The deck shifted under them. Spray hit the glass panel of the door. The captain watched the sea.

"Mr. Costain."

"Sir?"

"How do you find the passengers?"

"Fine, sir. Not worried."

"Very good."

57

The deck shifted under them. A thin cackle of Morse came from the doorway of the wireless-room. Outside, the gale sang in the shrouds. They could feel the ship meeting each sea and slowly overcoming it, wallowing to meet the next and overcoming it, until the quartermaster felt the great strain go out of the wheel as the bows began cutting into the waves and breaking their force. The sea was no longer pounding at the flat plates along the starboard side but was being brought obliquely across the bows; and the bows dipped and rose and ploughed the big waters and shipped them, tossed them and dropped them across the fo'c'sle and sent them washing into the scuppers and away.

"Ease her."

"Ease her, sir."

The light from the compass bowl cast a sick blue sheen on the captain's face as he watched the card. Mr. Beggs stood near the windows, judging the sea. Costain was by the door to the starboard wing, his excitement gone, replaced by a calm contemplation of this scene in here. The Skip was good to watch: he stood quite still and yet it seemed he was moving strongly with his ship and with the sea that was their enemy. Beggs loomed beyond him, with not a hint of movement in his big body; but when he looked once across at Costain, the third mate could see the thoughts there in the steady eyes of the man. Wide open and intelligent, they were reviewing the entire situation with an appraisal as primitive as an animal's. The sea had become a hunter and this brain was finely tuned to meet the threat.

"Midships."

"Midships, sir."

A wave caught the flare of her bow and she yawed to it.

"Wheel's amidships, sir!"

The *Whipper* was round, her head to the sea and the gale. The fo'c'sle was already lost in a smother of white.

"Steady . . ."

"Steady, sir." The midships spoke came up. "Course, sir! South, thirty-one degrees west."

Harkness stared into the compass bowl with a fortune-teller's concentration. In a few seconds he brought his head up and looked at the sea.

"Steer south thirty-five west."

"Steer south thirty-five west, sir." The quartermaster put the wheel down starboard. The captain watched the sea and the lie of it. "Course south thirty-five degrees west, sir!"

"Very good."

He moved to the telegraph and rang Half Ahead to keep steerage-way. It was no longer quiet in here. The gale hit the windows and they became semi-opaque under the hail of spindrift.

The second mate had moved away from the windows and stood watching the inclinometer. For a moment Harkness joined him. The list was fifteen degrees. Harkness said above the noise, "See how Mr. Turnbull is getting on."

"Ay, ay, sir." Beggs braced the door open against the wind's force and banged it shut behind him. Turnbull would be on deck for'ard with the bosun's team and all spare hands. That was where the crack had come from.

Harkness went into the wireless-room and said to Bond:

"To owners: *Position forty-nine ten minutes north, thirteen fifty minutes west. Am hove-to in south-westerly gale.*" He went to the doorway into the wheelhouse as the first mate came up. Turnbull's black oilskins were astream with water. He was breathing hard and there was a red gash on his hand.

"Shifting-boards gone in number two, sir. The grain's shifted. We're doing what we can to trim it now."

Harkness stood listening to the slam of the wind against the superstructure.

59

"What was the condition of the shifting-boards in Buenos Aires?"

"Good condition, sir."

"You checked them yourself, Mr. Turnbull?"

"Yes, sir."

Harkness watched the windows. The spray flew against them, bursting. "Do what you can."

"Ay, ay, sir."

When he had gone, Harkness turned back and said to Bond:

"Add to that message: *Cargo shifted. List fifteen degrees. No anxiety.*"

He watched the wireless operator working. When he had finished, Harkness said, "Send the same complete message to P.O. for distribution."

Bond's hands went to the dials. "Require assistance, sir?"

"No. All we want is some shovels, Mr. Bond."

The captain went into the wheelhouse and said to Costain:

"It's close on tea-time. I'm going below, to take some tea with the passengers, should you want me."

"Ay, ay, sir." Costain watched him walk down the tilt of the deck to the wheelhouse door. Before he opened it he turned his head and looked at the third mate.

"I'll send a steward up. Tea or cocoa?"

It sounded important. Costain's face lost its strain as he smiled. "Cocoa please, sir."

The captain nodded, and pushed open the door.

SIX

THE bosun had twenty-four men with him on the foredeck where the seas were coming in white-peaked mountains that shattered as the ship ran into them. As they shattered the wind tore the fragments away and drove them stinging across the deck so that the men would hunch and take the water on their backs and then work on again until the next wave crashed over the bows and the salt-blast struck at them and they stood with their feet braced in whirling water; then they worked on again until the next wave came, and the next, while the bows of the *Whipper* went into them and clove them and shipped them boiling white across the fo'c'sle head. The wind drove low, pressing the funnel smoke down to the lifting crests and howling through the shrouds and stays and aerials so that the ship was loud with hellish music as she wallowed head to weather, keeping her steerage-way and letting the seas come, and meeting them, sometimes lifting her bows above a wave as the last one ran astern and left a trough, sometimes butting her bows down and cleaving a wave at the base so that water came green against the winches and broke there in a burst of spume that could hardly rise before the wind struck and drove it across the foredeck and hatches and bridge.

Art Starley worked his men at the after end of number two hatch, above the hold where the grain had shifted. They had loosed the battens and drawn half the tarpaulin back, rigging it as best they could at an angle to protect the others as they worked in the narrow gap between the boards and the after coaming. When the bosun had piped them on deck they had fought their way against the wind to the forestore for shovels; now they were out of the wind, shielded by the rigged tarpaulin that took the main force of each ragged gust as it flung white water flat against it with a percussion that numbed the ears.

The men who worked with the shovels waded knee-deep in the grain, driving the shovel-blades down and turning them, shifting the grain from the port side to the starboard, digging and sending it flying in the half-light of the dying afternoon, digging and bringing it up and sending it scattering through the gloom until their boots sank deeper and they must drag them out and stand on the shifting surface and then slowly sink again as their shovels dug, and drove, and flung, dug, and drove, and flung the grain aside while their muscles burned and the sweat ran stinging in their eyes.

They were standing on top of a thousand tons of grain, ants in a sugar-bowl. Only now, after thirty minutes' toil, were they beginning to realise that this was a fortnight's job under their feet.

Starley clambered over the coaming and picked on two spare hands. "Go an' ask the chief engineer if we can have two shovels from the stokehold!" He watched them dart away, dodging through spindrift, then turned and shouted to Wilson and Copley; but water exploded against the tarpaulin and his mouth moved in silence.

"You two! *You two!*" They looked up, their faces bright with sweat and their chests heaving. He pointed to Mounsey and Smithers, who were braced with their backs to the edge of the tarpaulin, their hands dragging down on the ropes. "Change places, you lot!"

Copley, a five-foot-nothing deck-hand on his first trip deep-sea, stuck his shovel into the grain and scrambled out, catching his sea-boot and going down spread-eagled as another man brought his shovel back with a swing and deflected the blade in time. "Christ, I thought you was a beetle, boy!"

"Jump to it, Copley!"

His feet scattered the grain. Someone gave him a hand as Smithers dropped and took up his shovel. The tarpaulin above them cracked as the wind struck it; a rope skinned through a man's hand; he cried out in pain and grabbed the slack, lashing it round the crook of his elbow; the shovels hit the grain and lifted it in dull gold showers.

Copley clung to his rope, feeling the wind trying to take the tarpaulin. Was it strong enough, the wind, to rip the corner away and take him with it on the rope? The rope jerked in his hands; he took another bight when it slackened for an instant; if the lot went up he must go up with it, and that was that. He had to hang on, and bring his slight weight down when the wind tugged, and keep the rope like a live thing trembling in his arms, and feel it trying to lift him bodily and drag him upwards into the great strong flight of the wind and flick him into the sea. The bosun had given him the job and he'd have to do it, and when he'd done it he'd go below and sick up all the fright that was in him now.

He saw the banners of spray go flying against the superstructure and breaking to a mist that came sucking back as the gust blew out; he shut his eyes and took the sting of the water in his face; he clenched up his face like a knuckle and clung to the rope, and dragged on it, and felt it lift him, and dragged again while the spent spray went trickling down his neck, chilling him under the oilskin. He got his breath and opened his eyes, re-establishing himself in this vast explosive world of wind that could whirl him aloft, taking the tarpaulin, the rope and this whippet-thin boy before he could free himself. He felt it happening, time after time as the wind whipped and the rope went tight; and he wanted to be sick at the thought, and thus get rid of it. If the wind took him, the sea would kill him; but if he didn't hang on, the bosun would.

"Smithers! *Smithers!* Get back 'ere to the coamin'

before that shovel brains you! Keep over this way, you stupid git!"

The shovels went in, and lifted, slinging the grain aside while the ship wallowed and shifted it back. The men swore at the grain and the wind and the sea, and dug their shovels in, and turned the blades, and sent the grain to starboard while the ship took water along her side and shifted the grain to port.

"Let's see you bloody well work, then! Where's yer spunk, you bunch o' bleedin' sparrers?"

But Starley was working with them, harder than most; and they knew it, and drove themselves, with the tune and their own pet words to it running through their heads. . . . 'Starley is a bar-stid, a bar-stid, a bar-stid . . .' while they dug their shovels in and slung the grain aside, and the ship rolled, and slung it back.

They had worked for an hour. Two shovels were broken and a seaman had been dragged out of the hold unconscious, blood streaming from his head where it had caught the edge of the coaming as he had lost his balance on the shifting grain. Under a thick scud of cloud the light was fading. Water had been taken in as a wind-gust veered and sent a wash of it below the tarpaulin and into the hold.

Starley groped his way to where the first mate was braced against a samson post, and cupped his hands.

"We're not gettin' anywhere, sir!"

Turnbull jerked his head away as a drift of white spume smothered them. The water ran from their faces. He would have liked to tell the bosun to keep the hands working until the grain was back and the ship was eased from her list, even if they worked till their hearts burst and they dropped; but this hardness in him was not from any spite. In times like these Turnbull was at his best, and the ship was his only concern, and the men in her, even if they must work till they fell in order that she would be helped in her struggle with the sea.

"We'll never shift it, sir, in this weather!"

Turnbull opened the slit of his mouth. "Get them out. Get the tarpaulin back and batten down."

"Ay, ay, sir!"

They came out, bringing their shovels, exhausted as much by their knowledge that they had accomplished nothing as by the jading pace at which they had worked.

"Those two shovels, back to the stokehold. The rest in the forestore. Copley, what's the matter with you?"

"Nothing, sir." He was huddled over his stomach, a bundle of creased oilskins with a pinched white face.

"Get below." He swung round and saw the carpenters. "Take these two an' mend 'em, lively. We'll want 'em again, any time." He gave them the broken shovels. "Wilson!"

Wilson dodged towards him. Starley jerked a hand in young Copley's direction. "Take the kid below an' see he's all right."

"Yes, bose."

"Rest of you on the tarpaulin—lively, now!"

Against the wind and the torn water that was driving across the foredeck they worked while the daylight faded about them, putting the boards back and dragging the tarpaulin over them, slinging the battens down and making them fast. The wooden chocks were swollen with water, and would hardly budge.

From the bridge, Beggs and Costain saw the men finish the work and struggle in a group for the shelter of the companionway. Beggs turned from the windows and looked at the inclinometer. The mean reading was still fifteen degrees.

.   .   .   .

Captain Harkness had left his coat in his room before going along to the saloon for tea. He had also brushed his hair and corrected his tie. Along the alleyway he had filled his pipe and lit it, so that when he entered the saloon he was looking spruce and unworried. Persham, the chief steward, was handy to receive him formally.

"Tea, sir?"

"If you please."

But there was a bleakness about the saloon. There were only four people here: Mr. and Mrs. Jocelyn, Dr. Papasian and Major Draycott. The movement of the deck was not too bad, but the list was noticeable. Major Draycott, a thin yellow-faced man whose Army days had ended a long time ago, was sitting alone at the foremost table on the port side, reading a battered book. The Jocelyns were more at their ease, talking to the little Armenian, and when Harkness came in, Alan Jocelyn got up and met him amiably.

"Are you going to join us, sir?"

"If I may, Mr. Jocelyn."

Dr. Papasian stood up as they reached the table, his gold tooth winking its welcome. It was quite extraordinary, Jocelyn thought, how the rough weather had seemed to cure him of his sea-sickness. He had drunk three brandies and was ready for tea.

"Hello, Captain." Penny Jocelyn put a lot into it, making it sound as if she had said Cap, or Skipper. She liked Harkness; she considered him a really wonderful hunk of a male. He had a face like a slightly crumpled balloon and a figure that was dead square whichever way you looked at it; but there was so much strength in the man that it shone out of his pale blue eyes—not just muscle-power, but a bigness of will and spirit that was evident in his very calm. "Come and sit down," she said, and made it sound like Come and Sit with Me.

He turned a bland smile on her. "Thank you."

"What's it like on top?" asked Jocelyn. It was the first of the questions that Harkness was down here to answer. He was ready for them all.

"Windy." He left his bland smile on; it was correct wear for a captain taking tea with worried passengers. "Rather windy."

Penny Jocelyn said from beside him, "I'll bet it's a real whizzer, on deck."

He appeared to consider the word. "That would be a very fair description, Mrs. Jocelyn. A whizzer."

Two stewards brought trays and set them out. "I wonder," said Harkness, "if we should ask Major Draycott if he'd care to join us? He seems rather lonely."

The chief steward was ready to take the message, balanced on one foot; but Mrs. Jocelyn was slipping out of her chair. "I'll get him." The angle of the deck didn't seem to trouble her. Alan Jocelyn watched her lean both hands on the Major's table so that she could look directly and appealingly at him with their faces on the same level. From where he sat, Jocelyn admired the taut angle of her body as she leaned on her hands. She really was a lavish little wench; she used it on everybody, young and old, provided they were trousered. He watched the Major take his horn-rimmed glasses off and struggle to his feet; the book dropped, and she quickly stooped and laid it on the table still open. The poor old boy looked disturbed, as if his quiet reading had been interrupted, however pleasantly; except that Jocelyn knew that in the past half an hour he hadn't turned a page. Had his fine-boned face looked as yellow as that, before the gale had come? It was difficult to remember an exact shade of yellow.

When Draycott had sat down with them he seemed as lonely as he had been before, and less at ease. Penny said to him:

"The Captain's turned us round, Major. Back to the South American sunshine, since the weather's so filthy in England."

It was a silly enough remark but she had thrown it to him as a small lifebelt in his loneliness; he would have to think of an answer, and then she could pull him in. But the silence became awkward; he didn't seem to realise at once that he was being saved. He had clearly heard, for he was looking at her; but no faint change came to the yellow skin, no hint of a smile.

"You're not very well-informed, Mrs. Jocelyn." She relaxed. His voice was gentle, though it seemed a slight effort for him to use it. "According to the latest reports there were bright patches in Manchester, yesterday morning."

He blinked to the slight shock of the laughter that went round; his eyes had the defensive look of a man who shies from attention.

"Then we shall certainly turn about again," said Harkness, "as soon as we can. That shouldn't be very long, perhaps a few hours. I'm sorry, though, that we're meeting with this delay. The wireless-room is ready to send any messages to friends ashore, if anyone is being met at the dockside."

"I've always longed," said Penny, "to cultivate the kind of friend who'd wait for me on a dockside in winter at two in the morning." She crooked her hands in front of her dramatically. "Maybe it's because I don't *give* enough of myself."

Jocelyn murmured, "Oh, surely not." She gave him a quick fierce grimace. Major Draycott said:

"I assume the cargo has shifted?"

Captain Harkness turned his mild gaze on the man. He judged Draycott to be sixty, though long illness had aged him early. He looked a typical case of the man who serves his government either in or out of uniform, prodigally throwing down the vital years as the price of his promotion, quitting his own country and sweating the middle years away with a ration of gin and quinine, and returning withered by the black man's sun and by the first searing anger that he had nursed in silence against the petty shifts and subterfuge of white man's lordly government—an anger long since burned away and buried with its secret epitaph, *It wouldn't have Paid*. But a major now, and back to England with all honour. A job well done, and no trick left untried. A major, among the minors and sub-minors and the other majors and super-majors jockeying for their rightful position: at the top. But, failing the top, the prize. The pay-off and the pension, the yellow skin, and all the time in the world for self-pity and the search for friends, or, failing friends, people who would listen, or, failing those, just people, any people wherever they could be found and pinned down, in the club, in a bar, in a ship. Listen to my gallant past, and throw me the biggest biscuit of them all, and call me Major.

Almost typical, this man Draycott, except in one respect: he didn't want anyone to listen. He had kept intact his humility through all those regretted years; he needed his title only to show that he had not always been a sick old man with an unread battered book.

"That's quite correct, Major." The captain bowed his head in a careful nod. "The cargo has shifted. Not all of it, of course. The trouble is in number two hold—that's the one just forward of the bridge. The men are working on it now."

Mrs. Jocelyn said in a pleased voice, "And will the floor be straight when they've finished?"

"Until the gale drops, the floor will lie at all angles, according to the ancient traditions of the sea." He turned his head as he heard voices. The Sennetts were coming in, unobtrusively; their voices grew quiet as they chose a table, but before they had sat down Penny Jocelyn was hailing them.

"Captain's conference. Disciplinary action will be waived, in this instance, for late arrivals."

Unobserved by the rest, Major Draycott's face had

69

warmed to a wintry smile as he sat watching Penny. She reminded him of a girl he had known, a long time ago, before he had gone out to Kenya. But he could not quite remember her name.

Persham, the steward, was slipping the chains of two chairs and moving them to the table where the captain sat. Dr. Papasian was bobbing up as Mrs. Sennett neared. Harkness rose, moving his chair to make room. Jocelyn was slower. Major Draycott made every gesture of rising, except that of actually leaving his chair, delaying the moment until it was too late and Mrs. Sennett was putting her hand lightly on his shoulder—"Please don't disturb yourselves." She slipped quickly into her chair next to the Major. He was much relieved. Throughout this never-ending voyage he had carried the last words spoken to him on the shore, "And remember, no exertion." He would have wished for a more romantic farewell.

"We didn't know there was a conference on," said Sennett. He sat with his stiff left leg in front of him, his gloved left hand on his lap.

Harkness said, "In actual fact it's just a tea-party, but I expect you'll realise that Mrs. Jocelyn's flair for the dramatic has charged the occasion with solemnity."

Jocelyn beamed at the Sennetts. "You were going to be piped into the saloon, but Mrs. Jocelyn's psychiatrist has confiscated her mouth-organ."

Major Draycott's faint smile had gone, except perhaps from his eyes. He looked younger. Sennett noticed this. He also noticed that the banter seemed to be skating nervously across a very thin surface. The captain wouldn't be down here drinking tea for the want of something to do. Sennett thought there was probably a great deal to be done, on the bridge. He said when the moment was right, "I'm glad we've turned about. It was beginning to feel rough." His glance moved by degrees to Harkness.

"There's no indication," Harkness said easily, "that

this weather's going to fine down before noon tomorrow, even if then. We shall be delayed, obviously. As I was saying before you came in, messages can be sent to England to that effect, if there's anyone likely to worry." He swallowed some tea and pushed the cup away, keeping his finger-tips on it while the saloon tilted, and tilted back. Then he got up. "If you'll excuse me. I'll look forward to seeing you all at dinner."

When he had gone, the conversation stopped skating. Major Draycott was already asking a steward for a message-pad.

"What's the report?" asked Mrs. Sennett over-casually.

"Cargo's shifted," said Jocelyn. He looked at his wife. "You owe me five bob on that."

"I'll pay you in kind."

Mrs. Sennett said something quietly to her husband. Penny was watching them. They fascinated her. The girl was almost beautiful, with a long pale face that was so inanimate as to be uninteresting, until she spoke. She spoke with a sad timbre that was always there in her voice; even when she laughed there was a hint of wistfulness. Most marked was her devotion to Sennett, and her adoration of him. It would have been easy to conclude, at first sight of them, that because he was striking in his looks she adored him for his gold hair and brilliant ice-blue eyes and the chiselled fineness of his bone-structure, the firm set of his mouth and the sculpted shape of his head. When Penny Jocelyn had first seen him she had murmured to Alan in a deep velvet key, "Adonis, in person. It's not possible." Jocelyn had agreed. The least vain man would envy Sennett his looks. It would have been as easy to conclude, at first sight of these two people, that the girl was devoted to him because he was an object of pity, with his stiff leg and gloved hand, however much these injuries could lend a grim romantic air to his appearance. There was glamour, even at serious levels of thought, about a man who had suffered and emerged less whole.

No one on board the ship knew whether such first-sight conclusions were right; they had to settle for the obvious. It was assumed, understandably, that Sennett had come down in a blazing bomber; nothing less heroic could fit such a face; no other picture of his past was even sought for; but he gave no hint, even by the unconscious use of R.A.F. slang in his conversation. Nor was any light thrown by his wife. Most of their conversation was reserved for themselves; even in the throng of an after-dinner dance on board, when the full muster of passengers and officers seemed to crowd the small saloon, the Sennetts kept together, and danced together, admired for the picture they made of a couple in perfect love, and for the dexterity his practice and her harmony brought to their steps. The result of this withdrawal from other people was that they had become the immediate focus of conjecture and discussion during a long sea voyage. Penny Jocelyn had summed up the whole thing on the first evening:

"Well, obviously he's been through a bad time, and she's more in love with him than ever because she can now take over all the duties every woman yearns for—of wife, lover, mother, sister, protector and watchdog. She's obviously delirious about it."

"And penitent," Jocelyn had said.

"Penitent? What about?"

"Him. In some way. And he's up to his neck in self-pity."

"Well, he doesn't show it."

Jocelyn had shrugged. It was quite true—there had been no signs of self-pity in Sennett. He let her help him into his rain-proof coat when they went on deck, and find a cigarette for him when he began tapping his pockets, and sometimes light it for him; but these courtesies were returned. One almost began to feel it would be rather refreshing if one of them suddenly slapped the other one's face.

"Did the captain actually say that?" asked Sennett now.

"What?"

"That the cargo's shifted."

Dr. Papasian entered the conversation for the first time. "Oh, yes, Mr. Sennett. He did not like telling us."

Jocelyn grunted amiably. "And we did not like being told."

"We shall trust in our good ship," said Penny. "We shall face the future with strong hearts and quiet fortitude, so that with the help of the Lord we shall prevail."

It fell completely flat. She lit a new cigarette from the butt of the last, and started to tap her teeth with her thumb-nail. Too late to help her, but cutting the silence short, Alan Jocelyn said:

"Well, as long as they keep the bar open we shan't come to much harm. I'm saving the empties and putting the corks back. Lashed together they'll make an excellent life-raft."

"I imagine," said Major Draycott cautiously, "that if the cargo has shifted, we'll have signalled someone for assistance?" By the tone of his voice he imagined no such thing; he simply hoped.

"In this weather, yes." Sennett sat comfortably beside his wife. Whenever he spoke she turned her head to watch him, as to hear an oracle. "The cargo's mainly grain, which is treated as liquid. The only way to get rid of it would be to pump it out with special gear, which the ship doesn't carry. It's strictly a dockside operation." He spoke to no one in particular, though he was answering the Major's question. "So we shall finish the voyage with a fifteen-degree list. That's not awfully serious."

Penny said, "Is it fifteen degrees?"

"Approximately." His steady gaze was friendly but she

73

couldn't meet it for long. It was difficult to look at Sennett without losing grip on the libido. She said quickly:

"Have you spies on the bridge?"

His smile was charming. "Oh, no. We drew a circle on a piece of paper and then split it up into seventy-two segments." He looked, still smiling, at his wife. "It took half an hour before we'd got it right. Then we held it against a bulkhead, as near to the fore-and-aft line as we could judge." He was looking at Penny again. "If you like, I'll take over your five bob bet with Mr. Jocelyn."

Alan said straight away, "That it's fifteen degrees?"

"Well, we had to draw the segments freehand. I'll lay you it's nearer fifteen than ten or twenty."

"Taken. Where's the bit of paper?"

"I think we left it in——"

"I'll go." Mrs. Sennett was getting up. Alan said:

"Oh, no, don't worry about it now. Bring it when we meet at dinner——"

"It's no trouble."

"It'll give us something to play with," Sennett said when she had gone, "if the weather keeps us out here for a day or two."

Major Draycott's face had lost the last vestige of amusement. He looked old again. "You think it will?"

Sennett shrugged easily. "It's a comfortable ship, and very well run. I should think the worst we'll have to put up with is boredom."

SEVEN

Wireless-officer Bond had sent the messages off. The chief steward had brought them to him in a batch soon after the captain had come up from tea.

To Mrs. Draycott, 14 Pembury Crescent, Tunbridge Wells, Kent. Will be delayed. No cause for worry. Tom.

To C.M.O. St. Peter's Hospital, Weyland Street, Hampstead, London. Ship delayed. Do not know for how long. Will contact again soon as possible. Apologies. Good wishes. Papasian.

To Mrs. Timsett, Flat 5, Courtney Lodge, Bournemouth, Hants. Delayed. Will phone when landed. Please tell Mr. Sennett and Paul's firm. Lovely trip. Our love. Moira.

To K. Jones, 1 South Street, Kensington, London. See under ships overdue. Have borrowed galoshes. Don't flog furniture till executors say. S.W.A.L.K. Alpenny.

The first message given to the chief steward by the Jocelyns had read, *Ship sunk. Drunk as a skunk in funk in bunk. Gugnunk.* But Persham had suggested to Mr. Jocelyn that the information contained in the message concerning the ship was untrue, and that the wireless-officer, being an employee of the shipping company, would decline to accept such a mistruth for putting out on the air.

A message from Miss Brown had reached the wireless-room before tea-time, and had gone off. *To Miss Pierglover, Principal, Suretidge School, The High, Croydon, Surrey. Terribly sorry. Delayed. Will phone. Brownie.*

She had questioned Dodds, the steward, whom Peter Costain had sent to her cabin. "Is this what you'd call a bad gale?"

Dodds had issued himself with a tot of rum and had crept back to the fringe of courage. Orders had been

75

sent from the bridge that passengers must be reassured.

"Bad, miss? Bless your heart, no! Bit choppy, I'd say."

"But we've turned the ship round."

"Well, it's best." He grew confidential, screwing half his plump face into a wink. "We could've risked goin' on, see, an' ten to one we'd've done no worse'n break a bit o' crockery. But Captain 'Arkness, 'e's not a man to go an' take risks, for 'isself nor anyone else. 'E's the bravest man I've met in me life, but 'e plays safe." He screwed his face up another wrinkle and sank his voice still lower. " 'E plays safe, miss." There was a wistfulness in his face and voice to think of so brave a man, playing so safe. It was a Thought for the Day.

"That's nice to know." She was conscious of her red-rimmed eyes; their hot feeling reminded her that she was meant to be very frightened about the gale. "I feel much safer, now."

"Of course you do, miss. There's nothin' to fret about, you mark my words. It'd take a sight more'n a bit o' wind to send *this* ship to the bottom." That should reassure her.

"Well, that's—that's fine. I won't give it another moment's thought."

"That's right, miss. Now what can I get for you? Somethin' to drink, p'r'aps?"

"Well, no——"

"It 'elps, you know. It 'elps somethin' magical."

"I—I expect so, but I won't, just now. You've restored every bit of my confidence. But if we're facing the wrong way, it means we shall be late getting to England, won't it?"

Dodds shrugged off the thought as absurdly unimportant. "P'r'aps a few hours, p'r'aps a day, miss." So small a point. England could wait.

"Then I'd better send a message, by wireless. I can do that, can't I?"

76

"Why, cert'nly you can. I'll get the chief steward for you, an' 'e'll take your message to the bridge." He opened the door. "An' you won't have just one little . . . ?" He held up a finger and thumb enticingly. She smiled and shook her head.

"Not just now." It would cost as much as the message, and the message was more important.

Mr. Bond, sitting in the wireless-room, had dealt with the signals from the passengers and some of the crew. Should he send one to Thelma? She was expecting him home. Early tomorrow morning he should be going up Beaker Street, Bristol, his case in his hand, a present for her inside. How would he find 'things' when he got home? She was sorry about 'all that', her letter had said. She was all right now. For how long? She might run to the gate to meet him when she heard it open; or she might manage no more than a weary smile in the hall; he did not know and could not guess. Almost he would prefer her to leave him in peace, and ignore him while he was in the house; at least he could get on with the work on the new V.H.F. set he was building, without any pleas to go dancing at the Regency or to spend an evening with the Macrowans. Couldn't she get all the fun she wanted while he was at sea, and let him work in peace on his few days ashore?

She might, of course, have gone into his den and broken up the half-finished V.H.F. It had happened before, when he'd forgotten some friends were coming and had shut himself away with his beloved equipment. He awoke that night and heard it being smashed. He had not gone in to see what was happening; he knew what was happening. He should have changed his clothes, the evening before, and made sure the drinks were ready and the log-basket filled—"the simple duties of a good host," she had called it, standing there after they had gone, her hair shining in the light of the standard-lamp, her eyes

77

brilliant with anger, her voice rough with it. "I know you're a genius, Tony, and that God made Adam, and then Eve, and then a wireless-set; but couldn't you for once act like a human being and get your feet on the ground and have some fun before we're both too withered with age to enjoy ourselves in even the simplest ways? I know you can't stand the Regency—all right, it's fairly crummy and full of yobs; and you don't care for the Macrowans because Bill always gets a bit tight when we have drinks together—all right, he is a bore when he's tight and he doesn't know the first thing about valves or wavelengths and that sort of technical stuff; and the pictures bore you stiff because the acoustics want re-designing and most of the films are about mush and murder anyway——" And he had watched the light on her hair as she flung it about, and the flash of her eyes and the white of her teeth as she had gone on and on, her hands flying out, flying up to her hair, spreading and clenching as she stood in the dark blue dress she liked so much, the one he hadn't noticed when she had put it on for the first time . . . but she had so many. He had stood watching her and listening, just wishing it would stop.

"But for God's sake, Tony, give me a break sometimes! Just one week in a year, when we could do something for its own sake, for the fun of it—even a few days' fishing in the country by a river, or a night in London for a show or something—anything, *anything* except letting me sit here twiddling my thumbs while you shut yourself away upstairs and twiddle with knobs—Tony, can't you understand even a fraction of what I'm saying?"

She had stopped. He had understood a fraction. After a long minute had crept by, shy of the lamplight and her brilliant cold eyes, he said:

"I'm dull."

Her hands flew again, as if she were conducting the rhythm of the words she said, though they tumbled out

78

erratically in passionate fits and starts. "Not dull, Tony, because you're kind and have a really clever mind, and——" she searched desperately for another quality, but had to call in a vague generality—"you're a good husband and all that." She shook her head. He thought how pretty she was. "But you just don't see. Do you?"

"Of course I see. We'll go out somewhere. Now."

She looked at the clock. "But it's gone eleven."

"Tomorrow, then. Shopping, or—or something, in the morning."

They had gone shopping and she had spent seven pounds, five of them on things she didn't want. In the evening they went round to the Stapletons, who never got tight; but Thelma had put on her most extravagant off-the-shoulder dress and looked rather absurd beside Jean Stapleton's comfortable twin-set; and this time it was Thelma who suddenly wanted to get tight and managed to do it on the meagre supply of South African sherry they kept for Christmas and what they slyly called High Jinx. She was taken home from an atmosphere of gathering shock, and had been defiant and contrite in turn, cursing the stuffed-up suburbanity of the Stapletons and being sorry for smashing his wonderful gadgets last night after he'd promised to take her shopping. ("But I think it was the thought of shopping that hit me in the night, Tony—it was such a bloody let-down, really, and I couldn't sleep and I wanted to—to hurt you badly, and there wasn't a better way of doing it.")

The next day she showed no more defiance. She left him alone, and took lunch up to his den with hardly a word. Later, she said she had been thinking about 'things', and had decided they must 'finish all this'. He had never bothered to ask how, or why, because his ship was due for sailing and he left early, to 'pick up some things'.

He was prepared for anything when he went home next.

Late tomorrow, with any luck. The scenes would be the same, and they would be glad to say good-bye again. Yet what was wrong? 'Tony, you've a terribly limited imagination.' But surely his job alone required imagination?

He was staring up at the photograph. Love from Thelma. He looked down. The chair creaked under him as the ship heeled, and paused, and righted. There was less movement now that the *Whipper* was head-to-sea. She was turned away from land. Perhaps, with any luck, she'd never get there. There was a sulky triumph in the thought; but he was not so childish as to think vengefully how sorry she would be. He knew quite well that she would not be sorry at all.

. . . . .

"What happened?"

"You got knocked out, mate."

Persham snipped the lint strip and pinned it.

"Show me th' bastard, then! Who was it?" Harris tried to sit up.

"Lie quiet and let me finish what I'm doing!" Persham had a first-class proficiency certificate, and he was glad of a chance to practise.

"Who was it, then? Eh?"

"Oh, for Chris' sake shuddup, Harris. You knocked yourself out—that's the sort of prat you are. Now keep still."

Harris looked up at the chief steward, his eyes trying to focus; but they were deeply sunk into the white face, and he couldn't keep them open for long. He lay back as Persham swabbed the rest of the congealed blood from the side of his neck.

"Knocked meself out?" It was hardly audible. He watched Persham's fringe of red hair moving against the background of plates and rivets above his head. "Down in the grain?"

80

Persham said nothing. The swab in his hand was now pale crimson, and he took a new one from his kit. If only there'd been enough money. Christ, if only there *had* been. He could have finished his training by now; this year he would have been qualified, and working in a wonderful clean operating-theatre on a complicated case instead of down here in a sweaty cabin in a lousy cargo-packet with nothing more important than a stupid git of a seaman's flea-bitten head to patch up.

"Down on the grain, was it?"

"Yes. Now give over and keep still.'

Harris remembered the grain now, and the bright flying of the shovels and the hailing of the grain in the half-dark while the wind howled past the tarpaulin and bloody Starley yelling his bloody head off at them to keep on shovelling, when any half-witted clot could see they'd never shift that much grain if they worked all their lives, when the ship was pitching it back again as fast as she could go. Jesus, what a passage this had turned out to be, with the mate a tight-mouthed bastard and the bosun a bone-headed git, and the seas up and the cargo shifted and the gale getting worse! And not even a doctor on board, only this bloody longshore waiter who knew all there was to know about first-aid. First-aid? He couldn't stuff a duck.

His head throbbed to the rhythm of the engines. His brain was going to shake itself off its bearings. Men ran somewhere on deck, their boots thudding above the cabin, thundering across the top of his head. He felt chilled from his tongue to his bowels, and the cabin lifted and dropped, tilted and swung, and he was afraid.

"They'll never shift it," he said, not clearly enough for Persham to understand. He went on mumbling. Persham dropped the last swab and used the towel. There'd be no thanks for this. Harris wouldn't thank him, nor anyone else. No fee, and no thanks. But it didn't worry him. He could say it himself, 'That's a tidy job, Jack boy. Dr. Kildare couldn't have done neater than that.'

He packed his kit deftly. Money wasn't evil. You had to have it. People didn't realise. His father didn't. "I've talked to the matron at the hospital, Jack, an' she knows all there is about it. It's no go, boy. It'd cost a mint o' money. Even with the scholarships, you got to keep yourself, and nothin' comin' in to the house, no matter how hard you'd work. Not a penny. So you'd best forget it, Jack. There's plenty of other ways to make a good livin'."

"It's not a question of makin' a livin', Dad. It's a question of bein' a doctor." The gas-lamp flared above them. His father shrugged.

"We can't all be doctors, y' know. Rest of us has got to be the patients." He smiled. "Eh?" The smile died slowly.

"Yes, Dad."

He had not turned up for instruction at the St. John's depot, the evening after; but a friend of his, who worked at the hospital, persuaded him to finish the course; and he got his certificate, and showed it to his father, but—"It's no go, Jack. I realise you've got the ability. It's a question o' the money, see?" He had tapped the certificate. "If that were a hundred-poun' note, we could start talkin'."

Jack had torn up the certificate and dropped it down the lavatory pan; there had been a sour pleasure in pulling the chain on it. Before that year was out, he was at sea.

"They'll never shift it." The deck tilted to a roll, and tilted back. "See what I mean? You could work a month o' Sundays down that bloody hold, an' finish up where you started."

Jack Persham fetched a cup of water. Harris was still mumbling, his eyes open. ". . . just as well try an' empty th' ocean wi' a shovel." He laughed with slack lips; a bubble of saliva rose and burst.

"Take these, mate."

The eyes moved to look. "What're they, then?"

"Only aspirin."

"I don't want bloody aspirin."

"Come on. I've got some work to do."

"I don't take orders from a bloody steward."

The deck tilted, paused, tilted back. Voices shouted from above; one sounded like the bosun's. "That bastard."

"Come on, take these. I'm tryin' to help you, aren't I?" He had one arm round Harris's shoulders, lifting him so that he could drink. He was holding the cup near Harris's mouth. "Come on, mate. They'll stop a temp'rature, an' give you some sleep."

The smell of the blood and the antiseptic was sickly in the air. The water shivered in the cup as he tried to keep it steady. His arm was aching under Harris's weight. It was an ignorant, obdurate weight.

"Come on, it's not askin' much."

"You think asp'rins're goin' to help when there's a thous'n' tons o' grain down in number two?"

"Look, what've you got against me, mate? Aren't I trying to help you feel better?"

Harris managed another grunt, meant for a laugh. "All right, Doc."

Persham got the tablets into his mouth and held the cup while he drank; then he drew his arm away gently. When he had rinsed the cup and picked up his kit he took a last look at Harris, who had closed his eyes. Going out of the cabin, Persham was thinking, 'It's no good getting ideas, Jack, just because he called you Doc. He called you a bloody steward, too, and that's what you bloody well are.'

Art Starley had been down to see Harris, and Persham had told him he'd be all right in a couple of days. A couple of days were no use to the bosun because in the next forty-eight hours he was going to need every man's strength. Blast that sailor's eyes for his clumsiness at a time like this. He was just as useful now as if he was dead.

Someone knocked on the door of his room. He didn't answer. The bitch, the real bitch, was the grain. It was foxy tackle, once it took charge. If the seas got smaller they might shift the grain back with shovels, and rig a jury shifting-board to keep it there while the *Whipper* steamed for home. But the seas were going to get bigger. The forecasts said so. This lot was all over everywhere, from Hebrides to Biscay, and the *Whipper* wouldn't run through it with the grain like that. She could get home if the wind dropped to half, with the list that was on her now; she could get home in this full gale if the grain was trimmed; but until the wind dropped or they could find a way of trimming it they must stop out here in the deep water with the ship's eyes to the south, keeping steerage-way and meeting the seas, come as they might.

He felt jaded, sitting here in his own sweat with grain in his boots and salt on his face. He felt impotent. Stubbs was dead right. Call himself a bloody ship's bosun, did he? But there was nothing he could do until the weather gave him a break. Then he'd have them down in that hold and shifting the grain by the ton.

The knock at the door came again. His voice was sharp in the tiny cluttered room. "Well?"

When the door was wide open, there was no space for a man to pass between it and the bench, which was long and massive and buried beneath timber and paint and glue and ship's chandlery and tackle, with a space pushed clear for the bosun's paper-work.

Tich Copley said, "Can I see you, sir?"

"If you can't, you're blind." They stared at each other.

Copley was trying to shut the door, and Starley watched him. There was a rack of tools on the left of the door, with long handles sticking out so that they could be grabbed easily with no messing. With the door wide open at ninety degrees, as it was now, a man could stand here, just inside the room, as Copley was standing; but he couldn't go forward because of the bench, nor sideways to his right because of the door, nor sideways to his left because of the tools in the rack. He could go backwards, pulling the door after him, but there was no angle of less than ninety degrees at which the door gave room for a man to squeeze through; and the tools were stacked from the floor upwards, so that it wasn't possible to crawl under them and come up on the other side of the door.

Copley turned round, and tried to close it, fetching up sharp against the tools. A file dropped; he picked it up, and saw where it had come from; he slid it into the pigeon-hole and turned back and opened the door again, looking down at the bosun, who sat behind the bench.

"Shut that bloody door," said Art Starley.

"Ay, ay, sir."

Copley had broken out in a sweat. He backed, bringing the door after him until it was almost shut, so that he could try squeezing through the gap where the tool-racks gave more room. The bosun was watching a narrow strip of Copley, who was more outside the cabin than in it.

"Where the bloody hell are you goin'?" shouted Starley.

The deckie pushed the door open wider and ignored everything: the door, the tools, the bench, the bosun. He just pushed his way onwards towards the bench; but he didn't get through. A mallet-handle stuck him in the stomach and three or four spare timbers jammed the door as he knocked into them. He slid them back, and turned sideways, and sidled carefully into the gap until there was timber pressing against his buttocks and the door-handle was lodged in his groin. He breathed now with difficulty, saying over and over again to himself, 'God, why did I

85

come here? God, why did I come here?' The physical energy he was using would have been enough to fight a bull off; the nervous strain of trying to outwit the door and the tools and the bench was making his head pound.

He did not look at the bosun any more. He had his back to him now, and faced out of the room, pulling the door an inch towards him and then edging sideways between it and the bench. It was successful up to a point, the point where his body was squeezed so tightly in the gap that it forced the door wider again, until it pinned him as hard as a wedge.

"I can't think," Starley said, "what'd happen if anything man-sized came in here." He lit an American cigarette, and leaned back in his chair.

The smoke crept past Copley's face; he breathed it in. His scalp was hot and he was still saying the same thing in his mind, asking God why he had come here, but now he was stringing the question out with terrible other words, mixing them up with names for the bosun and his door. He freed himself, and turned round slowly, leaving the door wide open at right-angles to the bench; then he stood facing the bosun with his legs at ease and hands tucked behind him. He looked down at the bosun with his jaw tilted and his eyes gazing steadily into Starley's. There was no expression on his white pinched face, for the mouth was set and the eyes had gone like stones; but the bosun knew that Tich Copley was telling him carefully, 'I've tried all ways, and can't do it, so now I'm going to leave the door open, and you can stuff yourself.'

Starley's voice was quiet, but it came resonant from a big chest that made a magnificent sound-box for the lower register. He said, "That's how I feel about the grain."

Copley's face stayed set but his eyes lost their look of stones, and sparked with intelligence. He said nothing.

"Now you just give the door a shove, boy."

Copley pushed it. It swung away from him and banged

86

flat against the bulkhead, leaving enough room for a man to row a boat through.

"Now come on in."

Copley turned and walked past the front of the long bench, keeping his shoulders pulled back.

"Now swing it shut."

He swung it in one slow movement. It banged shut. The bosun said, "I keep the hinges oiled. That's why it's so easy."

Copley stood facing him again, balanced with his feet apart as the ship rolled; he bent his knees and waited; the roll stopped, and began again the other way. He straightened his knees. The bosun dropped the packet of Fifth Avenue towards him along the bench. "Have a fag, Copley."

"No, thank you, sir."

Starley grinned pleasantly. "Go on, son. You can do with it. Don't deny yourself just because I'm a bastard." He watched Copley take a cigarette from the packet and light it. "Now what d'you want to see me for?"

"I've forgotten which accident boat I'm in."

The bosun widened his stare. "You goin' to have an accident, then?"

"No, sir."

Starley's tone was reasonable. "Jesus, you can't come in here at the end of a two weeks' trip an' say you've forgotten which accident boat you're in! How many times have you done boat-drill in this ship?"

"I can't remember."

Starley tried to find a hint in the kid's expression that he'd gone mad. Copley said resolutely, "It's a lapse of memory, sir."

After a moment the bosun got up and leaned against the timber-racks. "What makes you think I won't murder you, for comin' in here with this bloody tale?"

Copley said nothing. He had smoked half the cigarette

already, pulling at it hard. He had needed it; he needed it still. The bosun said, "What's on your mind, kid?"

"Nothing, sir. I've just forgotten, that's all."

"You've jus' forgotten." He studied the boy carefully. He had a jockey's body, made of ribs and wire and knuckles and marrow bone; a gristly boy with a tousled head and a face nearly all chin, a body nearly all elbows and knees. All the vitality and expression was centred in the eyes: they could light up or dance or burn with anger or struggle to understand; they could go shut, without shutting. The bosun had known Copley three months, maybe less; but he knew what kind of boy he was. The good Lord had chosen gut for this one, thick gut for the sinews and fine for the nerves, and had afterwards tuned the instrument beyond the point of its ever going slack again. It rather frightened Starley to be in the presence of so much tension.

"You're a liar," he said.

Tich Copley did not answer. He was not interested. All he wanted to know was his accident boat station.

The bosun said, "Why didn't you ask your mates? They'd know."

"I didn't want to look silly, sir."

"But you don't mind lookin' silly in front o' me? You know I oughter sling you out of here for wastin' my time, Copley?"

The eyes went shut, without shutting. "I'd best go and ask my mates, then."

Art Starley was having a day of it. First in the Skip's room, with him and Stubbs stalking each other like cats round a chimney-pot; now in here with this kid. This kid was worse than the Skip, in some ways. You could pick him up and toss him through the porthole if you wanted to —but, flying through the air, he'd win. You'd be left like a fool, knowing it wasn't the answer. Shifting grain was a picnic, compared with this.

88

"Look here, kid. You often lose your memory?"

"No, sir."

"When did it happen the las' time?"

"I can't remember. I don't think I ever have, before."

The bosun said, "Are you scared?" Fright could do it.

"I don't think so."

"Aren't you certain?"

"I'm always sick when I'm scared."

"Most of us are." He stared at Copley as if he could see through his skull and read the bright worried mind. "How long've you been at sea?"

"Three years, sir."

"Then you've been in storms?"

"Yes, sir."

"Did they scare you?"

"Yes, sir."

"Well, you're normal, thank God. But what's so important about this accident boat? Why come here an' ask me *now*?"

"The cargo's shifted. If we've got to take to boats, I'll have to know."

"You think we'll have to leave the *Whipper* just because she's got a bit of a list?"

"I want to know, that's all. So I can be ready, like the rest."

"You're sick-scared, aren't you?"

"No, sir."

They held their feet to the next roll. It was a big one. A glue-pot shifted on the bench and Starley had to grab it. They waited, feeling the shudder of the engines as the screw came out. Timber was straining, as slowly as the creak of a footstep on the stair. The wind fluttered in the ventilator. The screw went back and the shuddering stopped. The angle eased suddenly as the ship came back from her roll. Starley took his hand away from the glue-pot.

89

"You're in starb'd, aft. Don't forget again."

"Starb'd aft, sir."

The bosun dropped his dog-end and stood on it; the last smoke floated round his face; he squinted through it at Copley. "You did right, to come an' ask me."

Copley opened the door, drew it right back, got on to the other side of it, and said, "Ay, ay, sir."

The bosun grinned. "Sod off."

When Copley had gone, Starley looked through the porthole. The sea was racing by in a long white parade of waves that boiled at the crests as the wind curled them over. A big one went by and broke astern of the ship as she lay wallowing in the trough. That was a seventh. He was awed by the sight of its breaking, by the white tumult as the wind knocked it down and smothered it in its own foam, big as it was. He'd seen waves sixty feet high—three times the size of that one. You get a seventh wave in a sea as big as that and you've got a killer. There were waves that nobody ever came back to tell of, yet you knew they were there, out there over this horizon or the next, by day or in the dark; giants, they were, standing up green and black and towering above you, coming for you, while you stood and watched them with their shadows coming over you and over your ship like the shadows of mountains over the land below, and you had to watch them come against the sky, leaning with the wind against their backs and scooped out dark underneath, until you tried to cry out and couldn't, and your bowels opened and you couldn't stop them; and underneath you was the deep, where you were going now, buried under the big killer when it dropped.

"Fester," he said softly, turning away from the port-hole, "fester." What did that stupid short-arse want to come here and talk about accident boats for? He should've skinned him alive.

EIGHT

DARKNESS had come down three hours ago; the sea and sky were black, with no stars to glint upon water, and no moon. It was a simmering dark, full of sound, covering the sea but leaving it alive; the wind clove through the dark, driving the sea and tormenting it so that its waters rose as if against the wind, to be whipped and sent down again with the waves' backs broken and their strength spilled in a flurry of foam, while others rose up and met the wind and were whipped down by it and scattered, while others rose, and others, in their tens of millions across the sweep of the South Atlantic; they ran their rising, falling race across the deeps below, where the wind could not go but where the big currents moved against the ocean's floor across the reefs and the ledges of sand and wreck and weed, journeyed through by the winter fish whose dark ways ran fathoms below the storm, and were not touched by it. The ocean worked its tides in quietness, only its surface in a rage.

The Breton fishermen have a prayer, as old as the sea it speaks to, "You are so mighty, and my ship is so small. Have mercy."

A ship is a mote in the sea. Be it a great ship with a royal name and a master strong and as one with the will of God, with huge dimensions and of a shape considered perfect by designers who have lavished their genius on its making, it is a mote in the sea. The sea is so mighty, and a ship is so small.

In this sea that was harried by the gale, Harkness kept his ship against the elements. He was a man of some faith in God, as a man must be if he leaves the safety of the land; but he had no faith in the mercy of the sea. It could not know of the things that died in it, nor wish for their death; it could only bury them quiet in its deeps. It was an insensate element, and it was absurd to speak of the sea as a cunning enemy; nor was the wind a friend if it filled your sails or a foe if it stripped them from you. But in any struggle between a man and some insensate thing the issue becomes personal, so that he will shout at it and curse it and give it foul humiliating names while he is fighting it; and sometimes it seems that the thing—be it the sea or the wind or flood or forest fire—has awareness of him and of his cunning, and answers with cunning of its own.

There was no cunning in the sea, this night. It came for the *Whipper* in her face, and pounded her as she lifted and shook the water down her sides, her sharp bows turned to face the sea and cut into it when she could. Her list had not worsened, but there could be no work in the hold where the grain had shifted until the sea grew less. Twice the bosun had taken men there, and the clusters had been lit from the deck-plugs so that in the blaze of light they could inspect the scene, and try to find a way of trimming the cargo.

From the wheelhouse Costain had watched the fore-deck, a pool of light in which stood the shadows of the mast and samson posts and the rigging's web. As the seas met the bows, white explosions bloomed enormously against the dark, and spindrift came in a blizzard from the fo'c'sle head, driving white across the deck and blotting out the scene below the high lamp-clusters so that in a moment all was lost—the deck, stanchions, posts, hatch-covers and moving men as the blizzard swept over them and reached the bridge and burst against the wheel-house windows with a rattle as of flying stones. Costain, keeping the first watch of the night, did not pity the men down there; they were seamen and there was the sea and this was their work; he was simply glad he was not one of them.

He could hear Tony Bond at work in the wireless-room; signals were pippling the closed-in silence here, as the frail communications were kept up from ship to ship and from the sea to shore. Captain Harkness was in there with Bond, after making a token appearance in the saloon for dinner. He had not been at ease; the passengers were worried and anxious to deceive him; he had been glad to leave them. He said to Bond:

"How's the *Valenca* faring, have you heard?"

"The tug's still searching, sir. She's not answered for the last hour, but she sounded cheerful enough when she gave a call just before eight. As I work it out, the *Abeille*'s nearly closed her, twice."

Harkness knew the *Valenca*, a German-built ship with Greek owners; she had a beautiful sheer and a long counter, and slipped through the seas like a fish. He could picture her now, with a deck-cargo of pit-props or perhaps soft timber, the uprights leaning out from the bulwarks under the pressure of the shifting cargo. She'd have a list on; maybe as much as the *Whipper*, maybe more, for a timber-ship was buoyant and could lean hard against the sea without alarm. But the hundreds of logs would be a worry by now, or she wouldn't have sent an S O S. Harkness knew her master, who was a Greek with a finger gone, and he was a man to keep his cargo on board until the ship was down. No carrier lightly jettisons his goods, any more than a tug deserts a tow. Socrates Nakonis would be watching his cargo at this minute, ready to give the order to knock off the slips and let the timber go; but his ship would have to lie over almost on her side before he was forced to do it.

Harkness did not know the *Abeille IV*, but like most of the deep-sea tugs she had a reputation talked about from Southampton to Sydney. She'd turn out in the face of a hurricane and bring back a cork in the dark if you threw it for her. Let her once find the *Valenca*, and she'd be safe.

That was the only danger: that the two ships would not find each other in the tempestuous night. For all the radios and direction-finders and radar systems that filled wheelhouse and chart-room with their magical presence in every fair-sized vessel afloat, the search by one ship for another was no foregone conclusion in the vastness of the deep and the dark. A ship was a mote in the sea.

"Trawler, sir."

The captain looked down at Bond. The voice on the radio-telephone was faint, the words fluttering through static.

'*Willow*', '*Willow*', '*Willow*'. '*Flasher*', '*Flasher*', '*Flasher*'. *Can you get us? Come back on the* 138. *Over.*

Bond said, "*Flasher*'s been silent for a long time now, sir. I've been trying to find out if——"

Hello '*Flasher*' *to* '*Willow Girl*', '*Flasher*', '*Flasher*'. *Are you staying out? Over.*

Bond stared at the dials, his eyes dreaming. One of his lost sheep was back. The *Flasher* was still sending.

'*Willow*', '*Willow*', '*Willow*'. *No, we are making in now, making in now. It's not worth it, Georgie. Keep wiggin'. Gone.*

Harkness said, "Who'd be in a trawler on a night like this?"

"It's the stink of the fish I couldn't stand, sir."

They listened again as a signal came through in code from a cruiser to Commander-in-Chief, Plymouth. Behind him Harkness heard the third mate giving an order to the helm. He left the warmth of the wireless-room. Costain had been joined by Turnbull, who was standing by one of the windows. Harkness glanced at the inclinometer and saw that the mean reading had increased a little. There was less rolling now that the ship was head-to-sea but she was putting her bows down heavily as the gale sent water rising for her.

He had been down to the engine-room and talked to the chief. The engine was turning at revs for nine knots but she wasn't making more than four through the water, keeping her steerage-way and burning coal and getting nowhere. The met. reports gave no hope of the gale fining down tonight nor even tomorrow before noon. They couldn't turn about and run for home; even if they could bring the ship round safely the list would remain and she'd be pooped by the following sea until her stern was smashed. Nor could they stay here much longer burning up coal until there was none left to turn the engines. Without engines in this sea they would be lost, with the steering gone and the ship broaching to and taking the seas on her side until they turned her over.

These thoughts were not only the captain's. Turnbull, at the wheelhouse window, was burdened with them. Costain's nerves were on edge as he stood by the binnacle, checking and re-checking the quartermaster's course as the seas thundered against the starboard flare and then the port and then starboard again, while Wilson brought the wheel a spoke down, a spoke up, watching his lubber-line and waiting for the third mate to say it again.

"Meet her."

"Ay, ay, sir, meet her!"

"Steady . . ."

"Steady sir."

As Captain Harkness came and stood beside him, Turnbull said:

"We've had it green, sir, over the fo'c'sle."

Harkness gazed through the window without answering. Spray came against the glass in a peppering of small white bursts; then the glass ran and cleared, giving them a hazy view of the next wave that was running towards them. They watched it gain height, a soft flurry in the gloom beyond the foremast steaming-light; then it hit, and was clove by the bows; it fountained on both sides, and the wind took it and the foredeck was a-smother. The explosions came again on the windows and they went blank. Under their feet they still felt the shock of the impact of wave and ship.

"I'm thinking about number one hatch, sir."

Harkness gave another nod. He was thinking about number one hatch, numbers two, three and four hatches, the bow-plates, the stern, the derricks, bridge, winches, ventilators and samson posts; he was thinking about four thousand tons of grain and ten passengers and forty crew.

The next wave was shipped green and they saw the black wall of it come up out of the dark and stand there and stagger in the gale until the ship drove into it with her head down and the screw coming out. They saw the fo'c'sle head vanish and then the hatch-covers and foremast and derricks and then the two big samson posts, and then they saw nothing, for the toughened glass of the windows were hammered as the water hit them and flattened so that the ship seemed suddenly to be deep in a drift of snow. She was still shuddering from the wave's brunt; the wheelhouse was loud with the din of the windows as they were smothered in the spray. Costain was shouting something to the helmsman and the helmsman made an answer. The faces of the captain and mate were a sick white in the glow reflected from the windows. They drained slowly.

Turnbull said nothing more to the captain; the captain was not in a talking mood; but Turnbull had a master's certificate, and he was thinking that if he were master of this ship he would have sent a signal by now, not informing the owners that their precious cargo was shifting but telling anyone who was within listening-range that the *Atlantic Whipper* was in need of help. The message was simple enough: *Save our souls.*

It irked the mate to be standing here, unable even to speak and get an answer, when he would have wished to go into the wireless-room and have a signal sent and at least know that he had taken what care he could, and in good time. He felt far out on a limb, his last touch lost with security. A signal would reassure him. It would do no harm. It could, if the gale worsened, save all their lives. These winter gales in the Western Approaches were as bad as any round the Horn; more ships had foundered in these waters than in the Pacific.

Harkness was leaving it late. It wasn't an easy thought, standing here and watching the big seas come, dropping their tons of weight across the hatches down there. There was grain in the holds below, and if water reached it each single pip would swell to twice its size and the ship would need the cubic space to take eight thousand tons of it instead of four. She would be split like a nut.

"Meet her."

"Meet her, sir!"

The wave struck. The bows vanished into dark water. Turnbull stood waiting for the shock to reach the bridge. The wind brought the water still black at the base with half the big wave still standing astride the foredeck as its top broke up into spray. The shock came, shuddering through the deck under their feet. The wave was only now dying, torn slowly apart by the wind; if it had done damage, the sound would have been lost in the tumult; it would not have been possible to know.

The windows went white as the water reached them and rattled with a crackling fusillade that numbed the ears.

"Steady." Costain's voice piped thinly above the din.

"Steady, sir!"

The ship staggered, falling into the trough and wallowing there. Through the clearing windows Turnbull and Harkness saw the foremast appear, and then the fo'c'sle head. White water was still draining across the scuppers. Below, a man shouted. They could not hear what he said.

Harkness had not moved. The feel of the ship under him was all the movement he wanted to ease his mind; there was strength in her, and he could feel it as she trembled; she was all alive, responding to the helm and to the sea. But he must send a signal soon, because that was only one big wave that had struck her just now. There were more coming, in hundreds, a dark pack of them driven by the gale; and the *Whipper* must meet them all, one by one as they came for her. But she could not meet them for ever; she could wait here with her head to them so long as she had coal left. At this speed she could keep steerage for another thirty hours. The gale could last a week.

Costain, being the officer of the watch, answered the telephone when it rang. Turnbull had moved his head to look at him. Harkness was still gazing through the window. Costain spoke into the phone, nodding. His face had gone white but when he turned to the captain there was nothing wrong with his voice.

"Bosun from fo'c'sle, sir! Number one hatch-cover's been stove-in by seas."

Turnbull dragged up the hood of his reefer and put his shoulder against the door to the bridge-end, pressing it open against the gale. As it slammed behind him a shower of spray came into the wheelhouse and spattered across the planks, flying against the captain's shoes as he went into the wireless-room and said to Bond:

"Signal."

"Sir?"

"*S O S.* '*Atlantic Whipper*' *lying hove-to approximately forty-nine-fifty north, twelve-forty west. Cargo shifted, slight list, number one hatch-cover stove-in by heavy seas and taking water.*" When Bond had transmitted, Harkness said, "Send a Mayday call to all ships and let me know immediately we have an answer."

He went back into the wheelhouse. White spray was

blanking the windows, and when the rattle of it died away there was left the sharp pipple of Morse from the wireless-room.

"Thank you, Mr. Costain. I'll take over."

NINE

ACROSS Cornwall the gale hammered at windows and sent
slates whirling away from roofs that were exposed to the
direct onslaught of it. The gale drove across dark wastes
of heather and rock and field, striking the walls of barns
and farmsteads, wrecking a hut and taking the splinters
with it until a gust died and they fell scattering along a
road where a man walked with his torch shielded with his
hand as rain came, stinging his face. Lights were uneasy,
shining from late windows, and doors banged, shaking the
houses as the wind rushed in and then was shut outside by
the nervy, rattling latch. It was as dark overland as on the
sea; but lights were more frequent. Sleep would be late
coming, tonight.

Where the sea met the land along the Cornish coast
there was a long smother of white as the waves staggered
home with their backs bent; they pitched headlong
against the rocks and were flung up in fountains that drove
across the shore and became mist, joining the soft salt
haze that drenched the wind over the land beyond.
Before darkness, rain squalls had driven people into their
houses; now the night was soaked and cobbles gleamed in
the light of fitful lamps. Paper went whirling from dust-
bins the wind had overturned, and fluttered past windows
where a candle burned and a child tried to sleep; in the
narrow streets of Hale and Helston and St. Mawes
people had to shout to be heard, though they walked
together side by side with their bodies bent against the
gale.

Along the coastline many of the land people thought of
the sea, for only a few of them had nothing to do with the
sea and the fish and the ships. There was worry for the

small boats that lay on the beaches, and for the trawlers in the bays towards Brixham. Down here in the foot of England the sea had claimed the land in subtle ways, exacting from whole families their lifelong dedication, giving them fish for a living and taking their sons away. On this night the sea was a hard bargainer, out for its price. But the people were safe, here on the land. The wind might blow an old one over, and break window-panes and send a bicycle sprawling from its perch on to the pavement; but the houses were safe; they would stand through this wild night as they had stood through others and worse; they could not overturn and drown in the deeps, taking their people with them; they were not ships.

But the people thought of the ships. Even those few who had no son nor brother nor friend who lived his life on the sea were thinking tonight of the trawlers up in the bay, and the traffic through the Downs and across the Irish Channel, and the *Valenca* in Biscay that Captain Tremayne had told them about when he had come home from the wireless station to look to his young wife, who had a five-day child in her arms that had not yet screamed shrill enough with its puny lungs to take the love-light from her eyes. "You howl," she had been saying to the child, "and let the wind howl, an' we'll all fall down an' call it a miracle."

Captain Tremayne was back at the radio station by nine o'clock this evening, with food in him and warm clothes on, for he expected to be here all night. He was in the station when at 9.23 p.m. another signal came in from the sea, from a ship two hundred miles away in the southern reaches of the storm.

The W/T operator shifted his log book an inch towards him and wrote steadily as he listened to the Morse.

S O S . . . S O S . . . S O S . . . DE GBAC/*Atlantic Whipper . . .*

He reached for a message-form and copied the signal, then passed it to the R/T operator beside him, who began speaking quickly but with careful emphasis into the mouthpiece of the radio-telephone:

"*Mayday* . . . *Mayday* . . . *Mayday! From steamship 'Atlantic Whipper'—'Atlantic Whipper' . . .*"

When he had finished speaking he got up and went into the next room and put the message into the teleprinter, and set off the automatic alarm system with twelve four-second dashes and the A.S. The alarm-bells began ringing at 9.26 p.m. on board the liner *Iberian Princess*, at anchor in the Solent, the motor-ship *Tribernum*, moving up-Channel beyond Portsmouth, the destroyer *Brindle*, steaming due north in the Irish Sea past Mizen Head in search of a crippled trawler, and the steamer *Angeles*, ploughing doggedly through big seas a hundred and thirty miles north-west of the stricken *Valenca*.

The Commander-in-Chief Plymouth had the message at 9.27 p.m. or a few seconds after, by land-line. The problem for him was whether to despatch a ship from Plymouth or to order H.M.S. *Brindle* to give up her search for the trawler and steam south to the position given by the *Atlantic Whipper*. The trawler had last signalled her propeller gone; she was in a critical condition. If the destroyer were called off the search for her, would she have sufficient help from other ships in her vicinity? She was in worse shape than the merchantman, which was still under command: but the trawler was nearer shelter than the steamer, and closer in touch with the emergency services.

The Naval Officer-in-charge set himself to solve this problem with the least possible delay. Meanwhile a request went out to shipping that radio silence be maintained during the first fifteen minutes of every hour except for distress calls.

Lloyd's of London picked up the Mayday alarm call as it

was put out by Land's End Radio. The Watson and Blount Sea-trading and Navigation Company's London offices had a message by land-line informing them of the position and condition of their steamship the *Atlantic Whipper*.

At 9.35 p.m. Watson and Blount were in touch by telephone with the Southern Salvage and Long-distance Towing Company, which had three tugs; but only two were equipped with deep-sea towing-gear and both were engaged already with casualties: the *Salvado* was closing the trawler in the Irish Sea and hoped to reach her within an hour, while the *Sea Horse* was in the narrow reaches of the Channel towards Dieppe, answering a call from a Swedish cargo ship that was in danger ten miles from the coast, her engines dead of a burst steam-pipe. The nearest available tug would be the *Abeille IV*, if she could soon take the *Valenca* to harbour and sail again for the *Atlantic Whipper*. The French company thought it unlikely that the *Abeille* could deal with her present casualty quickly enough to be of any help to the *Atlantic Whipper* before noon in two days' time at the earliest. Much would depend on the state of the weather in the meantime, and on how well the *Valenca* would handle in tow.

Watson and Blount sent a message via P.O. to their ship, saying that all available resources would be tapped. It did not add that there were no known resources available at the present time.

At approximately 9.30 p.m. the duty officer in the control-room at R.A.F. Redmoor, Cornwall, took a message from G.L.D. and within a few seconds the Tannoys were sounding in the airfield buildings—*Dinghy . . . Dinghy . . . Dinghy! Air-crew to briefing!*

Thirteen minutes after the master-pilot had taken his orders from Control, the stand-by machine was airborne and making south-west into the dark street of the gale carrying rescue-gear, flares, inflatable dinghies, life-rafts and hermetically-sealed food and comforts. The navigator passed the course to his pilot, according to the last-reported position of the S.S. *Atlantic Whipper*. It was unlikely that one aircraft, flying in bad weather and by night, could be of much use to a six-thousand-ton cargo ship still under command; but it was another link between sea and shore, between the danger-zone and a haven. If the chances had been a thousand to one against the possibility that the aircraft could help the ship, it would still have flown course 221 towards ship in distress 49.50 north, 12.40 west. The link must be made, however slender.

In the coastguard lookout huts between Land's End and Plymouth the duty wireless-operators were sending Z-series calls to establish the latest distress signal. There was nothing for them to do but keep watch at their radios and pass on information to land stations that others might have missed. Reception was poor. The network was by its own nature fragile, with its trembling web of aerial wires festooned in the dark above radio masts sent whipping by the gale; but many channels were duplicated, and there were many stations: civil, maritime, Naval and R.A.F. A breakdown of any size was hardly possible, though the gale shook even the buildings where the operators listened and replied. The call from the *Atlantic Whipper* had been established throughout the immediate network before 9.45 p.m., and acknowledgments were coming in from ships.

Tribernum judged herself to be too far up the Channel to help; but if no other ship were within shorter steaming-distance of the *Whipper* she would at once turn about and make for that position. *Sea Horse* was closing the Swedish timber-ship and must deal with this casualty first. *Salvado* had not yet located the crippled trawler in the Irish Sea but felt certain she was close and could help her. The tug was in contact with the destroyer *Brindle*, who was also trying to reach the trawler *Minniscoe*. There had been no orders from C.-in-C., Plymouth, for the destroyer to break her search and turn south for the *Whipper*. There was no immediate acknowledgment from the *Abeille IV*, who had now reached the *Valenca* in Biscay. Anchored in the Solent with a full complement of passengers, the *Iberian Princess* could offer no assistance.

But there was one call, a faint one whose message picked its way through the static and the tangle of other signals, that gave hope. '*Angeles*'—'*Angeles*'—'*Angeles*' to '*Atlantic Whipper*'. *Am steaming for you. Position about 47.50 N., 8.40 W. Will help you quick. A vous.*

It was the first comic note struck in the discord of signals this night: a message that started formally, lapsed into bad grammar and finished in French. It was from a Spanish ship. Such a man as Manuelo Lopez de las Castillas would send such a signal at such a time. His ship was an old one, as ugly to look at as a worn-out shoe, and he was already putting her into seas that had sent the crew praying hours ago for the salvation of all their souls and the eternal damnation of Manuelo Lopez de las Castillas for having brought them to these regions of Cain in a ship that bucked like a mule and shook like a jellyfish and stank like the summertime arm-pits of a Barcelona dust-man. Yet their captain had received the message from the merchantman, and had sent the only reply that was possible. He was coming. He would help quick.

Those who listened, in the wireless cabins of ships and in safe warm rooms of the land radio stations, at once began to measure the chances. Much of their calculation was necessarily guesswork: they judged optimistically that the ancient *Angeles* could make perhaps nine or ten knots through a storm such as this, and with luck cover the two hundred miles to the *Atlantic Whipper* in less than twenty hours. They could not hope to judge the direction or distance of drift that would be made by the distressed ship during those twenty hours, nor how long her radio would hold out as a guide to the *Angeles*. They dared not judge whether it was possible at all for the Spaniard to take his ship across an almost beam sea at force-ten strength. By logic the journey could not be made and could not even be dreamed of except by a fool. Only a few of the men who listened had personal knowledge of Manuelo, and knew the two things about him that at this moment counted most. He had no logic in him, but he was no fool. But this did not mean they believed he could get his ship to the *Whipper*. Their calculations supported the findings of all the other men who had no personal knowledge of Manuelo. They had set out to measure the chances, but now knew there were none.

If Manuelo had known these findings he would have gone on scratching his belly beneath the white silk shirt he wore. People, he would have said, were entitled to their opinions, but they must not ask him to be interested in them. He had many opinions of his own (he would have said), and they ranged from the convictions he had about flea-circuses and soya sauce and the laxative properties of the liquorice root to his bright high faith in the teachings of his Church; but he did not ask people to be interested in them. Likewise the opinions of others did not affect him. He could scratch his own belly and sail his own ship, and neither task could be accomplished better by any other man. It was a simple order of things so obvious as to be beyond argument, so that when one of his crew suggested that he was taking these many good men to their death without so much as consulting them he replied in rich Castilian that if he were a horse-knacker he would hardly consult the horses before cutting off their testicles.

Turning his ship westwards, he felt the seas coming to meet her a-beam and had to brace himself to keep his feet. There was shouting from below decks. He could hear things pitching and smashing and hoped that his servant had put away the big photograph of his family and also the hand-tinted photograph of the Christ in the Iglesia Parroquial de Santa Maya, before their glass was broken by their falling. Everything else could smash, and the sooner the better, for the *Angeles* would pitch and roll like this for the next twenty hours, and a thing could only smash once and leave peace afterwards.

Amid the noise of the shouting and smashing he thought of the people who were on board the vessel who had called for help. They would be frightened, perhaps, as many times he himself had been frightened by the sea. They must be comforted. He staggered across the wheelhouse to the wireless-room and let his big hand fall like a blessing upon the shoulder of the operator.

"Para '*Atlantic Whipper*': *No tiene miedo. Vamos rapidamente con Dios.*"

A cry came from somewhere below as the *Angeles* fell against a wave and shuddered as if sick, and as he lurched back to the wheelhouse he swore in his mind at a man who could cry out because he was merely uncomfortable. A man must make a noise like that, a donkey-bray, at respectable times when his mother died or his house burned down or his wife dropped a pitcher of wine; such a dismal trumpeting must be reserved for important times, and not spent on matters of discomfort. His ship and all in her must go like this through the night, and into the day, and through the day and into the dark again before they would come to the one they were to save. It was too early yet for twittering aloud like so many palsied pups of flea-bitten baboons.

At a minute to ten o'clock the *Atlantic Whipper* received the signal from the *Angeles*: *Have no fear. We are coming speedily, with God.*

Towards midnight a message flickered through the network of land-based aerials, from the destroyer *Brindle*. The trawler *Minniscoe* had been overwhelmed off the Irish coast. One survivor and two bodies had been picked up. The tug *Salvado* was still searching the area. Orders were requested from Plymouth.

Arrangements were made along the land-lines. Brief questions were asked and answered by the Admiralty, Watson and Blount, and the Southern Salvage Company, while in the windy dark the search went on for another bobbing head, an upturned face among the heaving trough and crest of the Irish Sea. It was perfectly simple, on paper. The destroyer was to attend rescue until relieved by the lifeboat now putting out from Wicklow, and then turn south for position 49.50 north, 12.40 west if she judged her remaining fuel to be sufficient. The tug was to leave the scene immediately and steam for the *Atlantic Whipper*.

On board the *Whipper*, Anthony Bond intercepted these several messages and passed them to the captain. They were reassuring; but they could not, even with the confidence expressed in their formality, more strongly sustain the heart of Captain Harkness than the signal he had been given earlier. *We are coming speedily, with God.* Now a crumpled ball of paper, it was still in his hand, buried in his pocket as he watched the white spray breaking on the windows of the wheelhouse. He knew what kind of a ship was the little *Angeles*, and he knew her position and course. Even with God, she would not reach the *Whipper*. Therein lay the strength of the message in his pocket, and its reassurance. On his behalf, a man was attempting the impossible.

TEN

THE three people in the lounge of the *Atlantic Whipper* had been silent for so long that it seemed deserted, and five minutes ago a steward had turned the lights out, not even troubling to look round the place. There were now only the smouldering points of light from the pilot bulbs to keep darkness away. In this faint glow their faces seemed to float in shadow and their hands to flutter up as softly as doves when they moved them to hide a yawn or light a cigarette. The glow did not define the unreflecting fabric of their clothes but only the pale skin of hands and faces, and the gold of Dr. Papasian's wrist-watch, and Major Draycott's horn-rimmed glasses, which he had not taken off although it was too dim in here now even to pretend to read his battered-looking book. Ann Brown was turning a small turquoise ring on her finger, slipping it round and round as she sat with her head back against the padded banquette, thinking of Peter. For a little while the Major had been watching the soft glint of the lamps on the ring as she turned it. He was becoming hypnotised.

She thought, 'Dearest Peter,' and felt the touch of him again and recounted the host of quiet intimacies, certain that she remembered each smallest one of them, and certain she always would.

The dim light gleamed again, again on the turning ring as her fingers moved, and the old man in the chair near-by dozed off, his waking worries turning to worried dreams.

Dr. Papasian took the handkerchief from the breast-pocket of his coat and as quietly as he could blew his nose. He was cold, but there was nowhere else to go. His mind was very alert; there could be no question of sleep; if he had wanted to sleep he would not have used the drug.

He put the handkerchief back, and sat for a long time without moving. The floor trembled under his feet but the small pilot lamps burned steadily, reminding him of the lamps that glowed in the early hours along hospital corridors. He would be there again, in St. Peter's, going along the corridors and into the wards and theatres, busy with work. There was nothing to worry about; he would soon be there again.

The floor trembled. The lamps glowed steadily. Draycott slept. Ann Brown's fingers moved, turning the thoughts round with the ring, turning them back, and round again, to gleam in the quiet of her mind.

Anthony Bond had sent a message to his wife, as soon as he had realised that the chance of sending private messages was thinning fast. He had simply said, *Will be delayed. Love. Tony.*

Love, Thelma, said the photograph. *Love, Tony,* said the telegram. The most abused dog-eared word in the language, used on Christmas cards by people who had nothing in common, certainly not love for each other; used on the telephone when the left ear ached to escape the pressure of the hard black bakelite and the monotony of the distant intimate voice—'Well, I've really got to dash now—remember me to Beatrice, and give her my love'; used as a quick paying-off when the pen neared the bottom of the note-paper with sudden relief. 'Affectionately' would be too personal a word, an obvious lie; but 'love' would be all right; it could be used for anything— disinterest, duty, habit, even hate.

But now he had forgotten about sending the message. There had been others since, much more important ones from Watson and Blount, and G.L.D. Land's End, and the *Angeles.* A few minutes ago there had been another:

'Salvado'—'Salvado'—'Salvado' to 'Atlantic Whipper'. *Am making for you now. Please give position accurate as possible.*

He had given the tug' their position from the precise figures that Beggs had written down for him. He had asked Beggs:

"What's it like up for'ard?"

"Dodgy."

Beggs went back into the chart-room. In the wheel-house Captain Harkness was by the binnacle again. The mean list on the inclinometer was still less than twenty degrees. The list was not so important now as the trouble in number one hold; but if Turnbull and the bosun and the men down there failed to check the water, the list would grow, and the small thin needle on the indicator would move hour by hour into the danger section. It was no good breaking the glass and putting a finger in and pushing the little needle round to zero. The ship would have to be moved round the needle. A cycle had started when the hatch-cover had been stove-in. Riding head to sea, the ship was taking water over her bows and it was flooding into the hold; in the hold it was surging forward every time the bows went down to a trough, so that, every time, the bows went deeper and shipped more water than before. Soon it would flood across to number two hatch where the barley had shifted, and if number two hatch were stove-in the list would increase and there would be no stopping it.

That was the black side. Harkness had assessed it and dismissed it. On the other side there was only a pattern of chance, but it was based on realities. The gale could drop: if only it dropped to force seven or eight they could weather it until help came. The *Salvado* could reach them in a day and a half, and she was built for these seas; they were her natural element. The *Angeles* would never get here unless the storm died, and if it died there would be no need of her; but she was the nearest ship and even her presence gave comfort.

Harkness had answered her second signal by saying,

We are all right. You should resume your course. We shall not expect you but send our thanks for your offer.

He had never met the master of the *Angeles* but he had met his kind. Manuelo Lopez de las Castillas would be very indignant at the reply from the *Whipper*. Spanish conceit would be sorely pricked. So the captain of the British ship considered the *Angeles* too old and feeble for the task of saving him? He would be shown that it is better to be saved by even a drifting hulk with a crew of leprous rubbish-pickers mustered from the stinking garbage-heaps of hell than to wait for a smart new tug that would arrive to find him sunk.

You should resume your course. No message could drive Manuelo more urgently to heap his coal on. But had Harkness said, *Thank you, we shall expect you*, the *Angeles* would have steamed precisely in this same direction at full speed. There were no words a radio-transmitter could ever send that would alter Manuelo from his course or purpose; but for the record and his conscience, Harkness had tried.

Spray hit the windows and they went white in the glare of the lamps. Afterwards there was silence, a deep uncanny silence that would have led a landsman to believe the gale had dropped suddenly and completely to leave a perfect calm. The ship was canted forward and for this halcyon moment seemed transfixed in the sea and the silence. Harkness went to the port wheelhouse door and opened it. A moment ago it could not have been opened without a man's shoulder against it. Now it swung easily and he went out to the bridge-end. A soft breeze whispered past his face, rich with salt. Above him there was a mist flying past the lamps, racing along below the greater dark; spangles of it were caught by the angular tableau of the direction-finder and aerials on the monkey island above him; their pattern was frosted by the mist that clung where the light fell. He looked down, across the foredeck to where the lamps shone and the men worked. He pitied them. They were working against hopelessness more than against the sea itself.

Reluctantly he raised his head, and looked at the sea. The ship was listed to port, so that standing level here he was looking down at the water. It was black and a man would think he could walk on it. This was the bottom of the trough between the last wave and the next and the silence would go on until that next came. It would be high. He could make out its height already. It formed a ridge as solid-looking as a mountain-ridge against the white salt sky. It was higher than the ship. He watched it coming. There was still only the soft fanning of air against his face, and there was still the silence. Standing here like this in the midst of a violent gale you could believe in anything, in God or ghosts or poltergeists; you could see a flight of angels go overhead or a flock of bats sent by the devil to take your soul to hell; you could believe that these were your last few seconds of life, eked out by your quiet watching of the wave that was coming for you and your ship and all in her.

Matthew Harkness had seen waves like this, coming for him through the years of his life; he was not afraid of them; but he was awed by them, and by the bigness of the sea. He never forgot how big it was, or what it could do if you turned your eye away or mishandled your ship. Those who forgot died early. Those who were afraid had reason to be, for a man in fear has lost nine-tenths of the fight; they were afraid of the sea, but their worst enemy was within. The deadliest fear of all was the fear a man had of himself, of his own weakness and of his inability to meet danger and shout it down and deal with it. Turnbull, he thought, was not afraid of the sea, but he had no faith in himself. He would be afraid of not acquitting himself in the sight of others. Only a vain man could have this worst of all the fears, a man easily slighted. Turnbull was down there now, with the bosun and the men, working with them and urging them on, and urging himself on, committed to the absolute necessity of proving himself and outlasting them in strength and breath and courage, so that they should never find out. That was the paradox. Only a coward could be braver than the others, having to deal with his fear as well as with the danger; he would lead them to the exposed hill-top where the enemy guns were trained and waiting, or take them into the jungle where the night was stealthy, or urge them to the task of saving their ship from the deep when the hurricane raged. The coward was the bravest of them all, when his vanity drove him to prove it.

The wave neared, rising taller and beginning to stoop as the wind pressed against its back and tore away thin water from its top. The white spray was flung out and began falling, pattering on to the superstructure as Harkness turned for the door and opened it. He knew how to time a wetting. He was in the wheelhouse with the door slammed tight when the wave broke against the bows of the ship and its white wreckage came spilling and boiling over the fo'c'sle head. The night exploded and it seemed there could never have been such a thing as the silence that had gone before. The windows shuddered as the water hit them and in the wheelhouse the sick radiance shone, the white spray reflecting the lamplight and draining colour away as snow will do beneath the window of a room.

Harkness thought of the men for'ard; they would have run for the fo'c'sle shelters before the wave broke. They would be waiting now to dodge back to their work while the ship laboured into the trough and gave them another chance. Turnbull would be. there, shouting obscenities against the sea and helping the men. There would be no time for prayers; a quick black oath worked wonders when the heart was sick.

114

Bond came out of the wireless-room. Pitching his voice above the dying tumult he said, "Main aerial's gone, sir!"

Harkness looked at Bond. His face was crumpled and he looked lost. His big toy had broken.

"Can you rig a jury?"

It was as if Bond had never thought of it. In the despair of this terrible thing he had not been able to project his mind even to the next obvious step. His face brightened and his voice was eager.

"Oh. Yes, sir!" He ran to the door. Harkness looked at the brass clock on the bulkhead. It was nearing two a.m. From two until two-fifteen, shipping would maintain radio silence and await calls from the *Atlantic Whipper*; now there would be none.

The door opened again and Harkness thought it was Bond coming back, but when he turned he saw the mate. Water fell from his oilskins on to the dark patch of boards by the door. He wrenched off his sou'wester and stood with it in his hand. The gash on his hand had opened again and it bled brightly. He stood getting his breath. He had run aft from the fo'c'sle while the ship was in the trough. Harkness waited.

"Two pumps are going, sir." He took another breath. "We've got timber across number one but we can't rig a tarpaulin because there's——" then the next wave came and he stood shouting silently to the captain while the snow-light bloomed in the wheelhouse and the windows trembled. When he could be heard, Harkness stood close to Turnbull and said:

"What's number two hatch like?"

"All right so far. We're going to reinforce it after we've finished the other." He breathed deeply again, standing erect in the belled-out oilskins. Water was still running from his sea-boots and a rivulet had formed and was tracing its way towards the echo-sounder stand on the port side.

"There's help coming," Harkness said. "The *Salvado*'s on her way. Tell the men."

Turnbull tightened his face in case it should show relief. He said, "We can get home without a tug." He was prepared to play this the way the captain wanted it. If he had been here as master he would have sent a distress signal earlier than Harkness had; the *Salvado* would now have been closer. But Harkness had waited, maybe out of pride. Turnbull could be proud, too, prouder than Harkness, than anyone. He had to be. Most vital of all, he had to show it. He had been in a rage with Harkness when he had left the wheelhouse in answer to the call from the fo'c'sle that had reported the stove-in hatch. He had cursed him aloud in the welter of the wind as he had dodged from shelter to shelter across the foredeck, because Harkness had committed him to courage, out of pride. His rage had hardened him, and he was ready for the challenge, as always he had been ready throughout his life, forced to meet the little and the big challenges that had been thrown to him by kids at his kindergarten and by the puffed-up gang of hoodlums in his street, by his father, and his family, and the war. He had met them all, from the threat of a thick ear in the playground when the girls had been watching and cat-calling their derision, to the threat of a German U-boat's torpedo that had riven his ship and spread its wreckage on the water where he swam among bodies and red unrecognisable shapes. Now he had grown weary of challenge, and must steel himself harder against it and whip up his nerves to meet it, calling upon reserves that must one day run out and leave him naked, no braver than the others. Somehow he must arm himself even against that day, and be ready when it came. Unless, by luck, death gave him no time, and there was no one there to see.

Harkness said to him, "Yes, we might get home without a tug, but only a fool would try. The important thing is to

116

tell the men there's help coming. Have you got any of the electricians down there?"

"I've mustered all hands, sir."

"Send the electricians up here. The main aerial's gone and Bond's rigging a jury."

The wheelhouse suddenly swayed. They shot their hands out for support and Turnbull's sea-boot slipped on the wet planks. Harkness caught his arm and checked the fall as he skinned his head across the door. The quartermaster had called something but no one heard him as the spray came at the windows and burst there. He dragged at the wheel, but the ship had taken the slack and was wallowing with a crest under her until she slid to the trough, half buried in water at her stem.

"*Meet her!*"

Harkness shouted it. The mate was against the bulkhead, his hands pressed against the graze on his scalp. Harkness left him and staggered to the wheel, bringing his weight to bear with the helmsman's on the spokes. The card swung in the compass. Something fell to the planks from the first-aid shelf. Turnbull was upright, hands down from his head; he shook his head slowly like a dazed boxer.

The wheel came round. Vibration ran through the ship in a wave and then stilled. Beggs appeared from the chartroom, saw Turnbull, and went over to him, but Turnbull put a hand up in a queer gesture of defence as if Beggs were attacking him. He went on moving his head while the second mate held him. A bandage-canister rolled down the planks and stopped against Beggs's foot. Turnbull said in the noise, "Leave me alone."

Beggs picked up the canister and took it to the first-aid shelf. When he came back, Harkness was with Turnbull, examining his head. Turnbull was saying, ". . . to get back down there, they'll——"

Harkness said to Beggs, "Jim, go for'ard and look to the men."

"Ay, ay, sir."

Turnbull tried to reach the door first, throwing one hand out like a toppling drunk. Harkness held him back as Beggs pushed the door open against the gale and went out to the bridge-end.

"It's my place down there, it's my place," Turnbull said with a thick tongue, petulantly. The captain shouted for the lookout. Smithers came in, a pink face propped up by stiff black oilskins. Harkness told him:

"Help Mr. Turnbull below."

When they had gone he rang down to the chief steward and said that the mate was going below with a head wound. Persham was good with medicine.

"Are we okay, sir?"

"Just a big wave. Look to the passengers and make sure no one was knocked over." He was thinking chiefly of Major Draycott. He had to repeat it as the ship ran into the next swell but Persham understood and said he would see to everything.

Harkness went back to the binnacle.

"Starb'd ten."

"Starb'd ten, sir."

He watched the compass card with its glow on his face. The illuminated figures meant little; he was judging the course they needed by feel and instinct as the deck trembled under his feet.

"Midships."

"Midships, sir."

When he was satisfied he moved to the windows and waited. It was half an hour before Beggs came up to the bridge.

"Well?"

Beggs was a shapeless hump in his drenched reefer. "Number one's stove in again, sir. Two men hurt, not bad." Water trickled down his strong blunt face as he waited for Harkness to speak. The windows thundered and whitened. After they had cleared Harkness said:

"I take it there's no point in working any more on the hatch."

"It'd be dangerous, sir."

"Are the pumps still working?"

"Yes, two of them."

"Tell the bosun to get the hands below. Take some of them to help Sparks rig the new aerial. Where's Peter?"

"In his bunk, sir."

"Let him sleep. While you're below, ask Dr. Papasian if he'd mind looking in at the sick bay. Persham's there with Steve. See how Harris is. Tell any passengers who ask about that noise that the gale's as bad as it can be, and it can only get better after this. You're not a good liar but make it sound convincing."

Beggs nodded. "Anything you want sent up, sir?"

Harkness looked at the water collecting messily against the port side bulkhead. "A man with a mop."

Beggs left him. Harkness returned to the binnacle. He did not like seeing water in the wheelhouse; it was untidy, even dangerous—as Steve Turnbull had found out. And dear Margaret would be dreadfully self-satisfied if she could see these messy planks. She had set out, eleven years ago, to show him that a gentleman's life was on the land in a clean safe house, and that she could keep a finer home than a ship could ever make. She had not spared herself in her pathetic competition with the sea for the comfort of his company through these eleven years, blindly un-convinced that he would never leave the sea until he was too old or died with it; but he felt he must at least compete in his turn with her, even when she could not know. He had asked for a man with a mop.

He checked the helmsman, mentally reviewing his position. There could be no more work on number one hatch; in a sea like this a man could go overboard without a cry, or spill his brains against an obstacle. The two pumps must clear what water they could from the hold. The list would now increase. The grain in number two hold could not be shifted back. If the gale held at this force, number two hatch would be stove-in unless the ship could keep her head up with slack water below. The engines were using coal, burning it away at half speed to do no more than keep steerage. She was moving no nearer the land.

The *Whipper* lay perilously beset. His duty, at this moment of his admission, was changed. The cargo had no value now; if he could, he would jettison it to lighten ship, enough to bring her head up. His task was not to deliver his cargo and passengers to harbour, but to forget the cargo and ensure the safety of the ship and those on board. If the *Salvado* or some other ship arrived in time he must consider the step of ordering his passengers to the boats, and the three injured men and possibly Steve Turnbull as well, if Dr. Papasian advised it. The tug would take them on board and they would be safe. If by that time the sea was too bad for the boats to be launched, or the list was too severe, the passengers must jump into the water with their life-jackets on and be picked up by the tug.

He hoped it would not come to that. They had their trust in him; to have to order them overboard into a violent sea would humiliate him; it was the least gallant way of saving life. But they would suffer no more than the soaking and the shock; in a few hours they would emerge from their blankets on board the *Salvado*, warm from the brandy and relieved of this nagging fear that must be in some of them now. But he would not let it come to that, if he could help it.

He crossed the slope of the deck and called the engine-room on the telephone. He was answered by János, the third engineer. Harkness asked him:

"Are you all right down there?" He could visualise the Hungarian nodding his big handsome head.

"We are all fine, sir, yes."

"Have you had water on the skylight?"

There was a pause. János thought slowly, double-checking his reply before making it, as a chess-player deliberates on his next move. "There was some water, sir. Then we covered the skylight."

"I see. Has the Chief turned in?"

There was another pause, then Brewer's voice. "Chief here, sir."

"János says you're all right."

"We'd rather be down here than up there." He knew what the captain had telephoned for. "I thought you'd want the latest figures on consumption, sir."

"I should."

"We'll steam twenty-three hours at this speed. If you could drop one knot we could make nearly thirty."

The gale was worse now than an hour ago. "We can't risk it, Chief, unless she pipes down a bit."

"It's twenty-three hours, then, conservative."

Before Harkness had rung off he had run the simple calculation through his head. The *Salvado* would take thirty-six hours to get here. So far as he knew, there was no ship nearer than the tug except the *Angeles*, who would never reach this far in this sea without foundering. So there would be thirteen hours for the *Whipper* to spend here alone in the gale, her bunkers empty and engines dead. She could not do it. The moment the propeller stopped turning her steerage would go, and she would swing slowly round and broach-to. The first wave against her side would fill number one hold and smash the after hatches. The second or third would find her with a dangerous list and within minutes she would lie on her beam-ends.

Mathematics was a wonderful science. You could divine the future with it. At fifteen minutes to two tomorrow night the engines would stop and the ship would move into immediate danger. She could perhaps last another hour, lying broached-to and receiving the seas as they chose to come at her, pounding her and filling her until she foundered. So that by fifteen minutes to three the seascape in longitude 49.50 north, latitude 12.40 west, would be unbroken by the *Whipper's* shape.

The gap of thirteen hours was no better than a gap of thirty. The vital hour would be that which followed the dying of the engines when the coal ran out. In one hour the sea could easily obliterate this mote.

The deck tilted.

"Meet her!"

"Meet her, sir!"

The thunder came, the burst of water against the bridge. White drifts of it went whirling by. Then there came the trough, and the wallowing, and the unearthly silence.

Thirteen hours; but if they could be narrowed to a few, and the gale eased a little . . . there was a chance. You had to weigh it all up. You had to conjure with unknown figures, and turn your mind against unreasonable hope. If you were experienced, and judged things right, you could save this ship, twenty-three hours in advance. And, knowing this, you must bear the appalling weight of the decision. There was no one to help you. The officers and the engineers could give you information, and help you carry out the decision once it was made; but only you could make it. You were supreme here, and alone.

The storm burst at the windows. He could see his reflection in the whitened glass. He stood like a faded photograph, a hump of dark and a peaked cap and a white face. He thanked God he was not Turnbull. Had Steve been standing here, that would be the enemy he would have to fight, the man there in the glass. The windows cleared and the silence came. In the silence of the deep troughs he could think better. There was only one thought worth considering at this moment. If he were to order the engine-room to slow, he would imperil the ship, leaving her less headway to meet the seas with; but the danger would not be certain. The danger would be certain if her present speed were maintained. It would strike at fifteen minutes to two tomorrow night. If the thirteen-hour gap could be narrowed there was a chance, involving a change in the gale that could only be prayed for; but with less speed and less headway than this, the seas could come at the ship more strongly, and a big wave could fill her decks and send her down at any hour— tonight, or at dawn, tomorrow noon, or evening.

The scales were level. Chance was heavy on both sides. There had to be the decision. He stood near the binnacle, watching it, for a few seconds prolonging the luxury of leaving all this to God. The wheelhouse door was pulled open on the port side and a seaman came in; he slammed the door and gave a cheerful grin to the captain and then began pounding his mop across the planks.

Harkness watched him for a moment and then went to the telephone and rang the engine-room. When Brewer came through he told him, "Chief, you can have your knot."

"Ease speed one knot, sir. Ay, ay."

He hooked the receiver back. The gap was closed from thirteen hours to six.

ELEVEN

COSTAIN came along the passage at a half-run and as the deck tilted he caught his shoulder on a fire-extinguisher bracket and span round under the impact. There were only the pilot-lamps burning and his eyes were still slow from sleep. He went on again and came to cabin nine, and knocked. There was no answer, so he knocked again very briefly and opened the door. It was dark inside. "Ann." He put his head out again so that he could take a look along the passage, both ways. This was very irregular. He looked into the cabin again. "*Ann . . .*"

The ship yawed and the door tried to swing away from his hand. He found the light-switch and flipped it and the light burst against his eyes, showing him an aching golden scene whose furniture took shape by painful degrees. The bed was empty and tidy; none of her clothes were about. He switched off the light and drew back into the passage, shutting the door. When he turned round he looked directly into Dodds's face. The shock of seeing his white face and white jacket floating there in the gloom was a fair one; on top of it, Costain shouldn't be coming out of a woman passenger's cabin in the middle watch.

His heart pumped badly but his tone was authoritative. He might have to slip the man a pound for this, but that must settle it. They were still officer and steward. "Is Miss Brown all right, Dodds?"

The white face and jacket swayed and hit the bulkhead but didn't fall. The small bloodshot eyes wavered with a kind of bodiless independence as they searched the gloom for the voice.

"Damn you, is she all right?" He was angry with Dodds for being drunk and finding him here and not answering.

There mightn't be any blackmail, now. Or would it be worse? The man might go shouting about, broadcasting with bawdy gusto the story of the Third Mate and the Frightened Lady. Costain was sweating.

"We'll all go down . . ." Dodds said suddenly and very loudly—"All go down . . . the bloody ship an' all, we will!"

Costain slapped his face hard and he stopped, and drooped against the bulkhead, shivering noisily. "You'd better go and put your head under a tap, Dodds. If the mate finds you like this you'll be slung overboard." He stepped past the man, angry at the delay. The big wave had wakened him and he had turned out half-asleep. He wasn't on watch but he ought to be on the bridge. The watch-rota had been shelved but they must all help. He had to find Ann first, though, and tell her not to be frightened. She would be very frightened by now, and probably crying again. He began trotting along the passage.

The smoking-room was dark but he put the main lights on in case she had fallen asleep in a chair. There was no one here. He heard footsteps and turned and saw two men staggering together along the passage from the for'ard companionway. Christ, was the whole crew drunk? He caught them up. From the twin lurching bundle of oilskins a face turned as he called to them. Smithers said, "The mate's hurt, sir."

"Who the hell's that?" Turnbull lurched on, not looking round.

"Where are you taking him, Smithers?"

"Sick bay, sir."

"Can you manage?"

"Of course he can bloody well manage," said the mate bitterly. "Where are you going, Mr. Costain?"

They kept together in a shambling group along the narrow passage. "Bridge, sir."

"Well, this isn't the way, don't y' know that?"

Costain turned back without answering. At the end of the athwartships alleyway he stopped and found the door of the lounge bolted open. He switched on the lights and saw three people sitting in the corner. Ann was one of them. He took a step inside, then turned back and switched off the lights. It would be better. He hit a chair, going forward again in the total darkness that followed the glare. Slowly the three faces became visible in the glow of the pilot-lamps. Someone asked what time it was. It sounded like Major Draycott; his voice was bewildered, as if he had been woken up. Costain had automatically checked his watch when he had turned out.

"Two o'clock, sir." He stood at a loss. He had to talk to Ann, but not in front of Draycott and Dr. Papasian. He could not imagine ever being able to talk to Ann again in front of anyone else.

"There's a message for you, Miss Brown." He said it quietly, bending over the chair near where she sat on the banquette.

"A message?"

"Two o'clock, what day?" asked Draycott from the gloom. He sounded worried.

Peter Costain said quietly, "It's been sent to your cabin."

"Tuesday," said Papasian.

More quietly still, Costain said, "Ann . . ." Surely she'd understand and come with him?

Papasian said alertly, "What was that sway?"

She had to come. He must get up on the bridge as soon as he could. He said, "Sway?"

The alert voice nodded. There was the gleam of a gold tooth. "The lurch. The ship lurched."

Ann was moving. He said, "We hit a wave, Doctor, that's all."

"Tuesday morning," the Major said loudly to no one.

126

"Tuesday *morning*." He coughed to clear phlegm that had gathered in sleep. "It's not Tuesday *night*?"

Peter stood back and shifted the chair as Ann got up; the chair would not move more than a couple of inches because it was chained. He put a hand out and guided her between the chair and the banquette.

"Has anything happened?" she asked.

"No." He went with her to the port-side doorway. She was cramped and lurched against him on the tilted floor and he steadied her, thinking, 'There's not time to go to the cabin.'

"Nothing's happened at all," he said when they were in the passage. The main lights were not burning and they were out of sight of the lounge doorway now. Her face looked very pale but she did not sound frightened.

"What message is it, Peter?"

"There isn't one. It's from me. I had to talk to you. You're not frightened?" He held both her hands.

"Why should I be?" Her hands were not cold. He didn't understand this. She had been so frightened, before, that he had found her sobbing in her cabin. The gale was worse now and there had been that terrific lurch.

"I—I just thought you might be worried." He wanted to kiss her, but it would be irrelevant and could lead nowhere. He had to be on the bridge.

"I'm perfectly all right," she said.

He was oddly disappointed. He had been ready to protect her and she did not want protecting. He should have been glad she wasn't frightened.

"I'm glad," he said rather bleakly. "You were scared, before."

"When?" She was still trying to talk like a passenger to a ship's officer but it wasn't going to work. "Oh, in my cabin." She smiled suddenly. "I wasn't scared, Peter."

"But you were crying. You said——"

127

"I was only sad about growing old."

He could think of nothing to say. She began laughing softly. There she went again. Why couldn't he ever see anything funny, when she was tickled to death? He had spent all that energy in reassuring her, trying every trick he knew that would stop her being scared of the way the deck was tilting after that hideous crack of the shifting-boards, and she'd been crying because she was sad about growing old. And she had humoured him, pretending she was being comforted.

"My God," he said, "what a damn' fool I must have looked!"

She stopped laughing. "Dear Peter."

As an afterthought he said, "But you're only twenty-eight!"

"Then I must have been sad about being twenty-nine. Did you come here to comfort me again, Peter?"

"Yes, but I'll know better in future."

"Don't be angry with me."

"I'm not angry with *you*!"

"Then who?"

"God knows! It's—it's just that I've got no sense of humour, or something." He must go. "Anyway, I shan't have it on my mind that you're worried. The ship's all right. As soon as we reach port we can really talk, and—and see each other." Still angry that she had made a fool of him, not angry with her but with—with whom? Himself, he supposed—and conscious that he must hurry away, and that the gale was worse and that damned steward was drunk and the mate was injured, he said urgently and not graciously at all, "Oh Lord, Ann, I'm in love with you, up to my neck." Ashamed of the way he had said it, he took his hands away from hers. "I've got to go now."

He wanted her to say something before he ran. There had to be an answer of some sort. Or would she just laugh

128

softly? If she did, he'd have to ask her this time what was funny. He wasn't going to be left out of every joke.

"You mustn't be in love with me, Peter."

He heard someone coming. "It's just one of those things you can't stop." He turned away and saw the second mate looming along the passage. Ann whispered:

"Thank you for coming, Peter. You're wonderful."

Jim Beggs reached them and said, "You seen Dr. Papasian?"

"In there. What's up, Jim?"

Beggs passed them and went into the lounge, snapping the lights on. Peter said to Ann, "Sorry." He hurried off along the passage. There must be a clause in the book about officers canoodling with women passengers when the skipper was on the bridge and the ship was hove-to in a gale. It was unthinkable. That was what she did to him. This was love, and, God help him, he was in it.

Persham was dropping down a companionway as he reached the end of the passage, with a box and some scissors.

"Pershy!"

He stopped and looked up from the bottom of the steps. Costain said, "That man Dodds is drunk. You'd better——"

"I've fixed him. He's got it all up."

"How's the mate?"

"Contusions, nothin' bad." He looked like a busy doctor itching to get away from a visiting director of the board.

Behind Costain, Beggs and Dr. Papasian were hurrying along from the lounge.

"Someone's going to tell me what's happened," Costain said furiously, but Beggs and the little Armenian went bobbing down the companionway and he was left unanswered.

He got a rich oath out and went on deck into one of the

silences as the ship lay wallowing in a trough. Before he had reached the wing of the bridge the next wave came and he arrived in the wheelhouse drenched. Captain Harkness looked at him idly, and said:

"The deck has just been mopped, Mr. Costain."

He looked down at the pool of water forming round his feet. He squelched towards dry planking. "Sorry, sir."

"That mop has been left here for our use."

Costain took up the mop and pushed it over the wet planks. How the hell could he come in here with his feet dry when the sea was breaking green over the decks? He opened the door when there was a chance and wrung out the mop, coming back and propping it head-up in the corner of the wheelhouse. His feet squelched in his boots as he came across to the captain.

"Is there anything I can do, sir?"

Harkness remained in the grip of his thoughts, gazing at the windows as the spray came and turned the glass opaque. His face went dirty white in the back-glare. Obliquely Costain was watching him. Would he ever come to look as experienced as this master, as resolute, with a face as lined? Surely there was nothing in the world that this man hadn't seen.

After the wave's sound had died, Harkness looked at the third mate. "Have you just turned out, Peter?"

"Yes, sir."

The boy's face looked so young; but it looked an intelligent face, an honest one. It wouldn't be a bad face to see, later, when the crisis was on them all. He realised that for the last few hours he had been studying the men who were with him on this mote in the sea. He must try to know what pressure could be put on this man or that, so that when the time came he could pick the best of them for the most vital work. This one was reliable. He said:

"Do you know the general situation?"

"No, sir."

"I'll bring you up to date. Number one hatch-cover's been stove-in again and we've stopped work on it, leaving two pumps going. Two hands are injured, and the mate. The main aerial's been carried away and Sparks is trying to rig a jury. Until he does, we shall remain cut off from signals."

The next wave came. He waited, watching the big smother of it blot out the fo'c'sle and foredeck. When he could be heard again he said, "We expect the tug *Salvado* alongside in thirty-six hours. Our coal will last us thirty, as we've reduced speed one knot. We'll do what we can about the six-hour gap when there's a chance. That is the present situation."

They bent their knees as the deck swung. Peter had the sudden dreadful vision of Ann floating in her life-jacket. Oh Lord, what a time to fall in love!

"Are the hands hurt badly, sir?"

"No, but I don't expect they'll be much use to us."

The next wave broke. He listened for the cracking of timber as the water fell across the deck. With every wave he listened like this, as the water dropped by the ton across number two hatch-cover. If it were stove-in, the six-hour gap would lose its importance; with both for'ard holds filling, the *Whipper* would not ride another thirty hours; there would be coal left in her bunkers when she sank.

The silence of the next trough came. "Dr. Papasian has been asked to look at their injuries. We're lucky to have him aboard."

"Persham's busy, too. I passed him as I came on deck."

"Yes." He thought of the chief steward; he was one of those he could rely upon. "Didn't he want to be a doctor?"

"I've heard him talk about it, sir. I don't think he could afford the training."

"What a stupid waste."

The next wave thundered out of the night. When the windows drained clear he said, "Get the Aldis. After each wave, turn the beam on number two hatch and let me know how it looks."

"Ay, ay, sir." He fetched the lamp.

Dr. Papasian straightened up. "Now you should rest."

The smell of medicines was heavy in the air, a smell to make ill even the fit. Turnbull hated it and was afraid of it. The Seaman's Hospital at Greenwich had smelt like this for seven months and he remembered only the pain and not their kindness. He said:

"I can't rest, Doctor." He stood up. Someone had a hand under his elbow to steady him. Persham's. He shook it off. He couldn't feel the bandage round his head; he could feel only the aching rhythmic beat of the dying-away pain. The Armenian shrugged.

"You will make the damage worse."

Turnbull walked carefully down the slope of the deck. He must get outside before the smell made him retch. Papasian grimaced, turning away to wash his hands. When they came to you for healing you knew better than they did; when you had healed them they knew better than you.

Persham had the tap running, and waited near the basin with a clean towel ready. Papasian bent over the basin. The water swirled to the vortex tinged with red. As the sick bay lurched, Persham put a hand out and steadied the doctor.

"Thank you. The gale is worse?"

"It'll blow itself out, Doctor."

He took the towel and dried his hands, glancing once at the steward. "You have worked in a hospital?"

"No, Doctor." He felt proud, and bitter.

Papasian gave him the towel. "There is nothing

serious," he said, looking round at the bunks. "Let them rest. That was the first officer, who went out?"

"Yes, Doctor."

"He will be back, I expect. Send for me."

"Is there any sign of concussion, Doctor?"

"No. Just stupidity." He gave a quick gold smile and Persham laughed. It was heady to discuss a case like this, and share a joke about the mate's stupidity. It made up for a lot. "The way out is up those stairs?"

"I'll show you, Doctor."

From his bunk Harris watched them. The bloody steward creep-arsing the little medico; it made you sick. But it was too true what they said about the mate: he was a sore-headed bastard now, all right.

When Papasian had gone up the companionway, Harris called out to Persham, "Come on, Flossie Nightingale, my nose wants wipin'!"

Persham came along to his bunk. "Why don't you shut up? The other blokes need their sleep, don't you know that?"

"I'm goin' to turn out, mate. I've 'ad enough o' this."

"You'll keep where you are. You don't know when you're well off."

"Well off? Down 'ere in this stinkin' butcher's-shop?"

"You're feelin' better, I can see that."

"Go on, you mus' be psychic, mate. Now 'elp me out."

"Listen, I've asked the doctor about you, an' he says you got to rest." He turned as someone came down the companionway. It was Stubbs.

"Look out," said Harris, " 'ere comes the fairy queen."

Stubbs walked carefully down the slope of the planks. His eyes were bloodshot and a mist of spray clung to the stubble on his face. His reefer dripped water. Persham's instincts rebelled at the sight of anything so unhygienic

133

coming into his sick bay. "What do you want, Stubbs?"

"I don' feel so good."

"You wanter tonic?" Harris grinned from the bunk. "Go an' take a look at the Ole Bull with 'is 'ead done up like a puddin'!"

"Look," Persham said, "these blokes have got to sleep. Now get off out of it."

Stubbs looked down at Harris and said, "All nice an' cushy, eh? Bosun's bleedin' darlin', all tucked up in bed!"

"Now don't get on my tits," Harris said. Persham left them, to tidy the medical kit on the table. He couldn't handle men like Stubbs. They were just animals. You couldn't make them see sense when it was staring them in the face.

Harris asked Stubbs, "You got that grain shifted?"

The pale stubbly face lost the last of its colour and the beard showed up a dirty grey. "Would she be lyin' over like this if we 'ad? You don't know much, do you, down 'ere out of the way? You should see number one hatch, boy, fillin' up quick an' nothin' to stop it." He looked directly into Harris's face, speaking urgently, persuasively. "She's down by the head an' she won't come up again. You know what that means. I don' 'ave to tell you."

Harris frowned. "Number one got stove-in, then?" He had been awake only a little while; he still felt lightheaded. He called to Persham, "Hey, did I lose much blood?"

Persham came over and said, "What sort of selfish bastard are you? If you don't shut your row an' let these blokes sleep, you can just clear out of here. They've been hurt a sight worse'n you. Don't forget, now. One more shout, an' you'll get out, and don't come back with your head split open, because I won't be interested." He left them. Harris said:

134

"What's the time, Stubby?"

"I got no watch. It's night." He put a hand on Harris's shoulder. "You want to know what I think? This lot's due for the bottom." Harris realised at last what was bothering Stubbs. He was scared sick. "Listen," Stubbs said. "We sent an S O S a long time afore midnight, because there was a plane over us, tryin' to find us. You don't send for bloody aeroplanes unless you're in bad trouble. That was hours ago. Now she's goin' down by the head. I tell you we got no chance, an' the bloody afterguard knows it, an' won't even warn the passengers."

"Well, what d'you think I can do, for Chris' sake?"

Stubbs lowered his voice. "Tell the Skip we want to abandon ship an' take to the boats."

"Who, me?"

"You an' me an' Dodds—he'll go with us. I been talkin' to 'im."

Harris leaned back on his pillow. He had used up his few reserves of energy. "What's this, then—a bloody mutiny?"

Drops of water fell from Stubbs's reefer. The lamplight touched his face; it looked dirty and afraid. "It's every man for 'imself, soon. Who d'you think's goin' to look after you, when she starts going down? Eh?"

Harris closed his eyes. "You talk a lot o' bull."

"Bull, is it? You don' know what's goin' on up there. You bin asleep. I s'ppose you know the aerial's gone, an' we can't get no signals out, or receive any?"

Persham was standing beside him, looking at Harris. Harris was spent. Persham told Stubbs, "Get out."

"What's the matter with you lot?" Stubbs said. "Don't you know when you're in a sinkin' ship?"

Persham was shivering and his eyes were bright. "Get out, Stubbs. This is a sick bay."

"Sick bay, is it? You'll be wantin' a sick bay when——"

"*Get out!*"

Stubbs stood over Persham, who was a small man. "Quite the little doctor, aren't you? Considerin' you're just a bleedin' flunkey——"

Persham had brought the scissors with him because Stubbs was twice his weight, and he jabbed with them because he must get Stubbs out of here, and because Stubbs had called him a flunkey, and it was right. He jabbed at the wrist and blood came quickly as Stubbs jerked back and stared at the blood and then at Persham. He made an animal noise of surprise.

"Now get out."

Harris had opened his eyes at the sound of the steward's voice. He said, "Jesus."

Stubbs held his wrist and looked at Persham. As if he had just thought of a good idea and was still surprised at the simplicity of it he said slowly, "I'm goin' to kill you."

Harris got on to one elbow and said, "Leave the kid alone. He's told you to get out, an' he means it."

The air fluttered in the ventilators and vibration ran through the deck as a squall rose. The tilt increased but Stubbs was no longer frightened. He came towards Persham very deliberately and Harris said quickly, "Leave 'im alone, you fool."

Persham did not back away. He held the scissors in front of him. "You'll get it again," he said, shivering. He hated the man in front of him, for his dirt, and stupidity, and ugliness, and for his being in here.

The tilt stopped and then came back almost at once as if the ship were stiff. Stubbs took his hand off his wrist and attacked, swinging a blow sideways because of the scissors. They leapt like a bright fish and Stubbs screamed, falling across the slope, holding his arm. A hiss of breath came from Harris. Persham's face was sickly as he watched Stubbs crouched over the wound in his arm. The wrist was bright with blood and it fascinated him, horrified him. Someone should pity him, even his enemy. "I'm hurt bad," he said.

"Get out." Oh God, he shouldn't have done this, shouldn't have done this. It wasn't the way.

"You got to do something." It was a whimper. Persham knew he hadn't struck the artery; the floor would be smothered by now if he had.

"He'll bleed to death," Harris said. He wanted to rest and shut his eyes and wait for the throbbing in his head to stop. He must not feel weak like this when the ship was going down. Was it going down? That was Stubbs's tale. Stubbs was going to bleed to death. The scissors were red and Persham's face looked dead; but his eyes were bright; he must be mad; he must do something to stop the blood; this was a sick bay; the kid had said it; it had sounded as if he was saying it was a church; the kid was mad; the blood dripped; his head beat and beat and his stomach was cold, suddenly cold, and sweat was crawling over his face as he watched the bright blood and the big man crouched there with the kid over him and the scissors red.

Persham heard Harris vomiting.

"Help me," Stubbs said.

The smell of the vomit came into the air. Persham looked away from Stubbs for the first time, down at the scissors. He would do anything not to have done that. Against the boards, the vomit crept down the slope of the deck, coming to the blood-spots and covering them. He looked at Harris; he was lying back again with his eyes shut; his face was wet.

He wanted to move and wash the scissors, but movement would make him aware of himself and he would be at the mercy of the self-contempt that was waiting to swamp him. The scissors seemed stuck to his hand as though he must carry them for life so that people should know what he had done.

He was standing like that when the bosun came down

the companionway. He didn't ask a question but flicked a glance at Stubbs, at the steward, and back to Stubbs. Persham moved at last, taking the scissors to the basin and turning the tap on.

"Stubbs, get up." Starley stood at the bottom of the companionway. Persham got a mop and began clearing the mess from the deck, taking the mop to the bucket-hanger and rinsing it, coming back with it. Starley said, "What's the matter with him?"

"He's bleeding."

The bosun came across to Stubbs and took his collar in one hand, yanking him up. His arm flew out and flecks of blood spattered the bosun's face.

"What are you doin' down here, Stubbs?"

"I'm hurt, bad."

"What was it about, the fight?"

"He come at me, with scissors——"

"You could've eaten him, otherwise, couldn't you? What did you come down here for?"

"I'm bleedin', bad. You can see."

"Get up on deck."

Stubbs looked bewildered. They didn't understand. He was losing blood and his arm had gone numb. There were tears of frustration in his eyes. "I been hurt, damn you, *damn your bloody eyes!*"

Starley said, "Get up on deck."

Persham wrung out the mop and came over to them. "I'd better see to him."

Art Starley was smiling. He shook his head. "No, Pershy. I've got a job for him. He's been down here before, hasn't he? I've told him what'd happen if I found him down here again." He turned his bright smile on Stubbs. "I told you, didn't I?"

Stubbs had a sob in his breath. "Christ, can't you see I been hurt?" He thrust his bloodied wrist in front of the bosun's face.

138

"That's nothin', mate. I've not started yet. Get on deck."

Persham took the bad arm and raised it. "Keep it above your head, high as you can reach."

"You got to do somethin' for me."

Starley told the steward, "You're wasting your time. I'm taking him with me."

"But he wants attention, Arthur. He'll lose blood."

"He'll lose blood all right. Stubbs, I'm counting three."

Stubbs kept his arm as high as he could. The numbness was worse. His hand was white.

"One."

Persham said, "He's not fit to work, Arthur. You're not daft."

"Two."

Stubbs began backing away. "You can't," he said, "you can't."

"Three."

"Arthur," Persham said, "for Christ's sake give him a chance and——"

Starley hit Stubbs and he fell. "You're soft, Stubbs. Get up. You're goin' on deck."

"You'll kill him," said Persham. There was nothing he could do now. Even scissors wouldn't help. They hadn't helped before; they'd brought things to this. He turned away and soaked a swab, and wiped Harris's face. Some of his colour was back but he was still unconscious.

"All right," the bosun said, "I'll kill him."

Stubbs was in a heap, looking up at Starley. "Haven't you got no mercy?"

"Not for lice." He pitied the man but was resolved. "This time it's a beating-up. You've had enough warning. If I took you to the captain again he'd murder me. They've got quite enough to do on the bridge. I don't put up with a parasite, even in good weather. Time like this they're a menace. Get up. You're bigger than I am."

Stubbs was holding his wrist and his face was grey. He looked old. Pity was nagging at Starley, so he got hold of the man again and dragged him to his feet and hit him down again. "Get on deck before I lose my temper." Stubbs was whimpering like a child and the bosun was furious with him for awakening his pity. Stubbs was a danger in this ship, adding to the danger of the sea. He had been trying to spread panic among the hands ever since the hatch was stove-in, and he had probably come down here to work on Persham. He would be best overboard; but that was murder.

Stubbs went on whimpering. How bad was he? The bosun had no medical knowledge. He had seen men looking a sight worse than this in a dockside shindy. Poor little Copley had been worse than this, outside Mickey Green's in B.A. Tich Copley was worth ten of this bastard. Starley knew he was strong enough to lug him up the companionway and sling him on deck; but he wouldn't work, he'd pass out first. It wouldn't be the best thing. He'd have to be strong enough to leave Stubbs down here and forget him. He looked round the sick bay. There were two empty bunks. He stopped again and knocked the man's hand away as he tried to shield his face. He hit his face hard, and heard Persham behind him saying, "Don't, don't." Then he got a grip on Stubbs and dragged him across the sloping deck to the nearest bunk.

"He's out cold, Pershy. Gimme a hand."

They lifted him and got him into the bunk. Persham was very quiet. It had been a terrible thing to do, with the scissors, and terrible not to have stopped the bosun hitting Stubbs. He was in charge of the sick bay, but had no authority. It was terrible to have no authority, even enough to match his small responsibilities here.

"I'm sorry he's on your hands, Pershy, but he'll be no

bloody good to me on deck. If he gives any more trouble, bash him."

When the bosun had gone, the chief steward made a bandage-sling and tied Stubbs's arm to the rail above, then cleaned the two stab-cuts and dressed them. Afterwards he got the mop again and cleaned the deck. When he rinsed it in the bucket-hanger the water was tinged with red, as it had been in the basin when Dr. Papasian had washed his hands. He went over to Harris and counted his pulse, and wiped the sweat from his face again. Then, when there was nothing more he could do for the moment, he sat on the stool near the basins and held his face in his cupped hands.

This had to be got over, but as he reviled himself he offered his own excuse, his voice trembling among the other uneasy sounds in the sick bay: the fluttering of the ventilators, the strain of timber, the bright tingling of a spoon in a glass, the open-mouthed breathing of sick men asleep. "I've got no authority . . . I've got no authority . . ."

He said it again and again with his eyes hot and shut, his face imprisoned in his hands with the guilt and the excuse.

Major Draycott had sat alone for ten minutes after Miss Brown had left the lounge with the young third officer and Dr. Papasian had been summoned by Mr. Beggs. The Major had not talked to them when they had been sitting near him in the gloom, nor they to him or even to each other; but when they had gone he had missed their company. The lounge was a place of shadows; even his own presence did nothing to keep away the feeling that it was now utterly deserted; he was a ghost sitting here, and if anyone came they would not see him.

He had come from the lounge to his cabin; it was smaller, and the lamp beside the bed was cheerful; he

141

was still alone but the loneliness seemed less huge to him.

He read his book for a little while, and then, because he had read it so many times before, he shut it again, imagining the dust that would be clouding out from between the pre-war pages. He had become increasingly conscious of dust over the past few years; he could smell it, or seemed to smell it, when he opened the door of his room, and when he took his shoes from beneath the bed where his uniform and souvenirs were stored in the shallow sagging trunk, and when he opened the glass doors of the cabinet to touch his ivory miniatures that turned more yellow as each year came, bringing its dust and its gathering army of regrets that had been on the march since his mind had stopped looking forward and begun looking back to find the missed turning and the sign-post that was now too far away to read. There was dust in his books and on his shoes; of late, it had begun powdering silently over his heart.

His brother had said it was unwise of him to have made the long trip to South America just to see him for a matter of days; but there was no other relative to see, and he was not sorry he had gone. There had been no sunshine, and the sands were not as golden as he had pictured them; but he had gone to see Clive, and Clive was well and prospering; he had shared for a few days in a life that had gone right all the way along, and his nature had little envy in it to sharpen the regrets.

But this storm was very troubling. Even the others were worried by it, even those whose luggage was free of the solemn advice for daily use: there must be no exertion. The words had gathered dust already but he must not ignore them.

He went to the cupboard beside the porthole after shutting his book, and took down his medicine bottle, and shook it as directed on the label, where the stuff had run down from the neck and stained it. The cabin swung again, and this time it was much worse than the other times, so that he reached quickly behind him for the small arm-chair and sat down in it with the bottle in his hand. The floor tilted very badly and his left hand gripped the arm of the chair; the chair was shaking to the vibration. Then there came the dreadful noise from outside—more than just water falling. The floor was a dangerous slope; the chair pulled at its securing-chain as he crouched deeper into it. The book slid off the bed-table, but he did not notice it in the midst of the dreadful smashing sound that was still going on outside.

TWELVE

AT daybreak, Tuesday, gusts of ninety miles an hour were recorded at coastguard stations along the Cornish coast. With the wind there was rain. Windows were still lit long after dawn, for it was a grey watery light that seeped from the tempestuous sky.

Land's End Radio was still calling. *GLD—GLD—GLD to S.S. 'Atlantic Whipper' to 'Atlantic Whipper'. Can you hear? Can you hear?* It had been calling at one minute past each hour since two o'clock in the morning, when the *Atlantic Whipper* had failed to send. She had been silent now for seven hours. At Lloyd's, members were conscious of the familiar pattern formed by the signals that had come from this ship, as it had formed many times before. At 4.17 p.m. yesterday the *Whipper* had sent: *We are heaving-to until the gale abates. Ship in good trim and all happy aboard.* At 4.26 p.m. the signal came, *Am hove-to in south-westerly gale.* It was a confident, reassuring message—the master had said that he was going to heave-to, and now he had completed the planned manœuvre. But three minutes later there was the unexpected addition to the last signal, *Cargo shifted. List fifteen degrees. No anxiety.* Still confident, still reassuring. For nearly five hours the owners and Lloyd's were able to comfort themselves with the old saw that no news is good news. Captain Harkness was on the spot; his ship was listing to shifted cargo in a south-westerly gale, but if he said there was no anxiety, then there should be none felt by those with their feet firmly on land. The five hours ended at 9.23 p.m. last evening. *S O S. 'Atlantic Whipper' lying hove-to approximately forty-nine-fifty north, twelve-forty west. Cargo shifted, slight list, number one hatch-cover stove-in by heavy seas and taking water.*

Confidence ran out, suddenly. Signals such as these had led so many times to disaster. When the markets opened this morning, Tuesday, rumours immediately circulated in the City among insurance companies and marine underwriting syndicates. The first reinsurance rate quoted was ten guineas per cent. It was widely believed that a total of half a million pounds liability was spread over several insurance interests. Cargo value was estimated at a hundred and twenty-five thousand pounds. The early quotation of ten guineas per cent was not due to the gravity of the last signal sent out by the *Atlantic Whipper*, but to the long silence that followed it. No news was not good news when a ship lay in this critical condition.

Lloyd's issued a brief report to the Press, simply repeating the S O S and giving the estimated time of arrival of the tug *Salvado* alongside the distressed ship. This was given as 2 p.m. tomorrow, Wednesday. News that the Spanish steamer *Angeles* was much nearer the position than the *Salvado* gave rise to hopes; but not in all quarters. There were those who from their personal knowledge of the sea were ready to declare positively that the *Angeles* would never reach the position, steaming at ninety degrees across the path of the gale as she must.

The first of the day's B.B.C. bulletins gave no indication that the winds would moderate before evening. No mention was made of the *Atlantic Whipper*. Her name, however, appeared in the stop press of a few papers: she was reported in trouble, and a tug was going to meet her. It was quite simple; and on the breakfast-tables where these few papers were propped the bacon was getting cold.

In the big towns of England the wind was a nuisance, blowing dust into people's faces and scattering paper through the streets. In London a crowd collected when a chimney-pot blew down and landed near a bus-stop without hurting anyone. It was the talk of the day for those who had seen it. A flag-mast in Manchester was broken, and hung across its wires until a fire-engine was sent for: another small crowd had dramatic news for those at home this evening. When the rain came, umbrellas went up and a few blew inside-out. The wind was a nuisance across the land—even dangerous, as the chimney-pot had proved.

The steamship with forty-three Englishmen on board had now been silent for nine hours. This was hardly news, so that there was no mention of it in the noon editions. The Englishman, the son of the island race that is said by foreigners to have the sea in its blood, is not half-hearted about his insularity. Anything over the horizon is out of his sight.

Only among those whose lives were directly linked with the ship was there any concern: they were the families of the crew and passengers, the owners, the interested parties of the insurance companies, and the officers of coastal radio stations and coastguard headquarters and other services devoted to the safety of shipping.

The telegram was delivered in Beaker Street, Bristol, with the first post. Thelma Bond was still in her dressing-gown, and the telegram was in her hand when she came back to the bedroom.

"Is it trouble?" her friend asked. She shook her head.

"He's going to be delayed. That's all it says."

He laced his shoes and stood up, lighting a cigarette.

"Probably the gale."

"Probably." She looked at him critically, without meaning to. Behind him the bed was in a mess, with the bedclothes spilled half on to the floor; there were cigarette-stubs in the ashtray. His eyes were a little pink-rimmed, and she supposed hers must be. They had slept no longer than an hour or two, kept fitfully awake by the wind and the passion. Had there really been much passion? He wasn't very attractive. She felt no peace in her mind or body, no lingering after-glow. She just felt unwashed in the bleak windy light of the morning.

"Is there a smut on my nose?"

She said, "What?"

"You're staring rather hard."

She managed to smile. "I was miles away. Sorry."

"Are you worried about him?"

It occurred to her that she might be, subconsciously. "I don't know, really. It's not a very worrying message." She thought it must be the sense of guilt, the degrading sight of the bedclothes, the long creases in the under-sheet where they had lain, the memory of the unfamiliar smell of his hair-oil beside her face in the dark. Tony had such a pink washed-looking face and clear eyes, and he didn't use anything on his hair. If only he weren't such a single-minded specialist with his nice head full of valves and soldered wires, she wouldn't have brought herself to this.

"There might be something in the paper," he said. "About the ship."

"You think so?"

"I wish to God you didn't look so wonderful, even at this unearthly hour. Women don't, usually, however pretty they are."

Why did he have to make a set speech? Did he always make it, between lacing his shoes and putting his coat on? A sort of gentlemanly farewell address? 'Women don't, usually, however pretty they are.' As if he were explaining the habits of the green-tailed parakeet. 'Their plumage turns mud-brown in the morning.'

"I'll get the paper," she said. She escaped from the scent of the hair-oil. There was nothing about the ship in her paper; it was one of those that didn't carry the few lines in the stop press; but as she was dropping it still open into the chair the telephone rang; and she was worried.

147

"It's Jean," the caller said. Jean Stapleton. "Have you seen the paper?"

"Is there something about Tony's ship?"

"Hang on a minute, dear." She waited, hating the drama in Jean's tone, and the taste in her own mouth of the night's lechery, and the way he talked about women as if he were making a mildly curious study of their habits. "Thelma?"

"Yes."

"It's in the stop press. Are you listening?"

She felt drained even of impatience. "Yes, Jean."

"This is it. 'Cargo ship *Atlantic Whipper* reported in trouble two hundred miles south-west of Land's End. Salvage tug *Salvado* on way to meet her.' Did you get that, dear?"

"Yes."

The voice sounded slightly indignant that she was not bursting into tears. "Well, I do hope Tony's all right. It's a pretty bad gale, you know."

"There was a wire from him, a few minutes ago. It just says he'll be delayed."

"A *tele*gram . . ." Her tone was ominous. "Would you like me to pop over and see you, my dear?"

It would be almost worth a laugh, to see Jean's face when she arrived here, to find she was—how would she put it, in euphemistic suburbanese?—*not alone.* But it wouldn't really be funny; it would just be part of the whole sordid pattern.

"No, I'm not worrying. They'll be all right with a tug standing by."

"But, Thelma, how can we know that? It might be very serious." The tone changed key to the motherly. "I don't expect you're wide awake yet. Give me a ring after breakfast, and if you feel like talking to someone about it, I'll pop across on my way to the shops."

She sensed him standing near her; or it was the faint

148

oily smell. She turned her head. He was looking at his watch, pointedly.

"All right, Jean. Thank you for phoning."

"My dear, I wouldn't not have. Now don't go worrying, will you?"

"No, I won't."

He was pacing with studied quietness up and down the narrow draughty hall. He looked exactly like every other small-time successful seducer, neatly dressed and with a homburg that had a brim just a fraction too wide.

". . . been through so many storms at sea," the voice chirped persistently, "that I'm sure he'll know what to do for the best."

"Yes. Good-bye, Jean."

"Good-bye—and don't forget, if you feel like talking to someone——"

"Good-bye." Only the receiver could stop it. He took off the homburg with pointed politeness; she was certain he'd put it on just so that he could go through the little act of remembering his manners, despite the urgent problems that were on his mind at the beginning of a hard business day.

She returned his kiss coldly.

"You were splendid," he said, with the generous overtone afforded by the imminence of their parting. "Splendid, Thelma."

She said that it was nice of him to have come. Lovers not in love must find words for good-bye, to round it all off for the sake of propriety.

The wind tore at the door as he opened it, and she stood back where she couldn't be seen from the street; though it hardly mattered. In the draughty reaches of dejection the worst catastrophe looked small.

The stray bitter thought that was in her mind as she went upstairs to run the bath was that instead of telling

149

her she had been splendid, he might have said he hoped the ship would be all right.

The day's light began lowering early in the afternoon. The rain was coming inland from the sea in long squalls that broke across the rocky coast of Cornwall and were gathered up by the higher wind that raced from the south. Visibility was bad wherever a man was, for if he were behind a window the glass was distorted by the rain and if he were in the open he must screw his eyes up against its sting.

The ether was charged with electricity that crackled among the signals criss-crossing the land and the sea, distorting them, blotting out a word and groups of words as men spoke into the radio-telephones. Silence was no longer requested of general shipping during the first fifteen minutes of each hour. GLD was still calling.

Land's End Radio—Land's End Radio—Land's End Radio to 'Atlantic Whipper' 'Atlantic Whipper'. Come in, please.

There had been no answer for fourteen hours.

Captain Tremayne said that she must have gone down. One big sea could overwhelm her if she were listing and the for'ard hold were filled with free surface-water. He had been quiet, during the snatched hour at his home where the five-day-old child still shouted at the storm in puling rage. His wife had asked about the ship and he had been glum, and she had said it was sad, but they must not take it so to heart. He had hardly glanced at the child, and she had been glad to be rid of him when he had put on his big coat and gone back to the radio station. Since the first cockleshell had been fashioned by barbarians, women had been jealous of ships, quick to see how men came to love the ugly things and give them girls' names—it was all 'she' this and 'she' that, as if they talked of another woman; and it was worse than another woman, for you couldn't scratch the eyes out of anything so big and cold.

Tremayne was back on duty a tired man; his ears ached for an answer from the sea, just a word to show him that the *Whipper* was not deep in the dark, deaf for ever to the quick tapping hand, *GLD—GLD—GLD—to 'Atlantic Whipper'. Can you receive me? Can you receive me?*

There was no comfort in the other signals that were threading through the tangle of the static.

'Salvado' to Land's End Radio. Position 51 north, 7.20 west. Speed thirteen knots. Heavy seas. Any signal from 'Atlantic Whipper'? Any signal yet? Cannot raise her.

'Angeles'—'Angeles'—'Angeles'. Position 49.30 north, 11 west. Where is 'Atlantic Whipper'? We must be near. We must be near. Wind bad. No visibility. Does anyone know where is 'Whipper'?

Nobody knew. She might be anywhere on the surface, or under the waves. It would have been heartening to realise how well the Spanish steamer had kept her course, how fast she had made through this bitter storm, but for the knowledge that even if she came within a mile of the distressed ship they would be blind to each other. The light of the bleak day was drawing down, and the rain cast a veil across the waves, merging with the spindrift that was torn from their tops to lay a screen from one horizon to the other. The *Angeles* carried no radar. Her signal was strong but she must have an answer from the region of 49.50 north, 12.40 west. How big a region was it by now? The *Whipper* could be drifting a long way north-east, her engines unable to give her headway in the sea. Already the *Angeles* could be steaming away from where she lay, and so could the *Salvado*, and the destroyer *Brindle*. Their reports to land stations gave their radar-screens as blank, still blank: *Still nothing, still nothing, cannot raise her, cannot receive her.* Part of the fragile network had broken down, the most vital part. There was a gap of silence, two hundred miles south-west of Land's End, the geographical point in the ocean that had now been extended northwards and eastwards to cover a half-circle. The ship was any-where in that area. She would not be south nor west of the geographical point 49.50 north 12.40 west, for the wind had not changed its direction. The drift would be north and east, towards the land, towards the barrier of rocks where the spume boiled and spilled flotsam into the caves and creeks—old shoes and fishermen's corks, split-open rancid oranges and the splintered skeleton of a deck-chair down from its summer in Torquay, and the remains of a broken ship that had gone down last year off the Lizard. If the *Whipper* were drifting, it would be towards this coast.

When night came, some gave up hope. There was a fuller report in the evening papers: some of them devoted nearly a dozen lines to the vague story of the ship that was in trouble. The news varied; you could believe which version you wanted to. Most of it was plain information: the *Atlantic Whipper* (or *Atlantic Whippet*) was a cargo ship of six thousand tons (or nine thousand five hundred and twenty-two, to quote a journal well-known for its insistence upon precise figures) and was carrying grain and other goods (or bales) from Buenos Aires to Avonmouth (or Liverpool). She had a crew of forty (and this was the only figure on which all were agreed) and ten (or a dozen) passengers among whom was Dr. Papasian (the name had five variations, for he was a foreigner and no one would know), until two years ago personal surgeon to the President of Brazil. From this general information the reports slipped freely into speculation, but no paper committed itself to facts, since no facts were known of the ship's whereabouts. She had sent no signal for 'some few hours' (since noon today, since midnight last night), and it was feared she had been overwhelmed.

This final item of speculation was innocent of any cruelty. It must have been clear to editors that among their readers would be friends and relatives of the crew and passengers, reading and re-reading every brief report they could find in any paper they could come by, pinning their hopes to a single word of good news if one were offered them. But the news must go through; the public was owed a solemn duty by the Press; so that if a junior editor who had spent six months at sea before being put ashore for reasons of chronic sea-sickness or hopeless incompetence now declared that he believed, from his personal experience of the sea, that the *Atlantic Whipper* must have foundered, the opinion must go into print. For the want of facts, a chance remark would have to suffice. The truth would not suffer for being printed in more formal language: 'I'd say she's had it, myself,' meant precisely the same as: 'It is feared she has been over-whelmed.'

It was not known, nor was it considered important to guess, how many people read reports such as this in the evening papers of today, Tuesday. There were fifty on board the imperilled ship. Even a friendless man with no more permanent home than the ports of the ocean has seldom fewer than two other people on the earth who love him; the average would be nearer six. So that there were some hundreds on this anxious night who were denied their sleep for thought of a friend's or son's or brother's death in the violent seas that were pounding this ship where she lay helpless or nursing her wreckage a score of fathoms down. Some telephoned the offices of the news-papers (for if they didn't know the facts, who did?); some made enquiries at the Admiralty, the radio stations and coastguard headquarters and harbour authorities. Some-one must know. But there was no news.

Official reports carried negative information. Twice during the day an aircraft had taken off from R.A.F. Redmoor to search the area where it was judged the *Whipper* must lie; but the sea had no visible surface any-where. Through the rain-distorted observation-panels and the rain-haze itself there could be seen nothing more than a desert of spindrift and the occasional white up-thrust of a wave-crest that became mist a moment afterwards. The aircraft had flown low, driving with flimsy strength against the gale, turning and drifting, flying always outside the limit beyond which an aircraft could not be expected to return to base without the extra reserve of skill and courage that danger brings to a pilot and his crew. It had come home, with no news.

The tug *Salvado*, at nightfall within a hundred miles of the point 49.50 north, 12.40 west, called up Land's End repeatedly for a bearing. There was none to give her. She altered course slightly to eastwards, her master certain that if the *Atlantic Whipper* still floated she must have drifted to north and east of her last reported position. The tug, within a hundred miles of that position, could be within fifty of the *Whipper* if she had a two-knots drift on her, northwards and east. In a few more hours there would be the danger of coming upon her in the dark and the blinding rain, with no warning of her presence until the collision came.

The *Angeles* signalled soon after dark that she was hove-to in position approximately 50 north, 11 west. Manuelo de las Castillas informed Land's End that he would conserve his coal until daybreak; meanwhile he would signal hourly to the *Whipper*. With naïve confidence he had ended, *We must be close to her, and she must answer soon.* There was the suggestion in these words that it was God's will. He was answered formally by Land's End; but from the destroyer *Brindle* there came the message: *You have done magnificently to have reached your present position. Have you cornered the market in miracles?*

It was two hours before Manuelo, in worried con-sultation with his radio officers and those on board who could muster a word of English, could make anything of the idiomatic signal from *Brindle*. There was nothing helpful in the phrase-books about cornered markets. It was decided finally that a corn-market must be alluded to, and the word 'miracles' suggested a biblical connotation. But none among the crew could remember a miracle involving corn especially. Did the British naval ship mean: had the *Angeles* as many miracles as there are grains of corn in a market? It was very worrying, this, for Manuelo, because the message from the *Brindle* was full of praise and kindness, and she must be thanked for it, and aptly. There must be a little joke, for cheerfulness.

Towards ten o'clock the radio officer in *Brindle* picked up a signal from *Angeles*. *Thank you. It was nothing. We have a cargo of marbles.* The Spanish letter 'v', virtually interchangeable with 'b' in both speech and writing, was responsible for the perplexity on the bridge of H.M.S. *Brindle*. Commander Lawson held the message-slip at arm's length, in case physical perspective might render the words more clear. "Marbles? What extraordinary merchandise some of these boys carry."

Half an hour later the *Angeles* received a signal. *Excellent. We'll give you a game when we meet.*

Manuelo Lopez de las Castillas hurried into consultation again with the more scholarly members of his crew.

It might have seemed they had forgotten why they had brought their ships here to this violent region where the wind and the waves attacked them again and again as they sent their little jokes to each other to pass the hours. The destroyer bore steadily south, nearing the area of search. The *Angeles* lay with steerage-way on her, wallowing, her ancient timbers with the ague in them as the sea pitched, and the ship pitched, and the sea fell away, and she fell away too, until a man rolled from his bunk below and cursed Manuelo, just as he had been cursing him in his dreams. From the north came the *Salvado*, so near the *Brindle* that they had each other on their radar-screens. Soon they would pick up the Spanish steamer, and at daybreak the search could begin. If the *Atlantic Whipper* could last the night they would find her tomorrow: but had she lasted even through the day?

There were no more aircraft despatched from Redmoor by dark. It would have been pointless. There were no fresh orders from C.-in-C., Plymouth, to *Brindle*; her course would bring her to the search area almost together with the *Salvado*, a little after noon tomorrow, or if the distressed ship had drifted more north than east they might come upon her as soon as it was light. There were these simple reckonings and these trumped up hopes to sustain them through the night. It was not known what Manuelo thought of the chances. Commander Lawson seemed confident that something could be done; but if he were asked on oath for the truth in his mind he would have said he was looking for wreckage and survivors. Captain Howes, master of the deep-sea tug *Salvado*, was of like opinion in the privacy of his own counsel. It was almost twenty-four hours since the casualty had signalled that she was listing and taking seas into her for'ard hold. In this gale her condition would not have improved. Had she been able to signal, what would she have sent? *List increasing. Number two hatch stove-in. Steampipe fractured. Engines dead and steering gone and men injured.* A dozen shades of darkening tragedy could have blotted her slowly out. The last signal, had she been able to send it, would have been: *Am sinking.*

Howes, like Lawson, would be looking for survivors when first light came, for wreckage, an oil-patch, a huddle of half-drowned figures in a boat. There had not been one spark of hope to brighten the long exchange of signals through the day and half the night. In the late evening the Admiralty had requested radio amateurs to listen for signals from the distressed ship and to report anything they picked up, however faint. There had been no reports from these wavelengths.

As eight bells were rung at midnight and in these three ships the graveyard watch began, hope had run out. In these first hours of a new day the heart of any wakeful man is at its lowest ebb, even on the land. In this cold heaving waste there was nothing to help Lawson or Howes or Manuelo to believe that anything good could come to this night, not even one grain of a miracle. But soon after two in the morning the gale began dying, and by three it was dead, and the sea quiet.

★
THIRTEEN
★

THE sea was inert. There were yellow scum-patches where the waves had brought up seaweed; in the pale starlight you could believe they were patches of sand, small low islands in the water. A flight of stormy petrels traced through the faint milky light, haunting the night to the north; and not far from their passage the ship lay.

She was dark. There was a gentle movement on her, a look of exhaustion about her as a low wave crept and lifted her bows and let them fall again, easefully. All the anger and passion had gone away from the sea and the ship; like lovers they lay quietly, saddened and exhausted by the orgasm. Soft light went rippling along her side when a wave stronger than the others broke a froth of bubbles in the shadows and the starlight caught them and lit them. Their sound was stonily musical, less easily heard than the stronger steamy sound of the water that fell to the sea from the two pumps that were still working in the for'ard hold. Where these two jets of water reached the sea a lacework of bubbles went spreading in a slow circle through the black.

Sometimes a flicker of light sparked from the darkened shape as a man worked; there were figures along the fore-deck and in the tangle of rail and wire and cable above the monkey island.

An hour ago, when the ship had been wallowing in great seas—listing badly and refusing for the last time to take a mortal wave, refusing again for the last time, each time seeming to have no strength left to deal with one more wave and yet refusing again, always for the last time—the lookout had come in from the bridge-end, his voice full of wonder.

"She's piping down, sir. She's piping down!"

Captain Harkness had looked at the man. The man was mad or mistaken; his wet face looked exalted as he stared at the captain. But behind him the door was not smashed shut as the ship staggered to the next crest and the wind came, and there was no blizzard of spindrift. Water burst lazily over the fo'c'sle head and fell away to the port scuppers with the angle draining it fast. The door slammed, but only as an angry man would slam it, and not a tempest in a rage.

For a few seconds Harkness did not answer. From the lookout's oilskins water trickled to the deck and ran down the slope, puddling in the corner that was already filled with water that had burst in through the smashed window. Since it had been smashed and then boarded up, water had sprung between the boards whenever a big sea broke at the bows; but none came through there now. The lookout, Mounsey, the tall man with the white grin, stood waiting, watching Harkness. The Skip must say something; something had to be voiced, about this thing that had happened to them all. He must say God had saved them, or must tell him he was wrong, tell him to get out of here before he was kicked out for coming away from his station with this bloody tale.

But he couldn't be wrong. It wasn't only that he had felt the drop of the gale against his crouched body, the sudden astonished relief when the next wave fell short of the bridge and didn't drench him. You could tell it was true: the windows were clear; the noise was less; the ship wasn't plunging into this trough with her head down and her whole length shuddering; she was wallowing into it with her screw still thrusting underwater. But the Skip must say something. Silence couldn't contain this moment. He'd come in here to tell the Skip the gale was piping down, after forty hours, and there'd have to be an answer from someone, from another human voice to

159

comfort his nerves after the loneliness out there on the wing between the black water and the black sky with nothing on his mind but the thought of death.

Harkness said, "Yes."

The deck tilted as the *Whipper* rose to the next wave; it was a smaller wave, pathetic after the others; it could hardly spill itself on to the fo'c'sle head. The screw came out this time, and the shudder came to the wheelhouse. They braced their legs and waited; the ship settled in the rough sea where the waves rose ten feet high and the wind tore the white from their crests: yet in comparison with the storm that had been here minutes ago it seemed they sailed through calm.

The second mate was near Harkness. Mounsey looked at him to see if he were going to say anything. Beggs was standing with his head lowered and his hands held loosely in front of him. Mounsey was embarrassed to see a man as big as the second mate praying. He turned away and opened the door when the ship began sliding into the next trough. Standing on the wing, alone again, he had the feeling of anticlimax, as when the surgeon comes past you in the corridor with his mask off and his hands pulling at the tapes of his gown, saying casually in answer to your frozen half-sick question, 'Oh, yes, she's out of danger now.'

The *Whipper* was still afloat, and the gale was dropping. Why had the Skip said nothing more than 'yes'?

Now the gale was gone. Under a soft breeze the sea had a swell across it, if you could call it a swell after watching the sixty-foot waves that had come at you like mountains in the dark. The men were working at the for'ard hatches, and up on the boat-deck where cables lay twisted and severed. The two lifeboats had been filled, smashed and carried away some little time after two o'clock, and the dreadful sound of their going had brought the passengers from their cabins; there had been a clamour of white-faced questions and one of the women had been crying and saying something about children; but there were no children in the ship. Some of them had asked why nothing could have been done to save the two lifeboats, yet no man in the crew had sworn at them. They were gathered in the smoking-room, most of them at the bar, where Tonio was serving drinks, and the woman who had cried before was crying again because the gale was over.

The passengers could not sit at the stools; and it was difficult to stand. The Sennetts' tattered piece of paper—named recently by Alan Jocelyn as the Longshoreman's List-indicator—now showed the angle of the ship as thirty degrees. Behind the bar, Tonio the Spaniard had stacked his bottles and glasses into corners to secure them; he still trod broken glass whenever he moved his feet. But he was very happy. It was startling to see his face, his smile, to hear him laughing as he spoke. He was the happiest man on board, because in the midst of the terrible storm he had been told by the third mate, who had come down here to look to the passengers, that a ship was coming to help them, that she was already nearer them than any other, and that the name of her brave captain was Manuelo Lopez de las Castillas.

For a long time Major Draycott had been crouched in the chair by the door, watching Tonio as a galley-slave in his chains would watch a sea-bird perched on the prow. Because of the storm and the condition of the ship, Draycott was chained to his fear as his chair was chained to the deck; but Tonio was free. His face was full of smiles. Only a few of his thoughts were in this ship; the rest were in the other, the *Angeles*. Manuelo—it was a good name; his own grandfather's name was that. He would be seeing his grandfather again; now he knew it. The gale was over and the *Angeles* was close. Soon he would be home; already he could smell the sunshine in this bleak swaying saloon where the passengers had come together for comfort. They were so white-looking and miserable; he was sorry for them; it was a sin to feel as happy as he did.

"I suppose he's been drinking," Paul Sennett had told his wife.

"He doesn't seem drunk, darling."

"I think he's drunk." Sennett had lost his golden colouring and the blaze of the blue eyes had dulled. He had passed the point when he cared whether the others saw that he was afraid or not.

"How do you feel, darling?"

He said, "Splendid. Why shouldn't I? There's nothing on my mind, except the thought that we're all going down."

His mouth had a twist when he spoke like that; she looked away from it. "But the gale's over, Paul. We'll be all right now." She must never be angry with him; not again.

"That's wonderful. It must be reassuring, having two good legs to swim with."

However much he reminded her, she must never be anything but tolerant; she could never atone. "We shan't have to swim," she said.

"Have you had confidential information about that?" He leaned his head forward; even in his fear he tried to talk sense. "The port boats have been washed away. We can't lower the other two, at this angle. When she goes down there'll only be a few bits of timber to hang on to—those of us who don't get sucked under."

She was chilled by his tone; fear gave it vibrance, as if he were only just in control of a passionate conviction. Perhaps he was: the conviction that he was going to die. It might be true. She might have only a few more hours left in which to atone. It wasn't long enough; it was unfair.

"Don't worry, darling. We'll be all right."

He leaned his head back, and did not answer.

Another glass fell from the bar as the ship lurched; but Tonio laughed ruefully and did nothing about it. A shout had sounded from above, from somewhere on deck, as if the noise of the glass had called for comment. A few minutes after, a seaman went at a jog-trot past the open doors. Any sound, any sign of excitement now played on the fears of them all. A ship could go down within a few minutes: if you had never experienced it, you had read about it or been told by someone. You could be trapped below deck without a chance. A final lurch as slack water shifted in the holds, then the plunge. You would have a minute to watch the others who were with you. They would not look pleasant; you would try not to panic when the bulkheads reared and the furniture went smashing against them and the water came in from the blackness outside, bringing the blackness in here.

The lights here had come on half an hour ago; they could flicker out again as they had before. You watched the bulbs, and the faces of the others, and the man running past the doors. Whatever happened you would not panic.

The seaman had climbed the companionway and joined the others who worked on the foredeck, now by the light of the Aldis lamp. There was a great comfort in the light, after the darkness before. The men worked steadily, slinging new timber across number one hatch. High above them Tich Copley came down the mast, monkey-quick and out of breath. Another man followed, looking down so that he should not put his boots on Copley's hands as they plucked at the rungs, one below one below one until he could jump. The two electricians stood by; they looked like dead men, with their eyes hollow in white faces; they had spent too many hours on their task to feel any elation now that it was finished. They had worked through the daylight yesterday, and much of the night; they and the others had rigged a new aerial three times in the last twenty hours and three times it had been torn away from their hands and the masts by the violence of the gale. Two men had been sent below for Persham and Dr. Papasian to deal with; one had been knocked unconscious, the other ripped across the face and shoulders when a taut cable had parted and whipped him with its torn metal end; he had been lucky, they all said, not to be killed or blinded.

When the gale had died they had rigged the aerial for the fourth time, and there was no wind to snatch it away before they could secure it. It was up there now, singing. There was no triumph in them; they wanted to go below and sleep or be sick or get drunk or just sit in the dark with a cigarette. There was no excitement in the knowledge that a signal would go out now, for the first time in twenty-four hours. Much good might it do to send a signal now with the ship lying in the sea like a half-dead fish and her crew sick with strain.

They were sent below and given rum. They went, some of them, into the sick bay to ask how their friends were feeling; but there was no comfort in there; their friends were feeling bad, worse than they were; it didn't console them.

Mr. Bond had come down from the monkey island to the wing of the bridge, and made his way up the thirty-degree slope of the deck in the wheelhouse. Turnbull was with him, his face pinched and bitter and his head throbbing under the bandage: he had worked with the men, driving himself, making them see that he could do it; and some of them had been convinced that he worked like this for the sake of rigging the aerial and saving the ship.

Captain Harkness looked at Bond as he went into the wireless-room. He did not ask if they could now send a signal; Bond would tell him. He must wait, composing the message in his mind.

It was a quarter past three when the call was picked up

by the major land-stations, twenty or thirty coastguard lookout huts, the Admiralty, the R.A.F., the *Salvado*, *Angeles*, *Brindle*, and close on a hundred and sixty amateur radio-fans tuned in to the distress wavelengths. In the quiet of the night, while surprise was still in men's minds that the gale had abated, the signal had the force of an electric shock.

DE GBAC—'*Atlantic Whipper*'. *DE GBAC*—'*Atlantic Whipper*'.

The quiet of the night had gone. Under the bright lamp-bulbs the operators reached for their message-pads, turning their heads to alert the others in the wireless-rooms, giving a quick word as their fingers touched the dials to strengthen the magic that was coming.

"*Whipper!*"

"What?"

"She's calling . . ."

DE GBAC—'*Atlantic Whipper*'—*do you receive me?*

The Morse picked through static.

"Quick—phone Tremayne."

"You certain?"

On board the *Angeles*—"*Capitano! Escuche! Escuche! El Wheeper!*"

"*No es verdad!*"

"*Es verdad! Venga—escuche!*"

DE GBAC—'*Atlantic Whipper*'—*do you receive me, please?*

In the high attics, the cluttered basements, the amateurs sat startled and could not call out to their families who were fast asleep—many of them had been told to go to bed, hours ago, because of school tomorrow or the early train to work. Some were half-asleep, sitting with an eiderdown drawn round them, sitting alone in the dark in defiance of the orders of a family that had never understood this unreasonable preoccupation with wires and valves and dials; but this was the moment, the grand justification. They were in touch with a miracle.

*'Whipper'—'Whipper'—'Whipper' to Land's End Radio . . .
Do you hear me, please? Over.*

At Plymouth, Staff Operations was given a message-form from the Main Wireless Office. H.M.S. *Brindle* had been on the R/T hourly since dark had come, and the message-forms made a little pile on his desk. Now the name was not *Brindle*, but *Whipper*. The operator left his office and hurried to the radio-room.

The owners were informed by land-line. A signal was picked up from the tug *Salvado* to her company. At R.A.F. Redmoor the duty pilot was called to the briefing-room; on the tarmac an aircraft was warming-up.

DE GBAC—'Atlantic Whipper'—do you hear me?

Many heard; many answered. At Land's End, Plymouth and Niton the operators were busy trying to clear channels. The ether was jammed for twelve minutes.

At 3.27 a.m. the first clear message was picked up by Land's End. It was the message that before dawn would be recorded in the offices of Watson and Blount, Lloyd's of London and the half-dozen major national newspapers with their headquarters in Fleet Street. This would be served tomorrow with the bacon and eggs. It was not headlines, but it was front page.

'Atlantic Whipper'—'Atlantic Whipper' to Land's End Radio. Approximate position 49.30 north, 10.35 west. Moderate breeze, slight sea. Number one hold filled to coamings, one pump still working. Number two hatch stove-in, pumps operating. Two boats washed away port side. Six hands injured, one badly, but doctor on board. Water in generators now cleared, jury aerial rigged. List to port now thirty degrees and ship down by the head. Will not withstand further heavy seas. Would not be able to lower starboard boats. Need met.-report and new E.T.A. of 'Salvado', please. Over.

Jim Beggs took star sights again as a double check while Bond was receiving from Land's End. Captain Harkness was in the chart-room. On Beggs's reckoning the ship had resisted the northward force of the gale and had even made headway a few miles south, but had drifted eastwards over a hundred miles, with the wind against her higher starboard side.

"Got a call from the *Angeles*, sir."

Harkness straightened up from the chart-table. Bond gave him the message-slip. He had almost forgotten the Spanish steamer; the *Whipper* had been out of touch with land and shipping for twenty-five hours. "So she's still afloat, is she?"

"Bit more than just afloat, sir."

Harkness read the message. *'Angeles' to 'Atlantico Whipper'. I am* 49.20 *north,* 11.10 *west. I am near you. I will see you. Your ship is brave.* The message was signed in full. Harkness looked up at Tony Bond.

"Is it possible?"

Bond said with his quick smile, "It's a strong signal, sir. I'd say they're close."

Harkness bent over the charts again, and said in a moment, "Forty to fifty miles." He looked at Bond again. "If that position's accurate, we were drifting a matter of ten miles north of them during the night."

Bond grinned again with his red-eyed sleepless face.

"Land's End gives the E.T.A. of *Salvado* and *Brindle* as eleven o'clock this morning, with the better speed they can make to our new position, now the weather's okay. But the *Angeles* can reach us by eight or nine."

It was a matter for pleased surprise, but Harkness went on looking at Bond as if it were tragic news. His voice was low. "But how did she get through that gale?"

Bond shrugged. "Manuelo Etcetera said he would. I suppose he knew he could do it."

"But it should have sunk her!" He put out a hand as the slight swell moved the ship but he went on looking at Bond. "And he tells us our ship is brave!"

A signal began pipping and Bond turned away to get it.

Harkness did not move for a moment. The lamp glared painfully across his eyes. He had reached the stage where a man knows that he is tired, where he feels the stubble on his face without touching it and sees the redness of his eyes without a mirror, the early stage through which he will pass to the much longer period when he will forget he was tired, and no longer think about sleep; but his brain was electrically alert as it considered this news from the *Angeles*. She could not be as near as this. There was a mistake. Something to do with her radio officer's lack of accurate English, or her navigation officer's reckoning.

He moved suddenly down the sloping planks and went into the wheelhouse. "Mr. Beggs."

"Sir?"

"Your bearing was accurate." His tone didn't lift it to a question, though it was a question.

"I double-checked it, sir." There was no indignation in the second mate's voice.

"Of course." Harkness turned sideways into the wireless-room and said to Bond, "To *Angeles*. Please repeat your position."

"Ay, ay, sir." He moved the dials, thinking, 'Is Thelma asleep now? Did the telegram mean anything to her? Would she be glad if we didn't make it, apart from the sadness of so many dying?' *'Atlantic Whipper'*— *'Whipper' to 'Angeles', 'Angeles'. Over.*

Harkness went back into the wheelhouse. Turnbull had come up, a clean bandage on his head. Below it his face aroused pity in Harkness.

"Get below, Steve."

"Air's fresher up here, sir."

"It's mutiny."

"Then string me up, sir."

Was there anything of amusement in those hard scared eyes? Harkness looked for it. Triumph, perhaps. What would happen if he made it an order, and sent Turnbull below? He'd go. And would never forgive him. Harkness told him:

"The *Angeles* reports she's close, south'ard of us."

Turnbull said, "She can't be."

"We're asking her to repeat."

"How close, sir?"

"Forty to fifty miles."

"Someone's slipped, then."

"Yes," said Harkness, "I think so." They braced themselves against the windows, watching the play of starlight on the rolling backs of the swell. In a little while Harkness said, "You're weighing up the chances, I imagine."

Turnbull watched the swell. "Of turning about, sir?"

"And running for home."

The slight wave reached the bows, a sinuous rolling of black water that was slowly pewtered by the stars; the ship moved gently; it was an easy movement with nothing of the shock and shudder that the waves had brought when they were hitting her mightily, driven on to her by the gale; but there was in this movement a heaviness, a dullness. Along the port bulwarks the water ran between the rails however slight the waves, because of the dangerous angle at which she lay. The two men felt the heaviness under their feet. The *Whipper* was lolling in the sea. She was no longer sensitive to its movement; she responded only with a slack movement of her own. Until the pumps could draw the free surface water from the two for'ard holds she would lie like this, carrying the extra thousand tons of dangerous cargo as painfully as a great fish about to spawn.

An extra thousand tons would not affect her trim, if it were well stowed and balanced; as it was she had left Buenos Aires with less than full cargo. But this cargo was water, and it was not well stowed. It had burst in through the hatch-covers and now it was free down there to slop about, its huge liquid weight exaggerating every movement she made: if a wave came under her high starboard bow it would lift her and lift the water in her and the water would surge against the port bulkheads and double the force of the wave. With a big wave, raised by even a force-seven wind, she would be in danger of rolling slowly on to her beam ends and staying there. The slack water in her was as dangerous as explosives.

Turnbull could see it, the dark water that surged below as each wave came and touched her lazily; he could feel how dull she was, how heavy. He said:

"It'd be a risk, sir."

"There'll be a risk, whatever we decide on."

In his mind, Harkness could see beyond the water in the holds. It could not all be cleared. Even if the pumps could draw up all the free water that was there, they would leave the grain behind; and the grain had been waterlogged for twenty-four hours; it was swelling, every peck of it, locking the water in; the pumps would not get at it, ever. So that if he decided against the risk of turning the ship about and taking a wave on her side that could roll her over, he must accept the other risk and let her lie here until help reached her. But it must reach her before the weather broke again, before the grain swelled and split her plates open to the inrush of the sea. There was no hope of making an estimate, in terms of hours. You knew how much coal you had and how much you would burn at a given speed; you could not know how fast the grain was swelling, how fast the pumps were drawing the water out, how fast the ship was settling by the head as more water was taken in across the sharp angle of the foredeck and between the cracks of the timber that was battened over the holds. You couldn't know when the wind would come again.

They would rather have stood here with their feet braced against the quicker movement of a stiffer ship, and feel her respond to the sea, than feel this dreadful sloth in her, this wallowing.

"We can last as long as the weather," Turnbull said.

"That won't be long. The met. gives a bad outlook."

"If we could get the passengers off . . ."

"Could we get those boats clear?"

"Starley's tried every trick he knows, sir. For all the good they are, we can say we've no boats."

The ship moved slowly as a swell rolled under her. A soft rush of water ran along the port rails and left a scum in the starlight. Both men automatically judged the height of the swell and its speed and its distance from the next one, and imagined a swell of this height and speed meeting the ship beam-on if she lay with her starboard side exposed as she tried to turn about. Their findings were much the same. If she had been turning about when that wave had reached her she would have been in worse danger than she had been when the storm was at its height. Turn her to starboard, and a wave could surge over the port-side bulwarks and cover the makeshift timbers on the for'ard hatches, and some of it get through. Turn her to port, and a wave could roll against her high starboard side and send her over to lie capsized in the sea.

If a ship reached the *Whipper* before the next wind rose she stood a chance of putting off her passengers and crew before she sank.

In the glass of the window Turnbull's reflected face looked back at him. He thought to Harkness, 'How proud are you now?'

A scuffle sounded behind them and when they turned they saw Bond fetching up against the echo-sounder stand. He grinned quickly, embarrassed. Harkness said to Turnbull:

"You see why you shouldn't be on deck, Steve."

Turnbull's head began throbbing badly as he watched

Bond stand upright again on the thirty-degree slope of the planking.

"He wants to learn to walk," he said with his mouth tight.

"*Angeles*, sir," said Bond. "She's confirmed her position." He gave Harkness the slip of paper.

"Then there's no question."

"It isn't natural," said Turnbull.

Harkness stood with the piece of paper in his hand. Less than fifty miles on their port bow must be the Spanish steamer, making for them through the dark. Manuelo had said he was coming with God. Surely he could never have come alone.

"Tony, repeat our position to the *Angeles*. Make quite certain she understands. And say——" what could possibly be put into words? Nothing of what he felt could be attempted in a radio message. "—And say that we shall be delighted for her to join us."

The Spaniard would consider the message stiff and formal, typically English. Well then, he must.

He told the first mate, "If she can hold her speed she should be within sight of us at eight, or not long after."

Turnbull said nothing. Watching the glint of starlight on the black water, watching it through the reflection of his face and the pale bandages, he wanted to lean his head forward two inches, and rest it against the cool glass, and let his eyes close. That was why he stood with his feet braced hard and his head up, well clear of the window. Harkness thought, 'Why don't you give in? I wouldn't think any the worse of you.'

Sometimes as they watched the swell they could see a ruffle of wind cross the slow rollers, chipping a fleck of white from their backs; but it was only a little wind. If it grew no bigger they would be here when the *Angeles* broke the horizon. But it might grow; it could grow in much less than four hours. Harkness had been in the North Sea on convoy in a dead calm and the calm had changed to a hundred-mile-an-hour blizzard within ten minutes, with the seas flying across the deck in iced fragments.

The *Whipper* could not take any more. A wind could rise and come for her and find her helpless and send her down and there would be nothing that anyone could do.

He turned his head to the door of the port bridge-end and called, "Lookout!"

Mounsey came in. "Sir?"

"A steamer will rendezvous with us at about eight o'clock. She should appear on the port bow. Be sure to pass it on to your relief."

"Ay, ay, sir."

Harkness turned away and telephoned the fo'c'sle, and then the chief steward. "My shaving things, and a tray of coffee. My compliments to Mr. Costain. Would he report to the bridge."

He moved close to Turnbull, so that they could talk without the helmsman hearing. "Steve, we might have to leave the ship at any time in the next four hours. You'll need your strength then. There's nothing for you to do now. Get below and sleep if you can."

"I might be needed."

"If so, you'll be sent for."

Turnbull would not look at him. His head had begun bumping with anger. Harkness said, "You're released."

The words came with difficulty from so hard a mouth.

"I'd prefer to stay on the bridge, sir."

The ship moved with her dreadful weight as the swell rolled under her; then she lolled easy.

"You are ordered off watch, Mr. Turnbull." He moved away from him to stand by the binnacle. He was checking the compass when the first mate went out and the door shut behind him. Costain came up a minute later. Harkness noticed the boy had shaved.

"Yes, sir?"

"How are things below, Peter?"

"Bit tilted over, but everyone's cheerful, sir."

"How is Dukes?" Dukes was the man who had been ripped by the parting cable.

"The Doc's got him under a drug, sir. He says there's a good chance."

"Does he need any supplies?"

"He didn't ask for anything. He's got a bag with him."

The movement came. They braced their feet. It ceased. They relaxed. "Listen, Peter. If this weather holds, we should have the *Angeles* alongside in four hours. If the sea gets up, we shall be in difficulties. I need Jim Beggs with me up here and I've sent Mr. Turnbull below to get rest. I want you to look after the passengers and also to co-operate with the bosun. He is lashing up life-rafts. Your job is to keep everyone down there in good spirits. If you can get them to match your own, that's all I ask. Some of the passengers are knowledgeable; they'll know the critical condition we are in, so make a great deal of the *Angeles*. She's steaming for us at full speed and is now less than fifty miles away."

The door banged open and a steward came in. Costain grabbed one end of the tray as the man slithered on the steep deck.

The man cursed quietly and then said, "Could do with one leg shorter 'n the other, sir, eh?" The coffee had spilled from the jug, a little of it, enough to make the tray look messy in this messy wheelhouse that Margaret would be disgusted to see, and triumphant. He mustn't hate her. He watched the steward put the tray down, propping it level with a box from the first-aid shelf. When he had gone he said to Costain:

"As soon as you've told the passengers about the *Angeles*, give them routine life-drill."

He felt the ship moved again by the swell. She felt heavy, so heavy. He said, "See they do it well."

FOURTEEN

BEFORE a ship sinks, she seems to die. The life and warmth goes out of her, even though people are still on board. There are draughts everywhere; there is wet, and cold. There is no more comfort in familiar things; at the sight of them there is a taste in the mouth; they seemed so important, before now, so treasured—a handbag, a pair of skin shoes, a favourite pipe, a photograph—but now there is no more comfort in them because you are cut off from the continuing sequence of your life and your place in it is lost. They become symbols, these prized possessions, for the comfortable orderliness that was your link with the world. Now they are not yours, nor anyone's; they are shapes drifting away from you until you stand naked of them; you don't want to touch them again because you know the feel of them will not be the same. You do not expect to touch a dead friend and feel him warm.

With the draughts and the cold there are the noises; and they are different; there is no more comfort in them either. They are unnatural sounds; you would rather not hear them but they go on; they are the sounds of a ship, sinking. There is wet, almost everywhere. Water is dripping from a skylight on to the fragments of glass where the rich carpeting has darkened and has a sheen made by the water; there are puddles gathering in corners; trickles and rivulets creep down the slope of the deck; somewhere there is the bleak drip of a leak in a tin bowl, a deserted sound, the sound of rain soaking into a derelict house from which everyone has gone. Only you are left behind; you go into a cabin or the smoking-room and find people and talk to them, but you know by the sickness inside you that only you have been left behind; these others are strangers, and you never knew them.

The cold is the worst. It is partly the draughts, partly the wet; mostly it is fear. Along with the fear, discomfort. The discomfort confirms the fear in little ways. You feel sweat on you but there's no time to bath; your shoes are damp because you walked through a patch of water in the dark, but there's no time to change them; there is a bruise, possibly a gash—tingling, going septic?—on your leg because you lurched into the table when the floor swung, but there's no time to look at it, and nobody would care; your face has a slight stubble on it that is itching, and your nails feel dirty and teeth furred and eyes sticky but there's no *time*. You won't shave or sleep or clean your teeth again because they are on the list of the last things, a remembered list of a thousand daily actions that won't be made again. Like the treasured possessions, these lifelong habits are drifting away, becoming symbols, showing you what you used to be, not what you are: dying.

There is no comfort, and no charity. The seamen have no civility left for passengers—passengers become a dangerous nuisance when a ship is sinking. The passengers have no respect left for a crew that has let this disaster come upon them all.

One constant is left, and that is the authority of the captain. Every man on board will leap to his slightest word. Whether they love him or think he is a bastard or a stupid fool or a gutless pimp they will obey him faithfully; because he is the only one in the ship who can save their skins.

Dodds the steward had said with his head buried in the grease-smelling curtain of the slop-chest scuttle, "We could've got in the boats, the bloody boats, while there was bloody time, instead of this . . . instead of this . . ." His breath trembled as he talked to himself and tightened his muscles to stop his water coming.

Stubbs had told Harris, "If we get out o' this lot, an' there's an enquiry, I'll be there, boy, I'll be there. I'll see this sod of a shipmaster don't get himself another ship, nor the soddin' bosun neither. Didn't I tell you? We could've taken to the boats, long before this." Braver than the steward, his fear was turning to anger and revenge as he sat on the bunk in the sick bay, short of blood.

Persham was not listening. He had been silent for a long time, moving busily about, collecting medicines and equipment, putting them into boxes, wrapping them in the green waterproof silk. He worked with devotion. Dr. Papasian had been down here, his eyes strangely bright. "I am told there are two rafts being made. We shall put these people on one of them, and look after them as best we can. I shall need your assistance. You will be in sole charge of them. I cannot be expected to do all this alone. I will come down again as soon as I have collected my things."

Persham worked steadily. He was in charge here. He had been given authority. He worked with devotion— not to Dr. Papasian but to a concept of humanity that he could never have grasped mentally, nor would ever have believed was in him, because of what he had done with the scissors.

"I'll see they scrag that stuck-up sod for this . . ."

Persham did not hear what Stubbs was saying. The patient was light-headed, short of blood. Soon he would be quiet, because Persham had got him to drink some 'water'. Stubbs had looked up at him with steady red eyes. "If this don't do me some good, I'll drown you when we're in the water, son. For what you did to me." He drank the sedative. "An' never swing."

Harris was talking again, but he and Stubbs kept their voices low because of Dukes in the end bunk. That kid had Harkness to thank for what had happened to him. If Dukes died, there'd be something to say at the enquiry.

Dukes had signed up under Harkness, had worked in the bosun's team and was now in the care of Persham. Those three had it coming to them if that kid died.

Harris looked up and said to Persham as he passed, "How's the boy-o, Jack?"

Persham did not answer; he was going carefully across the tilting deck with a glass jar. Stubbs told Harris gently, "He won't last, the kid won't." He looked down the tilted length of the sick bay to the hump in the end bunk. Dukes wouldn't have anything of a face left, even if he lived. It'd be worth him going. "He won't last, you'll see if I ain't right."

Harris pressed his hands to his face, bored with Stubbs and the smell in here and the thoughts of drowning. "You don't 'ave to sound so bloody pleased," he said into his hands.

A draught was coming through the sick bay, fluttering at the hanging edges of linen, touching Harris's hands. He shivered to it.

The bosun's mate came in to talk to Persham about the rafts, and moving the sick. He had changed into his number one rig, looking all wrong with his strained unshaven face and sleepless eyes below the neat blue cap; but these were the only clothes he'd get ashore with and they might as well be his best. Many of the seamen had put on their shore-going rig, slipping away from the work to tear the stiff stained trousers off and drag the smart ones on, punching their fists through the sleeves of the jacket and buttoning it with sore fingers clumsy with haste. Going back on deck they did not feel spruce in their creases and shiny buttons; there was none of the shore-leave feeling; the shore was a tidy way off and they might have to swim every mile. But they were practical men and had done a practical thing, and felt a little satisfaction in the midst of their anxieties.

Starley the bosun had not changed; there'd been no

time. The two rafts were finished; he wasn't pleased with them; already they looked like wreckage—a trellis of lashed timber with empty drums beneath. They'd float awash when they were loaded.

"Christ alive," he said, "they're rough enough."

"They'll float, Bose. They'll float."

The men stood round him in the light of a deck-cluster. The ropes had ripped their hands and one man was crouched by the companionway, ruptured when his sea-boot had slipped on the planking. His face was bloodless but he talked to the others as if he were resting: "Launch 'em with a bottle o' lemonade, Bose, launch 'em proper!"

"You better get down to the sick bay, Robins."

"Not likely! Look what 'appened to Stubbs!"

"You get down there. You're for a raft, mate—you can't swim with your guts half-out."

A man stood over Robins. "Come on, Rob, I'll give you 'and." Another came, ready to help.

"I don' wanter move. Lea' me alone. I'll move when I got to."

Starley came across to him. Robins had his hands driven hard against his groin. A voice as strong as this shouldn't come from a face so white. "You better leave him, then," said Starley to the others. "Put 'im on the sick-raft when we go. You want a drink o' water, mate?"

"If I see any more water I'll die o' mildew."

The bosun turned away and saw Copley climbing over the tangle of cable below the boat-davits. "Hey, Tich! You find him, did you?"

"Yes, Bose. He's comin'."

The ship moved and all the voices that had been audible a second ago were now silent as the throng of men felt the ship move and waited for her to stop. There was the distant rushing of the pumps and a soft whine of wind in the shrouds, but no other sound from anywhere. The water came quietly up from the sea as the ship wallowed with her port bulwarks leaning lower, lower into the quiet wave that ran through the rail stanchions and the tangle of cable just below where the men stood. They watched it. The sea was coming for them quietly, to play about their feet and swirl among the torn cables it had ripped apart when it had been angry. Now it was languid, reaching along the great hurt body of the ship as if to heal it with a soothing touch. The men knew better. The sea was coming quietly for them, creeping with the blind foul stealth of a fatal disease.

The ship stopped moving and lay for nearly a minute like this, with no strength in her to swing to starboard and send the water away through her wash-ports. She had passed the point where she could steady herself; she lay without dignity, wallowing in the sea. The wind stayed in the shrouds and aerial, a constant whine. One or two of the men looked up, as if they could answer the enemy by looking at it; but the wind was invisible.

The ship swung to starboard now, slowly, as the sea on her starboard beam fell away and let her fall there. She moved with an obedience that sickened the men; she was passive in the sea and it could do what it liked with her.

Starley looked at Copley. "What?"

"He's comin', Bose."

"Comin', is he?" The bosun's anger with the ship must vent itself on anyone, anything near him. "Where is he, eh?"

"Lamp-locker."

"Fetch him. Mac an' Yorky. Fetch him!"

The two big men left the group. They'd no stomach for the mission. Fred Sackett was a stupid bastard, drunk on a sinking ship. Better that he should drown when the lamp-locker filled and know nothing about it than meet the bosun again in this life.

They trod through water in the thwartships alleyway. Potatoes were tumbling down from the door of the galley and then bobbing as they reached the trapped water.

"We'll say we can't find him, Mac."

"The Bose'll tear our giblets out."

"I got no more use for mine, once this lot goes."

They stumbled on the potatoes and cursed the cook and the bosun and Fred Sackett and the wind that had started in the shrouds.

The wind touched the face of the lookout on the bridge-end and he could see it on the water below the steep starboard side of the ship. It was coming from the west; he could feel with his face where it was coming from; sometimes it shifted and he turned his head to keep with it; it would swing from sou'-west through west to nor'-west and then steady, moving about the night-sea with the stealth of a prowling cat, never going away—the cold soft music in the shrouds played a constant note. This wind would not pipe down; it had not awoken for nothing; it was here to try its strength. All this the lookout knew, and felt on his face; he had lived his life with the wind and tonight hoped not to die with it.

Near him in the wheelhouse they knew about the wind. They had watched the white coming to the top of the swell as each swell rolled quietly to meet the ship and move her. Harkness had a phrase in his mind now, all the time, a few words that made a statement and not a plea. *She won't stand any more.* It would be useless to say it to the wind or the dark or the sea or even to God; he said it to himself, to convince himself that what he was going to do would be right.

"Peter."

"Sir?"

"The bosun has the rafts ready?"

"Yes, sir."

A minute passed, while the ship was moved and they stood awkwardly, waiting, holding their nerves in a tight ball. She was so heavy.

"There's rough weather coming," said Harkness slowly. "It'll be here before the *Angeles*." Costain waited and said nothing. He would see that nothing happened to Ann. It was most important, almost all he thought about; it was dreadful to stand here close to the Skip and keep this secret: that he was thinking more about Ann than about the rest, about the *Whipper*. "I expect you can understand," Harkness said, "how difficult it is to abandon ship before we're forced to—I mean difficult to decide on doing it—like ducking before anyone lifts a hand. But we're going to do that. There's a gale coming, and the ship won't stand any more. In the shape she's in, she could go down very suddenly, and there wouldn't be time——" he turned and looked at Costain. "I'm telling you this because you'll be in charge of the rafts. Mr. Turnbull is sick and he'll be treated as a sick-bay case; I'll need Jim with me up here. You'll get plenty of questions. There won't be any trouble from the hands, of course, but you'll have to satisfy the passengers that we know what we're doing. If you don't, they'll make things difficult for you. Your job is to save life and you won't want any opposition."

Rain came against the windows, softly. They looked at the mottled glass. Rain would make no difference, really; but it wouldn't help to lift depression. "A reminder of home, Peter. You'll have to think of things like that. Down there you'll be a reassurance salesman. We'll all be home soon; meanwhile, salt water's wonderfully antiseptic and has tonic properties, and the fresh air's much healthier than stuffy cabins. Try to keep it cheerful. Actually it won't be so bad. Have you done it before?"

The rain pattered now at the windows but it did not bring a sense of cosiness in here, as it can to a house.

"I've never been in charge before, sir, but I've done a bit of swimming."

Harkness nodded. "I've complete confidence in you.

That's all you'll need." He realised he was trying to think of something more to say; it was a weakness, this hesitancy; there was no room for it. "You can start organising things now. Muster the passengers on the port shelter deck. They can take small personal possessions but no cases or trunks. Give them fifteen minutes in the baggage-room if they want to take anything small from their luggage. You will require absolute obedience, as this is an emergency. The stewards will help you serve out the life-jackets. A few minutes before the order is given to abandon ship I'll come down and have a word with everyone." The rain spattered, driven by the rising gusts. "That's all, Peter."

"Ay, ay, sir."

When Costain left the bridge the brass chronometer in the wheelhouse said eleven minutes to five. Harkness looked at it and realised vaguely that the gap was still too big. The gap had been thirteen hours, estimated by taking the number of hours the coal would last from the number of hours the *Salvado* would take to reach here. Then he had eased speed by one knot, closing the gap to six. The *Angeles* had thrown these simple mathematics aside as soon as the wireless aerial had been rigged and the *Whipper* could be told how near she was. Now the gap had narrowed from six hours to three or four: the *Angeles* was expected here by eight or nine o'clock. There was the unknown factor: how long could the *Whipper* stay on the surface during the storm that was coming? Not four hours, nor three. Two?

Perhaps two. From now until seven o'clock. That left the gap narrowed to one hour. From thirteen down to one. It was still too big. Any gap was too big: even a gap of one second between the going down of the ship and the arrival of help. Help must come before she foundered, if all were still on board.

"It's no go." He said it to Jim Beggs, who had come out

of the chart-room. He had to say it to someone. He was still not convinced he was right, for all his mental repetition of *she won't stand any more*.

"What's that, sir?"

He looked at Beggs. Beggs seemed larger than ever, his great hard rock-like face expressionless. You would have said he was witless. Even the eyes were quiet. Harkness thought, 'I'm going to miss you.' He said, "I've been working it out. She's got to stay afloat for three hours, perhaps four."

Their spines crept as the sea answered; it was as if he had called to the sea: *Are you going to give us three hours more before you sink us?* The deck was tilting slowly. A wave had flowed strongly against the starboard side and the ship was lolling to port. In the two for'ard holds the free surface water was surging and building against the port bulkheads and helping the sea to drive her over. The inclinometer moved from thirty to thirty-five degrees, to forty, forty-five. It took nearly a full minute. They heard the helmsman say something. A tin box came off the after bulkhead shelves and burst open on the planking. Below the port bridge-end there was water rushing against the base of the superstructure. It had not come so far inboard before. They listened to it. Then the starboard door came open and the lookout was shouting.

"She's going! She's going, sir!"

A flutter of wind came through the open door. Harkness felt it against his neck. His feet were about to slide; he could do nothing to stop them. Beggs put a hand out to the binnacle. He had stopped watching the inclinometer. A few drops of rain came flying through the doorway, spitting against his back. Vibration began as the screw came out. Everything tramped—the planking, doorjambs, window-frames, stanchions. Something smashed in the chart-room.

A faint chorus of voices came on the wind. It sounded

like a cheer, just as a moan of pain can sound like a moan of ecstasy. The bosun and his team, trying to save the rafts—or a man had gone overboard or was being crushed as deck-gear shifted. The sound was gone now.

The lookout said quietly, awed, "She's going over, sir."

Harkness had pain in his right hand; he was gripping the window-strap. "Get back to your station, lookout."

They heard him forcing the door upwards; he had almost to climb out of the wheelhouse; then the door slammed. The rain stopped pattering against Beggs's back. When the ship steadied he said, "That's all, sir."

"Yes."

She must start going back now, if she could. Harkness decided to give her one full minute. If she stayed at this angle he would use the whistle for abandon ship. His head was tilted to watch the brass chronometer. The vibration grew worse and then the deck began coming up, easing the strain on their feet. From the narrow puddle of water against the port bulkhead little waves crept, shivering to the vibration and spreading back. The needle of the list-indicator moved from forty-five to forty, to thirty-five; it stayed there. The vibration stopped.

Jim Beggs said, "List increased by five degrees, sir."

Harkness let go of the window-strap. "I've sent Peter to muster the passengers and get them ready for the rafts. Some may prefer to swim in their belts and leave more room for the women and the sick cases. Get down there and help him. I want to have every man off as soon as possible, before the lights go out or she rolls too far. Please hurry."

Beggs nodded. As he went out of the wheelhouse Harkness moved awkwardly against the tilt, reaching the telephones. He rang the engine-room. Brewer answered.

"Chief, you've got another ten minutes down there before we abandon ship. I want you to leave enough

185

steam for the auxiliaries and pumps, after we've finished with engines. Have you got that?"

"Leave ninety pounds, sir. I wish we could stay, though. We're okay down here, dry as a bone."

"You felt that last roll, and there's a gale coming. She won't stand any more——"

"It's a bloody shame. She's only young."

Harkness grew impatient. Did the chief think he liked doing this? "She'll be old before daylight. Just leave me ninety pounds, and when I ring Finished with Engines get your men out to the port shelter deck. Then over the side. You'll be the last to leave."

"That'll be something, then." He swore with the three most apt words he could use about the wind, and the calmness of his voice made the curse sound more vicious than had he shouted it. Then he said, "All right, sir. Understood."

Harkness leaned one shoulder against the bulkhead as a slight sea moved the *Whipper*. "There may not be time to see you, Chief. If not, good luck."

When he had put the telephone back he went down the slope to the wireless-room. Bond had a trickle of blood still oozing from the left side of his face; he had opened his cheek. He saw Harkness looking at the blood and said, "I slipped, sir." He gave the quick smile from habit.

"Wants some plaster on it."

"No, it'll heal all right. We're still in touch, sir, but there's nothing new."

Harkness felt confidence in here. You could be in touch with land, here, and other ships. You felt less sinkable. But it was an illusion. He mustn't go back to weighing the chances; he'd been doing that when the wave had come just now. There weren't any chances left.

"You're finished in here, Tony. We're going. Pick up what you want from your cabin and get along to the port shelter deck."

Bond wiped his bloodied handkerchief carefully along his jaw, below the gash. "I won't be in your way, sir, till you go. We might get a message."

"There isn't any message that would help."

Bond stood in front of him thinking of something to say, something to persuade Harkness to let him stay on for a while. This was the best home he had; there was no one who would feel any pain if it were his last.

"I can't swim," he said with the quick hopeful smile.

"You won't have to. The *Angeles* is coming. You'll float till then." He turned away from Bond. "Report to the shelter deck."

When he left the wireless-room, Bond was shrugging into his reefer. Half a minute later he came through the wheel-house. "Shall I see you down there, sir?"

Harkness was at the binnacle. "Yes."

There was only one wave, bigger than the rest, before Turnbull came up to the bridge. The wave put the list-indicator down to forty-five degrees; it returned to thirty-five. He had kept his balance by holding on to the binnacle. The quartermaster had spun the wheel, held it and spun it back. There had been an odd intimacy between the two men while they waited, an affinity that three would not have felt. Neither had looked at the other, nor spoken, but they had thought about each other clearly and consciously. They were the last two survivors of a wreck that hadn't happened yet, and they would have to spend the rest of their lives together, the whole of their ten-minute lifetime that was left.

Turnbull must have been outside on the bridge-end or on the companion when the wave had sent the ship listing; he came into the wheelhouse as soon as she had righted. The door swung shut behind him with the force of its own weight. He grabbed the storm-rail before the angle of the deck could take him down at a run.

"I'm all right now, sir."

His eyes were narrow with pain. Harkness climbed the slope from the binnacle. He knew Turnbull would force him to say something that shouldn't be said in front of the helmsman. Did these things matter at a time like this? More, he thought, than normally. "We're leaving her, Steve. You'll be on the sick bay raft."

Turnbull looked past Harkness to the helmsman, to the echo-sounder, the big brass clock, the telephones. Harkness knew he was thinking, 'We can't leave all this.'

"They said orders were to give me a knock-out drop, down there. Was that right, sir?"

Harkness felt impatient, as he had been with Brewer. "Not my orders, no. I expect discipline without resort to drugs." But he couldn't hurt this man more than he must. If the ship had had a face it would be as full of pain as this one. Steve couldn't stand any more. It wasn't only the wound on his head; he was knotted up; he'd been born with a cruel tightening-mechanism inside him and it had been stretching his nerves through the years.

"What do you want to do, Steve? Stay in the ship?"

"You're going to. Why shouldn't I?"

"Who said I was going to?"

"I don't need telling." The way he spoke, he might have hated Matthew.

"I'm not going down with her, Steve. That tradition's not practised any more."

A rattle of rain drove against the windows. Turnbull said: "Whatever you're going to do, you'll want help."

"Yes. But you're not giving me any. There's not much time left and you're wasting it."

Turnbull began breaking. His mouth lost its tightness. No man can plead stiffly. "I don't want to leave her till she goes. I don't want to. Not like a rat."

It was an effort for Harkness to keep himself from wrenching the mate's hand from the storm-rail and pitching him out of the wheelhouse. This was why

Turnbull had lost his command of a ship and why he was a bad first officer. He had more to deal with than his situation; there was the twist in him that he must straighten out, as well; and he wasn't big enough for both when they had to be dealt with together.

"Not till she goes, for God's sake." He was unused to pleading and the words wouldn't fit his voice, his voice wouldn't fit his face. Yet he was bitterly sincere. "You can't ask me to do this."

"Listen, Steve. I've sent Jim and young Costain down there to save lives. I don't consider they're rats. I couldn't do this without their help, but I can do it without yours. If you haven't got the guts to obey my orders and co-operate, then you can stay. But not on the bridge." He turned away from him. What had made him concede so much? Pity, he supposed. It didn't make any difference. There were only the two things, the ship and the sea. The sea was coming for the ship. Before it happened, life had to be safeguarded.

The door to the starboard bridge-end slammed. Turnbull had gone. 'But not on the bridge.' Had there been enough pride in him, then, to be pricked by that?

FIFTEEN

Tonio the barman was not smiling any more. He worked deftly, dispensing drinks, and was very civil towards the passengers; but he did not smile any more because they had come to resent it and to show him they resented it. He understood. Their grandfather's name was not Manuelo, and they had no trust at all in their own captain. They were ignorant people, but then all passengers were that. It did not matter. Soon the *Angeles* would come. Meanwhile he reaped a little harvest; the passengers did not worry about change when they paid for their drinks; their eyes were haunted by the future.

"Gin."

He poured it with a gesture. He could be generous too. Soon there would only be fish gliding here in the deep sea gloom among the bottles; the beautiful labels would come off because of the water and no one would know what was in them, and the fish would not care.

"That's all right."

"Thank you, sir." He must be careful. He had nearly smiled.

Sennett was in a chair, facing starboard so that he was pressed back into it. He had not spoken for a long time. His wife had left him, and talked to Penny Jocelyn, who was a little drunk. She was alone now, leaning with her back to the curtain on the port side. Dr. Papasian had gone away half an hour ago and had not come back. They said a man had died in the sick bay.

Ann Brown was talking to the Major. They were not drinking. "Said I mustn't exert myself, you see."

"You won't have to. We'll look after you."

But he said that he'd had a premonition of this, before he had come on board.

Sennett was sitting and looking with hatred at his wife, who still leaned with her back to the curtain, alone. The two young Mexican boys who had boarded the ship at Buenos Aires were nowhere to be seen; but then they had not been seen very often, except at meal-times. They were conspirators of some kind, people said.

"Even climbing a couple of stairs is an exertion, you see."

"We'll lift you." 'Lift' sounded better, somehow, than 'carry'. You lifted a child, carried the dead.

Jocelyn was also a little drunk, but he and his wife were quiet about it; it was obviously no new sensation and they were neither boastful nor obtrusive.

"He looks as though he hates the sight of her."

"He probably does," she said.

"Are you cold?"

"Yes. Alcohol lowers the temperature."

"I'll get you something else to put on."

"No." She touched his hand. She didn't want him to leave her. They mustn't be separated if anything happened. "I've been talking to her, Pooch."

"Moira?"

"M'm." Her glass was empty again but she didn't want any more. This was exactly the right state to be in. Paul should have got himself exactly like this, but they'd tried to make him drink with them and it was no good. "You know you said you believe she's penitent, not just sorry for him?"

He looked into his glass. How many more gins to the end of his life? Two? A thousand? There was always the last drink, the last cigarette, the last shave; very often you didn't know you should be savouring the taste, the smoke, the tingle, at this of all times, the last; but if you knew, the taste would turn in your mouth and the smoke choke you and the blade cut your face. But how many more gins for him? Should he be savouring this one?

"What?" he asked.

"Never mind, Pooch. You just dream."

With slow amiable impatience he said, "What were you saying? Something about someone being penitent. Who?"

"Oh God! Moira Sennett. Skip it. Another drinkie?"

"Listen. What about her?"

"You look like an owl when you're cut. What do I look like when I am?"

Working it out carefully as he went along he said, "I'm not cut enough to not want to know what you're talking about." He ended rather triumphantly, and beamed.

"Was that in Morse?"

"So I'm listening."

"Is it really going to be worth it, Pooch?" She looked past him, to Paul Sennett. "With a face like his I suppose any man would have trouble with women. Anyway, she said she drove a car at him."

Alan swung his head instinctively to look at Sennett, but caught it in time and gazed at the Major, who was talking to Ann. "Christ!"

"He was in the back of their garage and they'd had a pretty bad row again about his women. This was after they were married. She'd had some drinks because of being so bloody miserable and apparently it turned to anger. He'd blamed her for scratching the wing of the car or something, and that was the last straw. She didn't even do it just to frighten him."

After a moment he said, "She must've been very rocky."

"Living with a face like that and not having it to yourself exclusively would probably send you round the bend about it after a time."

"Poor little bitch."

She looked at him as if at a revelation. "I still don't ever know what you're going to say."

192

He frowned heavily, his gestures exaggerated. "Aren't you sorry for her, then?"

"I suppose so."

He moved his head again. Moira Sennett had gone away from the curtain; she was sitting in a chair beside Paul, talking to him. He was not looking at her. There was no sign that he was listening. Alan thought she was rather lovely, the long pale face and wistful smile. The man had been lucky, to get off with a hand and a leg. There was no need for her to be a slave for the rest of her life—worse than a slave, a penitent.

"What a perfectly revolting set-up."

Penny said, "I believe he rather flung them in her face. The women."

"What made her tell you?"

"She didn't. I just gathered——"

"No, I mean the whole thing."

"I think she wanted someone to hear it, in case anything happens."

"D'you still want to sleep with him?"

"You still want to sleep with her?"

Ann Brown had stood up and was looking at someone coming in. Costain, and a steward. He looked very white, coming awkwardly across the tilting floor, stopping, wondering which one to speak to first. Major Draycott was nearest.

". . . Anything in your luggage .,. . nothing big though . . ."

"What?" Alan said.

"We'd better go and listen."

"Every passenger will have two seamen with him," Beggs said. They stood like dummies in their life-jackets. The low wind moved Moira Sennett's hair. The rain was not reaching them here on the shelter deck but they could hear it hissing into the sea. The water ran by in the lights with a ruffle of white foam breaking where the rail-stanchions stuck up. They could smell it.

Jim Beggs looked enormous, standing with his back to the sea and the dark. They had heard him laughing a few minutes ago, a great-chested laugh very unlike his squeak of a voice. A seaman, a tiny man with a brooding face, had gone past the end of the shelter deck with an enormous sombrero on his head. Everyone was going to take something over the side with him: small presents for wives, children, sisters; small possessions they would never part with; packets of waterproof-wrapped cigarettes, cigars; a small flat box fastened to a man's groin with sticky tape because you could get ten years for this much heroin; and the tiny man with the brooding face was taking this with him, perhaps for his wife, this enormous sombrero. Hearing the second mate's laughter he cast him a dark indignant look, which made him funnier still. He had gone bobbing off like a busy candle-extinguisher.

What could be wrong with the barman and the second officer? Their laughter had been heard in this ship during the last hour. What sort of people were they that could laugh in a sinking ship? They resented Beggs's laughter; yet there was undeniable comfort in it.

"Your life-jackets," he said to them, "will keep you afloat indefinitely. In actual fact you'll be in the water less than sixty minutes. The *Angeles* will be making for us not long after dawn."

They looked beyond him. There was no light in the sky. Dawn might have been hours away. Something would have to happen. A radio message would reach the ship and they would all be saved.

If only the second officer would laugh again; but he did not laugh.

A steward checked Mr. Sennett's tapes, making sure they were not too tight.

A few minutes ago in the confusion of people coming on

194

to the shelter deck Peter Costain had spoken to Ann. He found she was not afraid. But she should be afraid. He didn't understand her. "I'll look after you, Ann."

"You'll have a lot to do. I'm going to look after the Major."

"He'll be on the sick-raft. I've fixed it. Ann, you'll be all right."

"Of course." The wind raced round the superstructure and cuffed their faces; drops of rain were torn from the paintwork and came flying on the gust.

"I want to marry you, Ann."

Men shouted, for'ard. Something splashed into the sea, a line of some kind. She turned her head back to look up at him. "Oh, my darling . . . no."

She mustn't laugh at his dear frowning face; he would be more hurt by that than by her answer. But he looked so very intense. He could think of nothing to say. She said, "Do you always propose on a sinking ship? It's like you. To hell with the weather, you've your own splendid directions." She felt a laugh coming, because she was a nearing-middle-aged teacher of deaf children who lived in a high mousey box among the chimney-smoke, and he was a ship's officer with all the world in his arms, and to stop the laugh coming she buried her brow against him and held on to him tightly.

"Ann. I love you. I've never wanted to marry anyone before. I'll give up the sea. If that's worrying you, I'll do it."

"This is a shipboard romance, Peter." Her voice was muffled, her face pressed against him. Past his rough sleeve in near focus she could see the dark water go rushing by.

"It's not. I've had them." There was no time to choose roundabout words. "Give me a reason. You don't love me?"

"Yes, I love you."

195

"Then . . ."

There was so little time. If she didn't convince him now, he would want to meet her in England. The dark water turned white as foam swept against the rail-stanchions.

"I'm married," she said.

"You can't be."

"I call myself Miss Brown because—I suppose I want to forget I'm married. But it doesn't change anything."

"Why did you leave him?"

"He left me."

"He must have been mad."

"You must help the others," she said.

Two seamen went clumping past towards the doors. Peter felt a slow fever mounting. There was no time to do anything now. But she had to promise.

"We'll talk about it later," he said. "I've got your address."

"Don't come there; it's a dreary place."

"I'll write and we'll meet. Promise."

Someone was near them; they sensed it. He turned his head. Major Draycott was making his way towards them over the tilted planking, one stiff white hand sliding along the rail.

"Ann. Meet me. Promise."

"There's nothing to talk about, darling." She moved away from him. She was chilled, now. It would be dreadful if they were to meet again, in cold blood, because they had said they would.

"*Promise.*"

The Major was saying something to her. For a moment she couldn't look away from Peter. It would be so easy to get this business off his mind and let him help the others.

"They've told me I must get on a raft." Draycott was appealing to her, oblivious of Costain. She had said she would look after him, and now he was lost.

"I'm coming, Major." She tried to turn towards him but Peter put his arm across; she heard his hand smack flat against the buttress beside her.

"*Promise.*" She was shocked by his urgency.

"I'll meet you again," she said. The chill rose in her body. Draycott was saying something again.

Peter said quite calmly, "It'll be all right. Nothing more than a wetting. We've got everything organised." He turned and looked at Draycott; he looked dead. He looked lost, and deserted. Costain felt a sudden anger against old people who clung on, who expected the whole world to rally to them because they had grown too feeble and selfish to help themselves.

He took the Major's arm. "You're on the sick-raft, sir. I'll show you where. Every modern comfort—you should see what they've rigged up."

Draycott walked between them for two or three paces along the dangerous slope and then shook them off with sudden impatience. "I only want to know where to go. I'm not injured. I don't want to go on the sick-raft."

They stopped. He looked less dead, less deserted. But there was no time to let him remember he was a soldier. The performance would take too long and be unbearable to watch.

"That's all right, Major. There's plenty of room, and you can help look after the others." *I'll look after you, Ann. I'm going to look after the Major. You can help look after the others.* But there wouldn't be much they could do, except look after themselves. There was a gale rising and the sea was deep, and sometimes a woman floated upright, trapped in the silent passages of the tomb on the sands, gliding from the lounge to the smoking-room on a gentle current, upright because of the air in her breasts, seeming alive because of her hair moving behind her.

"Williams!"

"Sir?"

"Help the Major. Sick-raft."

They picked their way among ropes. *These are my best green shoes.*

"My doctor says I mustn't exert myself, you see."

"Ann, I'll be back."

"Yes."

"You two, this lady's in your charge."

"Ay, ay, sir."

The water rose along the bulwarks and sent a smother of foam that was carried away in a dirty froth by a gust of wind that had gathered along the foredeck. There was the smell of seaweed, the childhood seaside smell. The bosun was clambering over one of the rafts—"Mac! *Mac!* Douse him with water. Get him sober!"

The long boxes in their row along the shelter deck were all empty now. There was no one without a life-jacket on. A man was moaning, sitting on the rough timbers of the sick-raft. Persham was with him. "You're okay, mate. We got you."

"I'm bad."

"We'll have you in bed, soon as we land. I'm going to look after you, see?"

Mac and Yorky held Fred Sackett by his legs and pushed his head into the next long roll of water as it came rushing over the bulwarks. "Poor bleeder. 'E'll be drinkin' quite enough o' this without our 'elp."

"Get that bastard sober!"

The rain hissed into the sea.

Persham held his patient. "You'll be okay, mate." He was in authority. He could heal a hundred men like this. Beside him someone was laughing, head on his knees. "You know something, Jack? I've bequeathed my body to a hospital. Couple of years back."

"Easy, mate. Don't worry about anythin'."

With the persistent obstinacy of the light-headed the

198

voice went on. "How're they going to find the thing, twenty fathoms down?"

"That's enough—he'll do!"

Mac and Yorky pulled Fred Sackett up the slope of the deck. He was shouting at them, cold sober and full of rage. They let him roll over and sick up the salt water, doubled on his knees.

Robins kept his head down, nursing the big pain in his groin. Persham had fixed him a truss, but he couldn't move. Christ, if anyone tripped and fell on him, what would he do?

"You feelin' easier, Rob?"

"Yep. Easier." The breath hissed through his teeth.

"A-way raft!"

Turnbull was on deck. Bloody Turnbull. They said he'd died in the sick bay. Wishful thinking. They must have meant Dukes.

There was a scream of timber as men moved, heaving. A line snaked across the planking and nobody picked it up.

"And again—*heave!*"

If they move me, I'm done.

A tin drum came away from the spars, wrenched free as the raft went up and was steadied and then was let fall. It caught and hung half in the water.

"Clear that line, some o' you!"

The deck-lights flickered and they were silent; the lights came on again. A man stood waist-deep in foam, hacking at the fouled line and parting it.

The rain hissed into the sea.

The second officer reported to the bridge and said the rafts were over the side and waiting. The passengers and the sick were in good care. Emergency equipment had been stowed.

Dukes?

Dr. Papasian was with him and would stay with him.

Where was the first mate?

On deck, in charge.

The helmsman listened. *Let's get off this ship. Just let's get off this bloody ship before she goes.*

His legs ached, keeping him balanced on the thirty-degree tilt of the platform.

All hands to be mustered excepting the engine-room. Get all away. And good luck.

At a few minutes after six o'clock Captain Harkness telephoned the chief engineer and asked him to keep his men on duty, ignoring the signal to abandon ship. A minute later the whistle sounded a series of quick short blasts and the sound flew away in the wind above the heads of the people who were clustered together on the port decks.

The last order to the wing lookout had been to hoist the daysign from the foremast: Vessel not Under Command. In the rain-haze that was turned a pale gold by the deck-clusters below, Harkness could see the daysign. In an hour, when daylight came, its message would be correct, if the ship were still on the sea.

He had been down to the shelter deck and talked to the passengers and crew. He had not stayed long, nor been consoled by the signs of first-class seamanlike organisation that were obvious to him. He did not believe he had let them suspect his humiliation. He did not apologise. There was nothing to be anxious about. They were in good hands. The rescue ship was due in these waters in sixty minutes.

They were in the water now, drifting astern of the ship. He had seen the dark shapes from the bridge-end. The *Angeles* would not be over the horizon yet, but every chance must be taken of guiding help towards the rafts and the swimming men. He sent up three Schermuly rockets from the starboard wing of the bridge, and for a few moments watched their red diffusion staining the scum of cloud. Then he came back into the wheelhouse and telephoned the engine-room.

It was warm down here among the machinery. The wind was hardly audible and the sea was out of sight. The beat of the Kincairds was steady. If they beat on, all would be well; when they stopped, all lost.

But there was no comfort in this sinking ship, even down here where it was warm. This place was a trap. You were in the bowels, here, already below the waterline. When she went down, filling and blowing, you would go down with her because there wouldn't be time to get up the ladders. You'd try, and that would make it worse. You were out of the wind and the cold, and the sight of the sea, but you were nearer the deep than the others, and you knew it. The place was a trap.

Water slopped below the metal walkways; you could hear it. She would turn on her side like a great dying fish and the sea would come in up there through the smashed skylight and the stove-in doors, solid water, black, filling this place and killing you slowly, giving you time to see it coming, time to shout and try to get clear of the deluge, knocked spinning and then up again drenched, frightened (*mother, mother!*) and the black water icy, freezing after the close air in here, and the air blowing out, escaping while you were cut off and had to fight your way to the metal rungs and climb through the downrush of the water until its cold dark weight tore your hands away and you went down with it; and if your back broke across the metal rails it would be merciful.

The whistle was piping, faint and urgent.

"That's for abandon, sir!"

"We're to hang on," said Brewer.

A bewildered face, oily, shining under the naked lamps. "Hang on, is it? For why? That's for abandon!"

"Rats first, then the Taffies. Aren't you proud to be in the Merchant Service?"

János came walking like a big bear along the rails, swinging against them to keep upright. "Ninety," he said. Brewer looked up at the gauges, and went to the telephone.

The water slopped below the metal walkways. A steam-valve whispered, high up the bulkhead in the gloom. The gauges were steady. The pumps were still cut in and the diesel hummed; but the Kincairds were silent. The men had gone. The telegraph stood at Finished with Engines.

In the lounge the main lights were out. Behind the bar a bottle rolled, hitting the leg of the stool and rolling back, hitting the leg again until it turned in line with the tilt and rolled to the other end of the bar and struck and broke. Along the passages the pilot-lamps glowed, shining against water that had gathered along the wainscoting; it rippled back and forth to the rhythm of the ship. A cabin door hung open; inside, a small lamp was overturned; its shade lay on the carpet; the heavy base was still suspended by the wire flex, and swung to the bulkhead and back, and swung again, tapping at the woodwork.

A box of pills was scattered in the passage; one of them that had rolled into a puddle of water had begun dissolving, to leave a powder-scum on the surface. A woman's glove lay at the intersection of two passages, fingers curled upwards. The door of the little library was open. Three books had come off a shelf and had fetched up fanwise. A deadlight banged on the ship's side as the water reached it. The sound echoed along the passage where the potatoes had rolled from the galley. They were now collected in the lowest corner, and jostled together; the water lapped at them.

Soon after the engine-room crew had been ordered over the side the helmsman was sent down from the bridge. He had been the last man to leave.

Not long before dawn a signal was picked up from the *Atlantic Whipper*.

Have abandoned ship, except master.

SIXTEEN

THERE was the smell of antiseptics but the room did not sway. There was no sound of the wind or the sea. Grey light came in at a window and outlined the high white ceiling. He knew what this place was. He'd been in one before, at Greenwich.

"Where's this place?"

A pulse began beating through his head until he could feel it throbbing on the pillow. The same smell and the same silence.

"Where's this place?"

The same kind of voice, motherly, admonishing. "You mustn't shout." Footsteps. They always wore thick ugly rubber heels and had strong capable bodies and smelt like everything else in these places.

His head rocked on the pillow so that the room seemed to be swaying. But there was no sound of the wind or the sea.

"Where's this place?"

"Plymouth." A cool hand.

"Hospital, eh?"

"Yes. How d'you feel, Mr. Turnbull?"

"What day?"

"Friday."

He tried to think back, but couldn't. "Where's Captain Harkness?"

"Still out there."

He closed his eyes. He couldn't stand motherly faces. He had to meet everything in life alone, and these people could just keep out of it.

"Now don't talk, and don't worry. I'm going to get you a drink."

204

"Out where, for Christ's sake?"

"You mustn't shout."

"Out where, then?"

"On the ship."

"What ship?"

"Yours. The *Atlantic Whipper*."

"He can't be. What day is it?"

"I've told you. Friday."

"When did I come into this place?"

"Yesterday." The pillow rocked. The bed rocked. He opened his eyes. A motherly face.

"When did she go down?" he asked through a tight mouth.

"Now you mustn't talk——"

"Listen to me. If you work in a seaman's hospital you ought to know what seamen are like. I want to know when my bloody ship went down."

The quiet voice went stiff. "The *Atlantic Whipper* is still afloat and Captain Harkness is on board her."

"She can't be. He can't be."

"Now please stop talking. You'll disturb the others."

He found the cool hand and gripped it hard. "Still afloat, is she? When did you hear that one?"

"You'll be in trouble if you don't behave." A mother's word, 'behave'.

"Who told you?" He had to shut his eyes again to stop everything rocking; but now the dark rocked.

"It's in the papers. They've taken the ship in tow."

The dark rocked and his nerves felt the water clamping his body. He was going down again, rising again as his numbed hand gripped the line that was lashed round the edge of the timbers. Someone on the raft was crying out; a woman; they could never be quiet, women. He was going down again, rising again with his cold hand like a hook. If he loosened it he'd go down and not rise again. Someone was prising his fingers open gently. He gripped harder.

205

"Don't worry. I'll get you a drink."

He gripped harder but his hand was too weak. The water rose over his head again and he clamped his mouth shut. His hand was forced open and he went down, and down.

The newspaper was on his knees. He had read it three times, just the report about the ship; and the news was stale. He would telephone again, in an hour, if he could keep his patience that long.

Thelma said, "Does it hurt?"

"No." She had brought more coffee for him. He looked up at her. She wasn't much like the photograph. "You look prettier," he said.

She turned away. His face felt stiff. He could feel the opened cheek healing, as if a benign current of electricity were flowing into it. He remembered hearing Peter saying to a passenger, 'Salt water's got wonderful tonic properties, you know.' Had he said 'tonic' or 'antiseptic'? It didn't matter. Thelma said:

"This is the kind of time when——"

He read it again, TUG REACHES CRIPPLED SHIP. He looked up and said, "What?"

"I don't feel very pretty, that's all." She was standing with her back to him.

He must be still rather light-headed, because he was saying things that would normally remain well battened down.

"When I came up the road, I had a job not to turn back and just disappear." There were raindrops on the window, and her hair looked as if it were surrounded by stars. "I was pretty certain you'd been hoping I'd be lost." But there had to be kindness even in cold truth. "Maybe not actually hoping—I mean just neutral about it. If I went down with her, it wouldn't be your fault. I mean you wouldn't have been exactly sorry."

Her shoulders were shaking, and her head went lower.

206

She was holding her hands up to it. He wished she'd turn round.

"Are you crying, Thel?"

How many years since he had called her Thel? She wasn't making any noise about it. That was like her. He felt perfectly unemotional, saying, "Cheer up. This is just a bit of sick-leave, nothing permanent. You'll hardly know I'm here, and as soon——"

"*Stop it!*" She swung round. Her dark hair span against the raindrops. They stared at each other. The cup of coffee tilted on the arm of the chair and slopped into the saucer. He saved it, and looked up at her again. She said, "That was an appalling thing to think." She really looked appalled, with wide scared eyes. With the force of an accusation she said, "I *want* to know you're here. I *want* you here."

She wasn't lying, he knew that. She was just conscience-stricken. "Thelma——" because 'Thel' had just slipped out, and mustn't be used again—"I don't regard myself as a shipwrecked sailor. It all went very smoothly, thanks to the Skip. Don't think it makes any difference. I shan't trade on it, and I don't expect you to treat me as—well, someone you nearly lost. I suppose it reminds one of the good points in people, when you nearly lose them; but it doesn't last long."

He felt bleak and a little sick. There wasn't any 'nearly' about it. He was going to lose her, soon. He shouldn't have come home at all.

Very quietly she said, "I'm not sorry for you because you've been through a bad time." She denied herself the relief of looking away from him as she cut the matter to the bone. "I didn't hope you'd be drowned. I didn't hope you wouldn't come back. But I spent a lot of time thinking about it—about losing you."

When he could say it steadily he said, "Any conclusions?"

"No." It was a relief for both of them to speak the perfect truth; the only difficulty was in knowing what it was. "But when I saw you, I was glad."

He stirred the film on the top of his coffee, and drank some. There was no sugar in it. "Glad I was alive," he nodded carefully.

"Glad you'd come home." It was odd, she thought, that one of the nicest things about him was that he didn't use hair-oil. "Jean Stapleton rang up, quite a lot—I mean after we knew what was happening to the ship. I don't think I've loathed anyone's voice so much in my life."

"You wanted to think things out, by yourself."

"Yes."

And suddenly the whole subject appeared to be closed, as if they'd reached some agreement. He knew agreement wasn't the right word. Understanding. He said, "I'm going to phone them again."

He finished the cup of cold unsweetened coffee. She must have been watching his face very closely, because she asked, "Was that horrid, Tony?"

"Was what?"

"The coffee."

"It was all right. I was only worried it might come out again through the hole in my cheek." Whenever he tried to give his quick smile it turned into a wince.

"I'll make some more," she said, and took the cup from the arm of the chair.

"Not unless you want some yourself, Thel."

"Yes, I do."

"You did very well, boy."

They stood at the bottom of the steps. Light rain came down from a thin mean sky. They breathed the air in deeply.

"I don't do anything very well," Copley said.

"Where d'you get that idea?" The bosun had his blue

mackintosh on, and looked smart, a smart seaman on leave. There was no sign about him that he had just come off a sinking ship, or out of a hospital ward.

"I'm too bloody small," said Copley.

Starley looked down at him. "Napoleon never thought 'e was too bloody small."

"An' look where he finished up."

"Listen, Tich. You can't expect to paddle about in a bad sea savin' everyone's life as if you'd been trained for it. We all got to do what we can, and leave the rest to some-one else."

"You did all right, anyway."

"I was lucky."

"You'll get yourself a medal, Bose."

The rain pattered about them. An ambulance came in and turned; the rear doors swung open. Absently the bosun said, "Nurses don't get prettier, y' know. It must be somethin' to do with the food. Listen, the last time I fell in the water they gave me the M.B.E. I s'ppose it's all right —you got an excuse for a bit of a piss-up at 'ome, an'——"

"They gave you the what?" Copley stood stiffly in his new brown gloves, his face awed.

"But where's it get you, boy? What's it for, eh? It makes your kids proud but they cheek you jus' the same an' you can never find an empty bloody chair to sit in. It doesn't get you extra money—but who wants extra money for savin' somebody's life? How would they ever work it out? Tanner for a tich your size an' a couple o' quid for a big 'un?"

He hit Copley in the stomach and nearly doubled him up. "Come on, I'm goin' to stand you a drink. You did very well—a sight better'n some other blokes bigger'n you are."

They watched a stretcher come out of the hospital into the ambulance. When the doors had closed, Starley said, "Anyhow, we all got through it, even Phil Dukes. That was a marvel, that was." They began walking down the short driveway to the road where the buses went past. Puddles were gathering. "You live in London, don't you, Tich?"

"Yes." The M.B.E. What did it feel like?

"You goin' home, then?"

"Not till they get the Skip off."

"You stayin' at the Mission, then?"

"Yes."

"So'm I."

They hesitated at the bus-stop, then walked on. The rain became steady, and the sweet fresh smell rose from the pavement. They walked for quite a time in silence like two old friends, content with each other's company.

"You think the *Whipper*'ll get in, Bose?"

A girl looked at them, hurrying past through the rain.

"If anyone can bring her in, the Skip can." He turned his head, and gave Tich Copley a nudge that nearly knocked him over. "Wouldn't mind a day at the races with that one, eh?"

Copley stepped right into a puddle and felt the water trickling down his ankle into his shoe. "What races?" he said.

"And how long were you in the water, Major Draycott?"

"About an hour, I think."

"It must have been a terrible experience."

The pencil waited. The bored young head was tilted. The curtains had a smell in this place, of old age and comfort and stale cigar smoke. Mrs. Draycott sat opposite. There were some muffins on the little table but the young man had shaken his head.

"Yes, I suppose it was."

"You must be feeling very relieved——" he turned his head automatically—"and you, Mrs. Draycott. Sometimes it's even worse, waiting for news."

She had a dry hard voice that seemed to call down a voice-pipe to a servant in the basement. "We're suing the company, of course."

The young man's pencil did not move.

"They speak highly of the captain," he said, and waited. Major Draycott gazed abstractedly at the muffins. Their butter had melted and run on to the plate and hardened. Where had he seen that girl, Mrs. Jocelyn, before? Or someone like her. It had been years ago, when he was a young man, so it must have been someone who looked like her. India? Ireland? The same rather mischievous eyes.

"If the captain could remain on board," said Mrs. Draycott, "I don't really see why the passengers had to suffer the severe ordeal they were subjected to. After all, the ship is now being towed in quite safely. We shall expect to be granted appropriate compensation."

Draycott was looking at her. She was attempting her social smile on the young reporter, quite certain he was in agreement with her point of view. He had a rather well shaped head and looked intelligent.

"I see," the young man said. He put his pencil away and folded the notebook.

She arranged her fur wrap. "You must have some more tea." Business over, her tone was arch. The young man thought, 'She must have talked like this on the croquet lawns, hundreds of years ago.' He must get away from the smell of these curtains.

"I wish I had time, Mrs. Draycott, but thanks just the same."

She folded her long pale hands. "Well, I'm very disappointed in you," she said.

Watching her, Major Draycott saw the faded vestige of mischief light her eyes as she studied the young man. He had only just realised how long a lifetime could be.

The reporter stood up, buttoning his coat. Draycott

was still watching his wife. Not Ireland, but India. The Mountridge Club. Christmas Eve. Out of the dusk, the soft blue mischievous eyes and then the dance.

She held up a long white hand. "We shall be here for a few days, until my husband feels fit again." She left it as a vague invitation.

Sennett held his left leg in front of him. His voice was crisp, his face fresh. The young man was made to be interested in the story by the sheer conciseness of its delivery. He wrote in shorthand, sitting forward on the edge of the chair.

"The whole manœuvre had the stamp of a military exercise. I had the impression of being in the hands of experts, and so my wife and I were never at any time seriously worried. The captain and crew inspired enormous confidence in us by the way they went about their work."

She stood sideways to the bar, watching him and the young reporter in turn. 'Save me, save me,' he had cried out to her when the raft had pitched them into the narrow waters between it and the side of the *Angeles*. 'I can't swim, you know I can't swim.' His hand had felt like a claw on her wrist and she had been afraid he would panic finally, and drag her down. The raft had smashed against the side of the steamer and there had been a moment when she knew she was going to die. 'Save me,' he had called, and she remembered how his face had looked.

". . . The bosun, I believe. Some of the others must have seen him do it. I don't know how many of us owe our lives to him, but the others might be able to give you a clearer picture. He behaved magnificently."

His face had looked two-dimensional against the background of the terrible wave, a white cut-out mask staring at her, choking; yet he was floating well enough.

". . . Although I can't vouch for that personally. My wife's not a very strong swimmer and I didn't have much chance of helping anyone else."

The pencil stopped. The young man said, "You don't feel there was any negligence, then, of any sort? One or two words have been dropped, on that subject."

Sennett appeared to consider it very carefully. The pencil waited. The girl took up her drink and lifted it. "I imagine there'll be an enquiry. If I'm asked to give evidence I shall say that both my wife and I are proud to have been present in a crisis where heroism, discipline and devotion to duty were the paramount features." He looked at the girl. "I can speak for both of us, can't I?"

She looked at the reporter, amused by something. "Yes."

The young man wrote and then put away his things and buttoned his coat. "You er—you were handicapped, Mr. Sennett, in the water. You did pretty well. The war, was it?"

The clean-cut golden head was bowed an inch: he studied the fingers of his gloved hand. It was Moira who spoke, very lightly and with nothing of the sad lilt in her voice.

"No, a woman did that to him. In the past they used to scratch, but these days they're tougher." She finished her drink and gave the reporter a quick smile. He was looking as if he had stepped on a rake.

"I've got no complaints."

"But you said you'd put the skids under 'im."

"That was a while ago."

Harris shrugged. "I'm easy."

They lit up another cigarette. "What changed your mind, then?"

Stubbs said, "Nothing. I'm glad to get out of it alive,

that's all. An' I'm not signing on again, not even in the *Queens*."

Harris grinned. The cigarette-paper stuck to his top lip and he pulled it away. "You think they'd have you in the *Queens*?"

"All I'm sayin' is they can stuff the sea. I'm done with it."

The rain tapped at the windows of the rest-room. Someone was making tea behind the hatchway, clattering about. Harris got up and flexed his shoulders. "Well, Stubby, look after yerself."

"I'll do that, all right."

Harris grinned again. He stuck his hands into the pockets of his mackintosh. "We'll meet again, in the sweet bye an' bye."

"I tell you I'm done with it."

"That's right, Stubby." He went to the doors and pushed the bar. "That's what they all say."

The doors clattered shut.

On the telephone Jocelyn said, "You can knock it into shape later. No one panicked. Who? No. There's something in the book about that—wait a minute. If a master is in difficulty and reasonable apprehension, his first task is to safeguard life. You'd better check on the exact wording. It's a good bit to put in, because Harkness certainly did just that. We had several sick-cases and one old boy with a dicky heart, and the lot came through. No, I'm sticking here till they bring in the *Whipper*. You got my number? Leave a message if I'm out."

When he came back into the hotel lounge, Penny was waiting for him. She had bought a pair of slacks and a duffle-jacket yesterday; the clothes she had worn in the sea were finished.

"You look rather delightful," he said.

She dug her hands into the duffle-coat pockets. "I've

just met a man who told me I looked *very* delightful." She still had the feeling that this was a holiday, a planned one, not the miserable tag-end of a sea-trip. The new clothes, perhaps, and a strange hotel in a town she had never expected to be in. And there was the blessing of still being here, being anywhere. "How's Barney?" she asked.

"Quite excited. We're front-page news. I've also been down to a local editor here and offered him my exclusive story." He beamed smugly. She asked:

"How much?"

"Well, I suggested a couple of thousand but he said his paper was very poor, and he only ran it because Plymouth was a place that deserved a newspaper like the *Argus*, and, after all, this was a heroic story and Plymouth had historic associations with the sea—he reminded me about Drake—and he was quite sure I wouldn't want to make profit from a story that was shining with the highest examples of——"

"How much?"

"A tenner."

"Well, it'll pay the bill here."

They found themselves drifting towards the bar. When they were perched on the stools she said, "Is there any point in staying on, Pooch?"

"I think so. The weather report's very mucky. There's a nice big story here, whether he brings her in or not." His bland face was turned to gaze at the rain on the windows. "The thing's this. There'll be a whole gaggle of blokes on the quay-side with offers for the story, and only one of them will be able to go up to Hárkness and talk to him before the press conference. Al Jocelyn."

"Don't hug yourself so hard or you'll bring on blood-pressure. Barney can't compete with the big Londons."

"He's told me to go to a thousand."

"The big ones'll make it twenty."

He shrugged. "I've got an ace."

She said in a sing-song tone, " 'I Was On Board'—story of heroic courage at sea by Ace Jocelyn."

He gazed at the windows for a moment more and said, "Of course this local chap was right, even though he wasn't there. D'you remember that bosun?"

She nodded. "And the boy on the *Angeles*, the one who jumped in." She picked up her drink a little impatiently. "Isn't it lousy to have to cash in on a thing like this?"

"You shouldn't have married a journalist."

It was still raining when dark fell, and the wind was rising across the town. In the evening papers there was a picture of Captain Harkness and another of the *Atlantic Whipper* showing her in the Mersey after fitting out, five years ago.

Many of the crew had left Plymouth by train—Brewer the chief engineer, some of the cooks, most of the seamen who lived in London, Birmingham and Cardiff. The second mate, Beggs, was drifting the bends through Dorset in his Aston Martin which he had picked up in Avonmouth. A few were still in hospital beds: Dukes, Robins, Smithers. Steve Turnbull was on his feet but not yet discharged.

Two representatives of Watson and Blount, the owners, had arrived in the town. Mrs. Harkness had been offered a car by a London newspaper and was driven down by a chauffeur to the Metropole, where one of the best rooms had been booked for her.

Tony Bond had gone home. Peter Costain was still in the town, trying to reach Miss Brown by telephone at the Suretidge School for Deaf Children, Croydon.

Wilson had been discharged from the Seamen's Hospital during the afternoon and had joined the steward, Tonio, on board the Spanish steamer *Angeles*, now lying in the South Dockyard. He had taken his guitar and was a hero among the crew for having nursed his precious instrument

216

in a waterproof parcel through the terrible sea. One of the Spaniards had an uncle who had met the mistress of the man who had made this very guitar—see, here was his signature inside it—and several of them had met Teresa in Buenos Aires, and were overjoyed to learn that such a brave Englishman was to marry her and save her from the life she was leading now. Wilson became rather subdued after this reference to Teresa, and passed out before midnight from the effects of strong Malaga wine and depression.

The wind rose to half a gale during the early hours of Saturday and gusts of sixty miles an hour were recorded by coastguard stations along the Cornish shore.

Only a few of these people heard the news when it came in by radio. They were the owners' representatives, Mrs. Harkness, Tony Bond—who had telephoned the radio station hourly since dusk last evening—and Manuelo de las Castillas, who had awakened from a long sleep to conduct the celebrations on board his ship in the South Dockyard and was now sitting in his cabin with his own radio tuned in to the shipping wavelength.

The others would not hear the news until they read the morning papers or were told by word of mouth.

The signal came from the tug *Salvado*, reporting strong gale conditions and heavy seas. The tow had parted and the *Atlantic Whipper* was lying over at sixty degrees with her port-side maindeck awash. She was drifting north-eastwards without lights or radio. The tug and the destroyer, still standing by, were trying to make contact with the casualty by radio and signal-lamps, but so far there had been no response.

The last message from the *Atlantic Whipper* had been flashed by Aldis lamp two hours ago, soon after midnight. Since then there had been no sign that Captain Harkness was still on board her.

SEVENTEEN

PAIN woke Harkness. He was lying face-down in the dark, and could smell salt water. It was washing in the angle between the deck and bulkhead, trapped water that surged and lapped against his chest. His face was close to it and so its smell was strong. The pain was in his face and head, in the cheekbone and brow—mostly the pain of pressure, for when he lifted his head it was eased. He listened, and the sounds were similar to those he had heard before he had pitched down, felled by the final onset of sleep that he had been fighting off for days. There was the wash of water, inside the ship, and the rush of it along her side, and the banging of a metal door, far away, as it swung on its hinges, and banged, and swung again as the sea moved the ship; and the smaller and more dangerous sound of a timber straining, a wire singing towards breaking-point, a loose piece of deck-gear sliding across the planks, ripping their soaked surface—he could visualise the wet dark wood torn slowly into fibres as the sea moved the ship and the gear slid again, grinding over the deck.

He could feel that his eyes were open but he blinked them to make certain. It was totally dark. His tongue was clogging his mouth. He felt unclean and humiliated, and the humiliation grew as he lay sprawled in the corner of the wheelhouse with his memory flying back—the helmsman perched on the wrecked boat-davits, staring up at him before he dived into the sea. *Has every man left her?* The white face staring up from the tortoise-like bulk of the life-jacket. *Every man's left her, sir!* And he had dived.

The humiliation was worse than the bruises on his face and head, worse than the taste in his mouth and the chill of his soaked body. They had all looked to him for their welfare, and he had ordered them into the sea.

He lifted himself until he was sitting cradled between deck and bulkhead. The *Whipper* was lolling badly. What did the list-indicator show, across there in the dark? Sixty? More? The sounds were going on all the time; it was like listening at the doorway of a torture-house as the sea worked on the ship. Water surged below-deck, hammering dully, and metal tore as rivets were sheared by the great slow weight of the sea. The sounds that unnerved him were those he couldn't identify—that one, now, was a strange one, a new one. The coal had shifted in the bunkers a long time ago, and just before he had sent the last signal with failing batteries there had come a hideous musical sound that had sent him below to find its cause, for he had to know everything that was happening in his ship. It had been a great crash, with splintering, and then the strange dream-like music echoing away and making him doubt his sanity. It had taken him a quarter of an hour to find the smashed piano in the smoking-lounge.

This one, now, had no music in it; but he couldn't identify it. It worsened his humiliation: something was happening in his ship that he didn't know about; it was like listening to unfriendly voices saying something about him in words he couldn't catch.

The humiliation itself was a danger, clogging his mind. He must be practical, and work, and not sit here in the dark with his sores. There were antidotes to his depression, very potent ones: the signal from H.M.S. *Brindle* that had come in the evening—*Plymouth reports every man safely landed by 'Angeles'*. He had ordered them into the sea but they were safe. Was that not merciful? And his situation at this moment: the ship was still afloat. She could have gone down while he slept and in his exhaustion he could not have roused his brain to save himself. Was it not merciful that he was still alive?

She could have gone down with all on board her, and there would have been heavy loss of life, but—*every man safely landed.* The seas could have come for her while he was unconscious, trapping him in here and taking him down (how much water now, Mr. Beggs? Forty fathoms, sir), taking him forty fathoms down to the sands where she would lie, keeping him with her until he was another skeleton captain with his crew gone and his engines cold and his bones picked clean by fish. Or would there have been air trapped in her? There were ships in the sea that never reached the bottom when they sank, but were left half-buoyant by air or cargo; and the deep-sea currents moved them across the ocean floor, great slow shadows with no direction of their own, their steering fouled and charts obliterated, the compass rusted in the bowl and the long aerial wires picking up nothing but the shreds of weeds . . . but still moving with the slow grace that a big ship has when the light is on her, moving down there with no fixed course and every harbour closed to her for always. When she went down, would she . . . ?

Morbidity. From pain to humiliation to morbidity. It was the lack of sleep: he had slept for long enough to let his brain register the pain in his face and head, so that he had woken to the warning. A few minutes of sleep, after how many days and nights? What night was it now, what hour?

He got to his feet and stood with his shoulder against an upright. His head swam; he waited until it cleared. His shoulder was hard against a flat surface, so that he knew he was leaning heavily and must judge the angle by his sense of balance alone, for he could not see the water. The flat surface was rough under his hand. His brain was shocked as it was forced to assess the ship's angle and he breathed quickly and deeply for minutes, steadying slowly. His feet were on the bulkhead, and he was leaning against the deck. She was nearly on her beam-ends.

When he moved his feet he kicked at rubbish—empty tins, a bottle, some loose candles. They fitted into place in his memory. And the signals that had crossed the mile of water, two nights ago (that was to say, last night—but which night was this one?)—*What do you need most?* He had answered, *Food, milk, candles.* And then the long hand-skinning business of catching the messenger-lines without losing his grip on the tilting rails. Two hours, perhaps more, before he could hack open the first tin of soup and drink it cold from the tin, cutting his mouth as the ship had rolled and sent him pitching against the bulkhead with the tin splashing away. Dear Margaret, with your elegant damask tablecloths and embroidered napkins, the gleam of the soup spoons under the gentle lights, where would you draw the line between sorrow for me and triumph for your perfectly ordered home?

The rubbish clattered as he worked his way towards the windows. One was broken: where was the wind, then? The other way, piling against the starboard side. He could hear it go whistling past. Now he could see the water surrounding the ship, a faint white haze lying like a scum on the dark shape of her.

There were lights suddenly to port, quite close. A ship had topped the swell and he could see her clearly, standing off to leeward. The *Brindle.* A lamp was flashing. He braced himself against the deck and watched. Sometimes the lamp dipped and was lost—for minutes he thought it was going out, breaking off in the middle of the message; then he realised the destroyer was vanishing into a trough. The swell was higher than he had thought. A—R—and then darkness—O—U—and a break and then—O—K— it made AROU break OK. They began again—A—R— E—and he got it. He had to think where his hand-torch was, had to climb back through his memory over obstacles (the batteries had failed and the Aldis no use—how had he signalled before he had been pitched into sleep?) until he could remember the hand-torch; and then he had to remember where it was. It was in his pocket. He pulled it out and even before he moved the switch he could feel the thing was smashed.

—O—U—break—O—K—and they began again. How long had they been keeping it up? He let the torch drop and it clattered about tinnily before it rang among the rubbish. Water slopped against his ankles and suddenly he was aware that one of his shoes was off. The foot was coming back to life, tingling. It was bruised. The shoe must have been wrenched off when he had fallen, when his brain had thrown the switch arbitrarily, blowing the fuse before worse happened.

He bent down and rummaged among the rubbish, finding a candle from the few that had spilled from the box. It had broken in many places but the wick held it together. Matches?

Back over the obstacles to find the matches among the memories of the rocket-line that had cleared the ship but fouled on the aerial, the net of supplies that had come down out of the dark, hitting his shoulder and nearly sending him down the slope of the deck to the smashed rails and the water, the rip of skin as his arm had grazed down the stanchion—back to find the matches. Had there been any? Where were they now?

—R—E—break—Y—O—U—

The flashing lamp sent a pale light into the wheelhouse, persistently flickering. The matches were in his pocket, like the torch; like the torch, useless, soaked. He struck a dozen and there wasn't a spark between them. He flung the box away with a jerk of his hand and then thought, 'Patience. Step by step.' Anger was a new emotion to him; it was rising to do battle with the humiliation: you could not feel humbled and angry; you had to win. But there was danger in anger; with the humiliation, reason went too. Step by step. Find the matches, light the candle, signal the destroyer, wait for daylight, rig a new tow and get home, get home out of this sick dark waste where murder was being done to his ship.

He had found the matches but they were damp. There must be more, somewhere.

He searched for an hour. At the end of his search he had not found matches, but knew every aspect of the wheelhouse, chart-room and wireless-room. The *Whipper* was rolling through eighty degrees and the sea was rising to the superstructure at minute intervals. He watched black water coming, on the other side of the port wheel-house door where the glass panel was cracked but not shattered. The water turned white as it boiled against the bridge-end and he heard the great hissing of it and smelt the rotten tang of weed.

He put one foot—the one with the shoe on—against the glass panel of the door and broke it, and stamped the fragments clear of the frame; otherwise he might step on the glass and not realise it, thinking it to be solid. The water lay below it.

—K—and a break—A—R—E—break—Y—O—

When his hand felt the cigarette-lighter in his pocket he was warned again of danger—the danger of not thinking properly. He should have thought of the lighter, long before this. An hour searching for matches, with no alternative in his mind . . . it was dangerous not to think properly. No batteries and therefore no Aldis lamp. The torch, then. Broken? A candle, then. Matches damp? Find more, then. But his brain had got tired. It hadn't thought of the cigarette-lighter. His brain mustn't get tired again.

He worked his thumb at the lighter and it sparked, and in a moment a flame lit, dazzling him with its light and its unexpectedness. The first sight of remembered things: soaked planking, the thick white-painted stand of the echo-sounder, blood on his hand, the glitter of broken glass and the wink of light on tins among the rubbish.

He could not show the candle from the wheelhouse door, because it was below his feet. The windows were taking the gale past them and he would have to hold the candle through the broken one for its light to be seen by the destroyer; but the wind would blow it out. The top of the wheelhouse was now a wall, tilted at twenty degrees from the vertical; and there were two small skylights, one at each end.

It took him half an hour to climb on to the echo-sounder, because the first attempt had knocked the lighter from his fingers and it had landed among the rubbish; he had searched by touch, thinking the word aloud, 'Patience'. When he had established his perch on the echo-sounder there had been the awkward business of staying there, gripping the candle under his arm and lighting it and then taking it out before he dropped the lighter again or fell off his perch.

The skylight in the port side of the wheelhouse deckhead was now at arm's length above him. It faced to leeward, towards the destroyer. It was hardly worth the effort. The outside of the glass would be thick with salt, and if in reaching up he fell from the echo-sounder he would pitch down through the door panel and hit the sea.

—U—break—O—K—break—A—R—E—

He could not see the lamp, from here, but only its flickering reflection in the windows below him. He must make the effort.

He leaned his back against the deck, and slid his body upwards, inching it slowly by straightening his legs. The round metal stand was hard under the arch of his bare foot and he had to come down again, and move his foot at an angle, and then push himself up again, slowly, stopping when the sea came under the starboard side and sent the ship rolling, pushing upwards again when she

steadied. Then he raised his arm, and felt the hot wax
dripping from the candle down his wrist. He moved the
flame higher until it reached the little skylight, and
lowered it, and raised it, and lowered it, working steadily
until the wax was caking his wrist and his whole body was
shaking with the need for relief. He gave it no relief until
the *Atlantic Whipper* had completed the first signal she had
sent since midnight, five hours ago.

·   ·   ·   ·

The lamps in the lounge of the Metropole Hotel were
still burning, two hours from dawn. The main entrance
doors had not been locked all night. Sometimes a car had
pulled up outside; people had come into the hotel or left it,
hurrying down the staircase with a coat half on, cigarette-
ash dropping, or hurrying in through the main doors and
glancing quickly about them in search of the face they had
come to see.

"I'm Scott. The Elk sent me . . ."

"You're welcome. Nothing's happened. What'll you
drink?"

The big doors brought a draught in. The chandelier in
the domed ceiling was faintly trembling to air currents
that were never still as the young, thin-faced, badly-
dressed men went out, came in.

"Where's Henry?"

"For Christ's sake, I don't know."

"This is nothing to do with Christ. Harkness is the
name of the century, just for this week. You want me to
spell it?"

"I haven't seen Henry. Try the Gents."

The brilliants of the chandelier trembled in the ceiling.
A telephone rang and was answered at once because there
were very strict orders that the Residents must not
have their Rest Disturbed by the comings and goings
of the Gentlemen of the Press. The atmosphere of

traditional quiet must be maintained in the Hotel Metropole.

"Hey, Mac! There's a wire from London, says he's been drowned."

The doors swung shut. The chandelier sent sparks of light reflecting across the dome.

"Please, gentlemen," the night-porter called, "I keep on telling you there's residents trying to sleep——"

"They're lucky they've got beds, old sport——"

"It's a phoney, I'd say. How does anyone know?"

"You might at least lower your voices——"

"They're lucky they're not out there on the *Whipper*. You can remind 'em of that."

The doors opened. A car sped away from the pavement outside.

"Where the hell is Henry?"

In the far corner where the wall-lamps were out sat the slim woman in tweeds, alone, watching the doors, the glimmer of light in the dome, the pale faces of the hurrying young men. The early arrivals knew she was here, and had not bothered to tell the others. They'd had her statement ("You call that a statement, Henry? What's the Elk goin' to print it on—bus tickets?") and had decided to leave her in peace until some news broke. When some news broke, they said, she'd have to talk. Even a woman like this one would have to *express* something sooner or later if only to keep her face pliant.

Her face was calm as she sat watching the doors and the lights and the men. There was detachment in the angle of her head, the stillness of her folded hands, the neatly crossed ankles.

"Quite a dish."

"Too strong and silent for me."

"I mean in a regal way."

"I like them alive, myself."

The doors opened, swung shut. Cool air touched her

face. The thing she expressed so clearly in her eyes and face and whole body as she sat here alone had no news-value for them; it was detachment.

"Call that a statement? You'll have to blow it up twice the size to rate a single in the Agony."

"Forget it. It's her old man that's news, not her."

"But the human angle, the anxious wife who——"

"Human? Her?"

She watched them. Had there been a tank of tropical fish let into the wall she would have watched them as steadily.

Possibly they resented her attitude less because it had no news in it than because it had dignity. They had not tried very hard to melt her; they knew by their long experience when they were striking rock.

"You must be counting the minutes, Mrs. Harkness."

She had lit a cigarette.

"I mean, it's going to be a race against time and tide."

She had asked pleasantly in her low hard voice, "Isn't that what they call a cliché?"

None of the four had answered that question. They had their own kind of dignity, comparable with the retreat of a hermit-crab into its shell. Like the hermit-crab, they stole out again, warily.

"At least you must be thankful they were all landed safely. That news must have cheered you in your anxiety, Mrs. Harkness."

"Of course."

"Did you go to see any of them? I mean the passengers?"

The tendril of smoke rose from her cigarette, exquisitely detached. "Why should I?"

Henry was looking nettled, the other three noticed. A private car and chauffeur at her disposal, one of the best rooms in the hotel. She didn't seem to recognise any of the rules.

"Anyway we're glad to have you here, Mrs. Harkness, right in the front row, so to speak. We shan't ever regret asking you to come all the way to the coast—we knew it was what you wished for."

The silence was awkward. They were all back tight in their shells, even Henry. Should he have said that? To hell.

"I was told there was no obligation. Has there been a change of policy?"

They had counted five before Henry stood up and excused himself.

Without Henry, maybe a little diplomacy might take a trick or two. In a frank open-hearted way, of course.

"Now, Mrs. Harkness, we don't pretend we did you anything of a service. Possibly it might have been more convenient for you to accept the little we offered than to take a train and book a room for yourself, but we hardly feel we've helped you as much as we could, by affording you mere convenience. What we regret is that there's nothing really valuable we can do for you, when you're going through an anxious time like this, waiting and wondering, hoping and praying . . ."

Mac was no better than Henry. Just losing himself in his own diplomacy and coming up against the old-fashioned sob-angle before he had the sense to go round it.

She had said nothing. Vosper tried:

"Mrs. Harkness, you're too intelligent a woman——" he was in his fifties, old enough to have been her father, and only he among them could try this kind of approach—"to mistake this situation. Whether the Captain brings his ship home safely or not, he's already endeared himself to the nation not only by making the terrible decision of ordering those people off his stricken ship into a bad sea, but by remaining on board himself. In brief, he is a hero. His countrymen want to know more about him, more

228

about his background, his home, his wife—about you. Now is that wrong? Is that surprising?"

Pause. Don't spoil it. But she said nothing. He leaned forward. "At any moment we might hear that the *Atlantic Whipper* has gone down. We might hear that she has been taken in tow again and stands a chance of getting home. We might hear——"

"I'm not interested in the ship."

Just a detached remark.

"I don't quite see what you mean," said Vosper. He wished he were alone with her. There was a story here that went down deep; not necessarily one he could ever print; but it would be interesting. He was constantly having to make a distinction between what could and could not be printed. He passed news to his editor, and kept back the real stuff for his own reading and re-reading. People were his life. When he found out what went on in them it made him feel sick, or cheered, or warmed or frozen stiff with astonishment or horror or cold fright. Mostly, sad.

"It's just your husband that's on your mind—what might be happening to him."

She said casually, making his seriousness seem like an act, "What does it matter if a ship sinks, as long as there's nobody on it?"

He had forgotten he must look for news. He was now looking for Margaret Harkness. Even the tiniest clues had value: for instance she called a ship 'it'.

"The Captain wouldn't agree with you," he said.

"No."

If the other two were called away, he could talk to this embittered woman, and make her talk to him. She was dying to talk to someone. To tell them what?

He listened for the telephone, the noise of a car, the doors. Wouldn't something happen to call the others off?

She watched him thinking, and knew he resented the

two younger men being here. What was this man Vosper really like, when he wasn't raking his nose along in the gutters for the little victories and failures and indecent secrets and plain honest-to-goodness human weaknesses that could be twisted into Human Interest? He looked middle-aged and had the hard stamp of the news-hawk on him; yet something told her that he had kept a part of him clean, over the years of muck-spreading in the great Sundays.

Mac said quickly, "Your only concern is for your husband. My God, that's natural enough, Mrs. Harkness!"

"But scarcely news."

Vosper waited impatiently.

"And you're confident he'll make it," said Mac.

She saw it in print. *My only concern is for my husband, but I'm confident he'll make it.* The brave little woman, chin up, faith steady in the man she loved.

"No," she said.

"No?"

Vosper wanted to smile. Mac sat back, giving it up. She said, "He's out there on a sinking ship and there's a gale blowing——" and Mac leaned forward again as if she had drawn him on a string—"and the nearest ship is a mile away. Why do you want me to say I'm confident he'll make it? I think the chances are that he won't, but you won't print that. You won't print anything I can tell you. It wouldn't have—what's the word?—an angle."

Her eyes, Vosper noticed, were green. Had he failed to observe this before, or were they now lit with anger?

"Come now, Mrs. Harkness," Mac said. Silence would have had as much meaning.

"Please get one thing clear, gentlemen. If you misquote me by one word, I shall sue. My friendly advice to you is to go and find someone with the right angle. Otherwise you'll be in real danger of printing something straight."

Two of them just got up and walked away. Vosper stayed where he was.

After a minute passed he said conversationally, "You don't like newspapers."

It was extraordinary how she could keep that beautiful dignity and yet say things like, "I think they're appreciated wrapped round fish and chips but I doubt if they keep the stuff any cleaner."

She said it with no animosity, no contempt. It was a detached remark. That was how she did it, kept the dignity.

With a tone of detachment that matched hers Vosper looked at his nails and said, "Newspapers, and ships."

Behind them the doors opened. Someone came in. If it were anyone to see him, he could blow. He'd got his baby alone now.

"Also," she said, "break-back mouse-traps, race distinction, garlic sausages, television parlour-games and burst pipes. I could extend the list but it wouldn't be news."

As if she hadn't spoken he murmured, "Especially this one. The *Whipper*."

"Naturally."

"Because?"

"It's liable to cost him his life. So many thousand tons of rusty iron lying waterlogged out there, and any minute it can sink, and take him down too. He could have been safe on land now, with the others."

Vosper let another minute go by, and selected his answer from the half-dozen that occurred. "There's nothing I can say, is there? I mean, apart from the obvious things."

"You don't seem a very obvious man. Try something."

"All right. It's difficult not to over-simplify, but it'll be a start. You look as though you might be going to lose the fight, after all these years. How's that?"

"Wouldn't it be a laugh if you went and printed it?"

"No. People would understand."

"Then print it."

"But it's not the kind of thing they *want* to understand." They were both leaning slightly forward now and spoke more quietly. The press interview was over and they were just two people putting in time until the news broke. "It's like that cancer-of-the-lung scare, you see. Most people understood the situation. About two per cent of all cigarette-smokers gave up smoking. The rest argued the point, because it wasn't the kind of thing they *wanted* to understand. We were glad to stop printing the facts and opinions. Bad news is no news." He shrugged.

She said nothing. He moved the ashtray towards her and she put her stub into it and leaned back into the chair, and he knew the interview was over.

"It's been nice talking to you, Mrs. Harkness." He stood up, straightening his worn double-breasted jacket. "And I hope you win."

That had been hours ago. She stared at the same ceiling now and sometimes caught a glimpse of Vosper going through the lounge or talking to the others. From this distance he looked a very tired man, tired with a long-term beaten-down fatigue, not just with the long night's waiting here.

The wall-clock said five. Her eyes felt heavy. Vosper had spoken to her again, for half a minute, coming over and giving his worn grey smile. "There's nothing come in yet, but when it does, I'll let you know. If you're upstairs asleep, I'll phone."

"I shan't leave here."

He had shrugged, and gone away again.

In the absence of news there were rumours. The only facts were figures: the force of the wind out there, the height of the waves, the angle of the ship, the number of hours and minutes that had gone by since there had been a signal from the *Atlantic Whipper*. Four hours, fifty-two minutes. The hand on the wall-clock moved. Fifty-three.

The rumours contradicted one another. A body had been picked up, believed to be Harkness. He had left the ship and swum for the *Salvado*. He had signalled that he intended to go down with his ship. The *Atlantic Whipper* was still in complete darkness. A light had been seen on board her.

Margaret Harkness watched the clock on the wall, the light in the dome of the ceiling, the doors and the young men who came and went, bringing a new rumour and scotching the last.

If the rumour were right, the one about a body being picked up, it could only have been Matthew's. How long ago? When had the clock stopped, for her? She did not look at it again, but concentrated on the talk of the journalists, catching a word here and there, building them into sentences. Rumours were still coming in; you could take your choice.

God, bring him home. Never mind the ship, bring Matthew. Let me see him again.

"Hey, Mac!"

"Quiet, will you? People're trying to sleep."

"There's something come in."

"From where? Delphi?"

The doors swung shut. Cool air moved against her face. The one called Henry, the huffy one, was driving the night-porter behind the reception desk where the switch-board was.

Vosper and two others had turned their heads. They watched the porter plugging in the leads, saying something to Henry. She didn't have to lip-read to know he was saying that he didn't like newspapermen. Suddenly she felt sorry for them all.

A car pulled up outside and a door slammed. A young

man came in with a girl in a duffle-jacket. Someone waved a casual hand. "Over there."

Henry was talking into one of the telephones, very quietly with his body crouched over the receiver like a monkey with a big special nut. She couldn't hear one clear word.

The young man and the girl were coming between the chairs, picking their way to the unlighted corner of the room.

Without meaning to she looked at the big gilt clock. It was ten minutes past five.

"Mrs. Harkness?"

"Yes."

"My name's Jocelyn. This is my wife. We were passengers on the *Atlantic Whipper*." He spoke like a silenced machine-gun. "This message has just come in by radio. It's authentic."

He gave her a slip of buff paper and she turned it to catch the glow of the main lights. He clicked his cigarette-lighter and held it near the paper. "Thank you," she murmured.

To C.-in-C. Plymouth from 'Brindle'. Signal received by flashing light from 'Atlantic Whipper'. Begins: Sorry, fell asleep. Ends. Time of origin 05.01.

EIGHTEEN

AT the Hub Club, London S.W.7, Jim Beggs had eaten a good lunch but passed the next few hours in the grip of indigestion. On his table there had been four noon editions of London papers, still neatly folded because he was interested only in the front page. At four o'clock he was sitting in his Aston Martin half-way along Buckingham Palace Road. Newspapers were on the seat beside him and on the floor below his legs. Two others had been blown whirling out of the car as he had driven hard along Kensington High Street. His destination lay south. He had telephoned his parents, saying he would be with them in the evening, and he had telephoned a girl in Mitcham saying he would collect her tomorrow morning, Sunday. Now he was parked in Buckingham Palace Road. This was as far as he could go, southwards, and he knew it. He left the car, found a telephone-box, cancelled his appointments and went back to the car, turning it towards Hyde Park Corner and heading west out of London.

He felt happier: the decision had been made. Through Kensington again he slowed only to pick up the wording on newspaper placards with a glance. At lunch-time they had read variously: *Tug has 'Whipper' in Tow*—100 *Miles to Plymouth*—*He Says he can Make It!*

As the Aston shot along through the west-bound traffic he became practised in picking out the white placards and getting their gist. *Still in Tow*—*Keep Your Fingers Crossed!*— *Seventy-five to Go.*

There was no other news on the placards. In the head-lines of the popular papers there was no pretence of formality. A spiritual touch-line had been set up and the people of the country were crowding along it, ready to cheer. Jim Beggs had intended driving down to Plymouth tomorrow afternoon, but this was more than he could bear with.

He pulled up at a chemist's shop in Staines and asked for bismuth—yes, in a glass of water—and the girl couldn't get the cap off and turned indignant when he grabbed it in a great fist and dealt with it. She watched him obliquely as he drank the mixture—big men always ate like pigs and this would teach him a lesson. He picked up his change but left the bottle on the counter and was swerving away from the kerb when she came to the door and called out. She hoped she wouldn't see him again. There seemed little chance: the thin howl of the engine was already fading in the drizzle.

He took on petrol in Basingstoke and bought a paper.

Homeward Bound at Three Knots.

He drove on, now behind headlights.

Steve Turnbull had been down to the harbours three times during the day, walking slowly with his collar turned up against the rain. He had been on his own since he had left the hospital. He knew where Starley and Copley were, where Costain was staying, where Beggs had gone; but he did not go to see anyone among the crew. He wanted to be as alone as the man on board the *Whipper*.

It wasn't easy for Turnbull, but he was getting round to a grudging acceptance of what had happened to him. He had met his biggest challenge yet: he had been asked to play a minor part in a major affair, and he had come through it with the knowledge that he had at least obeyed orders.

There was only one rather bitter consolation. He said quietly through a tight mouth to the rain-squalls, "You wish to God you had me there with you now, bloody Matthew."

He knew what Harkness was having to do, single-handed. That new tow hadn't been rigged easily. The wind out there was force six and the sea was toppling. The tug and the casualty must have been hard put to it even to close each other. The first rocket-line wouldn't have landed right, nor the next nor the next. Matthew had had to fight for that line, and fight to hold it when he'd caught it, and fight to bring the thicker one aboard, and then the tow, sodden with water and twice its dry weight. But he'd got it round the bitts. There wouldn't be much skin on his hands by now but only God knew how proud bloody Matthew must be. He'd wish there was someone there with him—not to help him, just to see what he could do when he'd got his proud mind made up to do it.

The rain beat in Turnbull's eyes. Matthew had it coming to him; he was all right. They were putting flags out, in the harbour, and the Mayor and Corporation were going down there. They'd got bands practising, and you couldn't move along the pavements even now. Cameramen everywhere, and police to see no one got killed in the rush to welcome bloody Matthew home.

The rain was cool on his face as he stood alone watching the sea and the battered *Angeles* lying in for repairs. There was the hero, if you wanted one. Picked up fifty men from a murderous sea after steaming through a gale that had left her plates stove-in and her foremast splintered in two. If he had gone to see anyone, Steve Turnbull would have gone to see Manuelo de las Castillas, and the deck-hand who'd jumped into the water because he couldn't wait to get his hands on all those lives and save them. But you couldn't move on the pavements here, and they were standing with their backs to the *Angeles*. She wasn't all that much to look at and she was a foreigner anyway. "*We want the 'Whipper'. We want the 'Whipper'.*"

They could bloody have her, and Matthew too.

But he was beginning to feel better. There wasn't the throb in his head. If his body mended by the time the ship

237

came in, much of his morbid jealousy would perhaps be eased.

"Mid-day tomorrow," the bosun said. "That's if another gale don't come."

Tich Copley sat on the bench against the wall, jacket open, hands stuck into his trouser pockets. There was another pint in front of him—the third or fourth?—and he was going to have to drink it, or the Bose would grin and tell him he couldn't take his liquor, and give him a playful punch in the stomach, and that would bring the lot up, that would.

"It'll look a treat, Bose. A treat. Eh?"

Starley had a moustache of beer-froth. "You know what I heard? Goin' to be a message from the Queen read out to 'im by the Mayor, when he lands."

Tich looked away from his vast glass of beer, his spirits lifting at the thought. A message from the Queen. The *Queen.* What would it feel like?

"He'll get the Silver, too, boy. Automatic."

"What silver?"

"Lloyd's Silver Medal. Outstandin' courage an' devotion to duty, see?"

Tich belched carefully, letting the wind out as quietly as he could. He'd have to make room somehow. "He ought to get everything," he said. "Everything there ever was."

He lifted the glass. It must be a good six inches tall. And full. Slopping over. Six foot to a fathom. Jesus, this was a twelfth of a fathom deep. You could drown yourself in this.

" 'Ere's how, Bose."

"Mud'n yer eye, boy." When he had wiped the froth off, Art Starley said, "You never been in a ship that's in tow, have you?"

"Not yet."

238

"It's murder."

"You been in one, then?"

"Yeh. Sea was like it is now. You close to somethin' like a hundred feet, so you can fire the line, see? Then it's a bear-dance. One minute the tug's on a crest an' lookin' down the ship's funnel, nex' minute the ship's on a crest an' lookin' down the tug's. God, never again. Then you start towin'. You'd think she'd follow the tug like a bitch on a lead, wouldn't you? She don't, y' know. She starts sheerin', first port, then starb'd, right out, she goes. You think she's gone mad. You can't see the tow-rope—it's under water. By God, though, you can feel it. You think you've got a live whale on the end. You ever see a whale brought in to the fact'ry-ship?"

"Not yet. Have you?"

"I'll say. Twelve months down in the Antarctic, me, 'fore the war. Can't stomach even the memory. But that's what it's like, Tich. A live whale, fightin' to free itself."

Copley had taken an inch of beer off the top of his glass. Five more to go. He'd have to do it somehow. He said, "Were you in the tug, or the casualty, that time?"

"Me? In the tug. Deckie."

"God, it's special sailoring, tug-work!"

"I'll say."

"Where *haven't* you been, Bose?"

"Now come off it. I'm on'y tellin' you what it's like out there now, with the *Whipper* in tow an' the sea like it is. Murder. An' only the Skip on board. Christ alive, I wish I was out there with 'im."

"So do I." He belched again. "But I'm glad I'm not."

In the evening, Tony Bond made up his mind to go down to Plymouth. He had been out of the house for an hour, and when he came back he found Thelma on the landing.

239

She called down the stairs, "Did you get wet?"

"Not very." He stood in the dark little hall. "What's up?"

"Nothing."

"You look guilty."

She had a duster in her hand, and waved it casually against the door of his den. "I've been dusting. But I was careful."

"Dusting? In there?"

"It wasn't locked."

He thought it was stupid of him to feel like this, just because she'd been dusting his clobber. He managed his quick smile without hurting his cheek. "I'm going down to Plymouth," he said. "Tonight."

"Oh."

He could see a little way up her skirt as she stood on the top stair. He could remember thinking, a long time ago, that she had wonderful legs. God, what a waste! Surely there was a good shore job for him, in wireless?

"I'll find out the trains for you, Tony." She began coming down.

"I've hired a car. Small one."

"Oh."

He climbed the first few stairs. "There'll be a hotel, without booking."

"The town's filling up, Jean told me. Everyone's making for Plymouth. You'd better try booking."

"All right." There was one more stair between them. "Come down there with me, Thel."

"What for?"

"Oh, I dunno. The ride."

He knew that she was pleased at being asked. He mustn't expect her to show it, at once. The past was meant to be dead. (*For God's sake give me a break, sometimes, Tony. Stop burying us both in this place while you shut yourself up. Can't we go out somewhere, anywhere, just for a day even?*)

240

"The Wallaces are coming in for drinks, before lunch tomorrow." She didn't sound very excited.

"They can go to church instead."

"D'you honestly want me to come?"

He turned and went down the stairs. "I'll phone the Wallaces to put 'em off, and then book a room down there. Room with a view." He picked up the telephone and while he was waiting for the line to open he looked up at her through the banisters. It made him feel almost sinful to think he was going to be in a strange hotel-room with a girl like this. Oh God, she mustn't kick him out now. He'd considered spending the rest of his life married to Thelma, when he was in the water keeping his weight on the raft-ropes to help steady it, and listening to someone's hysterical voice calling 'Save me, save me!' He'd thought about his marriage, almost all the time until the tall bows of the steamship *Angeles* had cut their way through the mountainous seascape and they all knew they were going to live. If he were going to live he must think what to do with his life; and he had thought it out, bobbing in the water watching the others go up the rescue-nets of the ship's battered side.

I'm dull . . .

No, not dull, Tony . . .

He said, "The best room they've got."

The odd thing was that he wasn't doing this because he must force himself not to be dull. It was coming naturally. Would it last, this careless excited feeling? Lord, make it last, and don't let her kick me out.

Looking down at him, Thelma said without speaking, 'You've changed, haven't you? What made you change? Being nearly drowned? I suppose it would change most people. You look very boyish, standing there with your bandage on, enthusiastic about the trip—not a bit like . . . with his little black business-man's hat with the hair-oil patch inside the crown. He's a comical person, I can see that now. I don't want to think about him again. It was filthy and dreary and very dangerous. It'd be terrible if you ever found out, because you'd think there was a great deal to it, and there wasn't.'

Looking up at her, he thought, 'What's made this difference in me? Being shipwrecked? If so, everyone should do it, once in their life. It ought to be made compulsory.'

"I'll go and get ready," she said.

He felt a thrill in him. It was bloody silly, really. It was bloody magnificent.

Click. "Charles Wallace here."

"Hello, Charles. How are you?"

"Who's that?"

He wanted to say, 'The new Anthony Bond.'

Jim Beggs arrived in Plymouth at a quarter to twelve on this Saturday night with a thick mud-film on the Aston. He called at the hospital first to see how Dukes was getting on. Dukes had regained consciousness during the afternoon and was off the danger-list. Mr. Turnbull? No one had seen him since he had left here. Harris? Discharged. Robins? Still dopey after the operation: he could have visitors tomorrow.

Beggs phoned five hotels and drew blank. The town was full. He booked in at the Y.M.C.A.

Mr. and Mrs. Bond had arrived in the evening. Stored furniture had been moved out of a top room in the Beacon Hotel and Guest-house and a double bed moved in with three hot-water bottles to air it. They were sorry to give so much trouble. It was no trouble, bless them—anyone in the crew of the *Atlantic Whipper* could have the run of the Beacon Hotel and Guest-house, and welcome. Mrs. Bond must be very proud of her husband. Yes, she said, she was.

They could see the end of one of the jetties from the cracked patched window. They couldn't ask to be much nearer the centre of things than that. It wasn't very romantic, he said when the proprietor had left them. She said it was the most romantic place she'd ever been in, ever. But they forgot about the hot-water bottles and stung themselves, and hurriedly threw them out.

Starley the bosun and Tich Copley had found a wet hunched figure on the harbour wall. "You drunken son of a whore!" shouted Art Starley, making him spin round startled.

Fred Sackett grinned sheepishly. The three of them stood together in the rain by the harbour wall. They'd not see the *Whipper* tonight, but this was the nearest they could get to her.

At midnight there was no change in the news, except that H.M.S. *Brindle* had been relieved by the destroyer *Vixen*, which had been lying at Plymouth under immediate notice for steam since Friday morning. The *Atlantic Whipper* was still in tow at a steady three knots, listing badly and down more by the head; but if she could maintain her reserve of buoyancy for another twelve hours she would make Plymouth.

The weather report forecast gales.

In the town the streets were deserted. Earlier rumours that the three ships might be visible on the horizon before nightfall had been discounted, and the crowds had gone home early to bed. Alarm-clocks in a thousand rooms had been synchronised to ring at dawn. The telephone exchange had put two extra men on duty in the early morning shift to cope with the plague of requests for alarm-calls at seven o'clock tomorrow.

In the docks, lights burned all night. The Southern Salvage Company had already arranged berthing facilities. A salvage vessel was standing by. Three divers had arrived in the town and would be ready with their equipment tomorrow morning.

At the closing of the markets the re-insurance rates had

fallen to ten guineas per cent in the City, where prophecy cost money. There was no more practical a statement of hope in any other quarter. The City thought Harkness could make it. So did Fleet Street and so did Plymouth, where decorations already hung limp in the rain from lamp-posts and flag-masts, windows, balconies and the rails along the jetties and quays in the South Docks. Most cheerful of all were the members of the Southern Salvage Company. The cost of maintaining a tug of the *Salvado*'s type ran to something like five hundred pounds per week— when she was lying idle. Three times in the last month she had been out deep-sea, reaching the casualty's position too late to save her, or in such seas as disallowed the passing of the tow. But she was bringing the *Atlantic Whipper* home on the same no-cure-no-pay terms; and this time there was hope. The financial reward to the salvage company was estimated at between five and six hundred thousand pounds.

A message came in at one o'clock on Sunday morning from the *Salvado*. She had been in contact again with her tow. Captain Harkness was tired but confident. He wished to thank all concerned for their messages of good will. Captain Howes, master of the tug, sent a personal message to the Mayor of Plymouth. *We shall try to deliver the 'Atlantic Whipper' into Plymouth at some time tomorrow if conditions permit us to hold our present speed.*

This was the last signal received during the night, but the silence brought no anxiety. Had any trouble developed, the *Salvado* and the destroyer *Vixen* would have signalled shore.

The wind drove the rain through the empty streets, and sometimes a gust stirred the soaked bunting that hung along them. The policemen on the beat, looking up at their bleak fluttering, had the impression that the celebrations were already over, and not waiting upon the morning to begin.

NINETEEN

THE tug's course was roughly north-east and the wind was in the west, coming on to her port quarter and sending sea after sea across her towing-deck. A thousand yards astern of her was the *Whipper*, sheering to starboard of the *Salvado* as the seas drove her that way. Half a mile to windward of them the *Vixen* was steaming with her lights bright.

Towards dawn a lookout in the destroyer reported a light to the north; but it could not yet be landfall. There were other ships not far away, riding between here and the coast; but there would be no collisions. There was no ship in these waters that did not know her precise position and the position of the others. There were to be no errors now, for there was no margin for them.

The *Atlantic Whipper*, her head down under the weight of swollen cargo and slack water in her two for'ard holds, was under tow stern-first, so that Harkness could not see the lights of the tug from the wheelhouse. Sometimes he could see the destroyer when she rode a crest, and at these times he feasted on the sight of her glimmering lamps through the rain-haze, because his worst enemy was now loneliness.

It would have seemed impossible for a man to feel lonely within a thousand yards of two other ships, and with the knowledge in him that so many millions of people were thinking of him at this moment, praying that he should win this fight he had taken on with the sea. But in all his life Matthew Harkness had never felt so lonely as this, had never known that loneliness could be so terrible. He knew that to a great extent it was fatigue, a middle-watch morbidity spreading from his blood to his brain; but to know the cause of an illness is not to cure it.

He had not slept since the pain in his face and head had wakened him, earlier this night. He felt now that he could finish his whole life without sleep, but knew that he would prefer death to a lifetime of consciousness such as this. He was alone in the torture-house and in the dark, listening to the sounds that a ship made when she was breaking up.

Sometimes he found himself raging with helplessness, beating his hands, talking to the sea, to God, to the ship, begging and cursing and demanding that the sea should now leave his ship alone. She was in safe hands and she was going to harbour. The sea had tried to take her down but it had failed. Now let it abate.

These fancies—this logical view of the situation—ran through his mind until he could see nothing but black and white, right and wrong, good and evil. Possibly had this mood of his remained as it was now, he could have un-seated the greatest judge in the kingdom. There was wisdom in him, and he seemed able to stand back and to see everything in perspective. There must be a natural law, somewhere in the cluttered archives of the universe, that would dictate that the sea be calm, now that the ship had refused to sink into the depths of it.

At intervals in this stream of wisdom he realised that he was thinking like a drunken Irish poet. He must get his mind clear. The job was not over. She could still go down. But God knew his ears were alert enough to this warning. There was no minute went by but it did not fill the wheelhouse with the sounds of the *Whipper's* dying; and Matthew could do nothing more to help her. A long time ago, when she had given up responding to the sea's movement, when she had lost all movement of her own, he had known that though she still floated she was alive no

246

more. Now he had the feeling strong in him that he was to lose her soon. This great and still graceful shape on which a man looked like an ant was lying in agony, and soon would go, and be seen no more. The waves would close. A scum of débris would float and slowly disperse. When day came, the ship would not be here. There would be nothing in the world with the name of *Atlantic Whipper*. Her name would be struck off the books; her crew would forget her and find berths in other ships. They would forget how slim she looked and how clean her bows cut the sea and furrowed it white so that as she slipped horizonwards she left a milky wake; would forget her great engines with their steel strong and the copper gleaming, the brass bright; forget her white and gold paintwork below deck, the rich carpeting, the gentle movement of her as she left harbour with her lights tracing through the dark and voices quiet.

'This is senseless!' Aloud, or to himself? He didn't know. 'This is murderous, murderous! Leave her alone!' His voice became just another sound of agony in the darkness. 'God make this foul black bastard of a monster leave my ship alone!'

A plate screamed as the rivets went. Water rushed in, the sound of it sending him sick in his heart. He cursed again, shouting, beating.

At other times he was normal again, as an epileptic is eased after the terrible paroxysm. 'Dear Margaret, stop praying for her to sink. Keep on praying for me, but let me bring her home. I can do it. We can all do it. There's only you among all of us hating this ship.'

He knew his wife very well. He knew what she was doing at this moment. Poor Margaret. Her mother had told him of a conversation, years ago, because now it was too late for the truth to matter. Her mother had said to Margaret, 'You'll never make him give up the sea. You've married a sailor, and you'll have to accept that.' And

Margaret had said, 'I can do it, in time. Give me five years, Mother.'

Longer than five years ago. Much more like ten. She had never understood the unspoken terms: love me, love my ship. At first she had been very confident, giving him freedom, pretending to be interested in the sea and often making long voyages with him as a passenger, delighting or seeming to delight in the strangeness of far places. But her father had warned Matthew, even before the marriage, 'She's a girl for home. A home's her element.'

Poor Margaret. The cost had been mostly hers. She had lost her only love, but he had kept the sea.

The water rushed below, to surge and hammer for escape against the weakening structures. It could do it, in time. Any ship could be attacked like this, and in time, however long, could be broken and taken below. Give it another day, for the *Whipper*.

Give me five years, Mother.

He hated her.

'Steady,' he said, 'steady. Patience. We're under tow. There's land coming, and daylight—daylight will help us all after this blindness of the dark. Patience.'

Often he found his body in a sweat and his hands shaking; but these bouts were understandable. He lacked sleep. His nerves were keeping his eyes open and his legs straight when his eyes tried to shut against the blood-red sparks and the whirl of images and his legs tried to buckle and pitch him down; at one time he had seen a snowstorm of flying white against the cracked windows of the wheelhouse, but the flakes had not settled and he had closed his eyes and then with enormous effort opened them again and the snow was gone.

A light flashed.

He answered with the hand-torch that had been sent across to him with the last batch of supplies: biscuits, chocolate, condensed milk, matches, cigarettes, and the

248

hand-torch, a long black rubber one, waterproof and shock-proof, the best. He was grateful to them. He flashed the torch at the windows. *O—K . . . O—K . . . O—K . . .*

He mustn't fall asleep again.

A flood of white light suddenly bathed the ship and for an instant he was afraid his eyes were burning away and that blindness was going to be like this, a flare of white instead of darkness; but it was the *Salvado's* searchlight. Captain Howes was checking on his tow, having a look at her. What did she look like, from a thousand yards ahead? Her stern would be high, her rudder clear. She would appear to be almost on her side, with the water rushing white past her superstructure. How confident was the master of the *Salvado* now? How confident is any man at sea, in this last hour before the dawn?

After a long time the light went out and the night turned pitch. He was alone again, listening to the shrill tearing of metal as the sea hammered, pounding and surging back and charging again, little by little breaking up his ship. But he mustn't sleep, nor be angry. Keep patience and he would bring the *Whipper* to harbour, as that magnificent Spaniard would say, with God.

With the morning, the miracle. There was rain on the sea but the sea was dark, with no whiteness anywhere on its waves. There was a wind but it was low, and had no strength in it. This was a grey day, a dull one, with no character in the skies, a day you could forget about while you got on with your business.

'So much for your careful forecasts, gentlemen!'

Matthew was beyond the point where he could feel elation. He accepted the miracle with no marked feelings at all. His emotions had long ago become dulled and he did not see this peace upon the waters as anything strange.

He merely observed a wind force two or three, sea smooth to slight, steady rainfall, visibility fair.

H.M.S. *Vixen* signalled: *Top o' the morning!*

He replied: *Thank God.* But he was not moved to any reverence in his mind. God had two faces, and this was the one with the smile.

When the daylight strengthened he clambered on to the starboard wing of the bridge, using the rope he had rigged there yesterday. Hoisting himself upwards he clung for a moment, staring across the rail, northwards. He could see the land. He said: "England." It meant nothing. He must get his ship to the land, and then it would be over. He must bring his ship to harbour safely, and then ... and then nothing. For six days he had never thought beyond that point. "England," he said; but it meant nothing.

He slid down the rope. The palms of his hands were hard with dried torn skin; he was no longer troubled by their condition. *Salt water has antiseptic properties, Peter. Tell them that.*

The *Whipper* was well out on a sheer on the tug's starboard quarter with the tow-rope drawn taut and flinging up spray. The strain was in the region of forty tons and both ships felt it. He was reminded of his duties. He must drop from the bridge and make his way along the afterdeck, and inspect the shackle and tow, see that the terrific friction was not burning the rope away as the *Whipper* came back from her sheer and followed astern and then sheered off to port, wallowing through the sea. He must see to it that she made the land over there, before God showed His other face. Matthew did not trust God.

At fifteen minutes past ten on this Sunday morning the message came from H.M.S. *Vixen* to shore stations: *Wind force four, sea slight, rainfall, visibility fair. Tug and casualty appear well. Captain Harkness signals he is in good spirits.*

There had been no message from the *Salvado* since dawn, when she had reported her position, course and progress.

By eleven o'clock the tug, casualty and escort were reported to be fifteen miles from Plymouth. The rain had eased. The wind was rising in gusts and was backing south-west. The casualty's starboard plates were already exposed to the great blows of the waves and it seemed impossible for her to ride like this for another five minutes; yet she had been at this dangerous angle all through the night when the seas had been bigger than these. She had found a reserve of buoyancy and was trying to keep it.

On board the destroyer and the tug no one was anxious. Masters and crews felt they could bring the *Atlantic Whipper* through a hurricane, with land now less than fifteen miles away.

At noon: *Wind strengthening, sea slight to moderate.* But after the gale it seemed as if the water were almost calm.

A mile from the three ships was the Plymouth lifeboat, standing by to landward. A helicopter from Redmoor had been over twice, hovering within a dozen feet of the crippled ship. Harkness had waved, indicating that he was all right and certainly had no intention of being taken off his ship now that she was nearly home. Back at the R.A.F. station the crew of the helicopter reported Captain Harkness as 'looking just about all-in.'

The wind blustered but did not strengthen again. There was white on the wave-tops but there were no big curlers. The miracle, now with the shine off it, was nevertheless still operating: the ship was being given more chance than she could expect, with the barometer falling and the south sky dark.

At about one-thirty Matthew opened a tin of fruit-juice, squatting in the wheelhouse among the rubbish, holding the tin steady and waiting for the ship's movement to ease before he drank, for the cut on his mouth was festering and gave him pain. The noise came from for'ard, below deck, muffled at first and then thundering, and with it there came the vibration, a gigantic shuddering that knocked the tin of fruit-juice from his hand.

He began shouting in a kind of mad protest, his voice drowned in the din of metal being torn apart, of timber splintering. His body trembled with the ship and he shut his eyes, and shouted again, as if his voice were the voice of the *Whipper* in her pain.

When the shuddering stopped, silence did not come. There was the rush of big water, for'ard in the ship. He listened with his head couched on his doubled-up knees and his eyes still shut. He was muttering. A single shudder ran through the ship, and all strain was gone. The waters had met.

He pushed himself upright against the planking and then the ship lurched and threw him against the echo-sounder. Light flashed in his head and he caught at the stanchion and clung there until his brain could clear; then he moved, with his left shoulder numbed and the arm useless. The shoulder had taken the impact of his weight against the stanchion and he wanted to be sick, but there was no time. He knew that he must hurry now.

When he had raised himself enough to look through the salt-filmed window he saw the big fissure across the fore-deck where the water had surged through. He felt for the grabbing-rope and climbed to the starboard bridge-end, his left arm dangling. The wind came fresh against his face. Twice in his journey aft from the wheelhouse he gave himself rest, gathering a little more strength. The second time it was difficult to lodge himself against the wreckage of the after derricks, for the ship was lurching with her head going lower. He took in deep breaths, watching the foam being left on the hatches and then being whipped away in the wind. A parted wire was swinging from the mainmast. As it passed near him he

252

could hear it whining. Débris was falling down the steep angle of the deck and floating off. Watching it, taking the slow deep breaths that must give him the steadiness he needed, he saw a terrible thing.

One piece of the débris was moving strangely with a seeming motivation of its own. When it struggled clear he saw that it was a big brown rat. In a moment it had darted down towards the ruff of white water that was sluicing along the hatches; now it dropped into the sea, and for an instant he could make out the wet sheen on its fur as it began swimming.

He looked away, sickened.

At the stern of the ship, now higher above the water, the big towing-shackle was swinging and then drawn rigid as the tension eased and returned. He had left the steel mallet wedged inside the base of the winch, and had to sit down and brace his legs against the steel flanges before he could drag it free. He lifted it, rising to his feet by pressing upwards against the winch, and moved forward until he reached the shackle.

He had worked, yesterday and again during the night, to secure this shackle with the tow round the bitts. He had worked beyond the point when he knew he must fail, the point when the mind backs out of the job and the will has to take over. Two hours, the first time, with his hands raw at the finish. The second time much longer, because the seas had been worse and it would have been so easy to get his hand or leg trapped under the big steel shackle and lose it, and lose the tow, and lose the ship.

He made all fast, and had made all fast the second time after the first tow had parted. He had brought the ship to within the sight of land, and the sea had calmed for him. But now the brown rat had dropped overboard, preferring the sea to the ship.

He lifted the mallet and brought its head against the quick-release pin of the shackle, and missed, and swung

253

it up, and hit square, and swung again, and hit again, and the pin was driven out and the shackle rocketed away, smashing a path through the chocks.

Two minutes later the tug signalled the destroyer in surprise:

Tow's parted.

H.M.S. *Vixen* was already swinging her bows to starboard and closing the casualty at full speed. She signalled the tug as she came:

'Whipper' sinking. Am going in for captain.

TWENTY

In the streets the rain had eased, and down by the docks people were closing their umbrellas. Educated in the cinema, they felt it was quite right that the rain should stop, now that the *Atlantic Whipper* was due to arrive among them. Rain would spoil the grand occasion; therefore it was easing off.

A brass band was waiting at the water's edge. It had been there for three hours and was now drenched. It looked forlorn, and people had been giving buns to the bandsmen, and someone had brought along a canteen thermos-flask of tea.

The Mayor was at the Town Hall, waiting for the news. Two B.B.C. mobile transmitters were down in the harbour. A newsreel van with mounted camera was still crawling through the narrow ways, and every time a group in the crowd was photographed it cheered self-consciously.

Peter Costain was down at the South Docks with some of the *Whipper's* crew. He had made his fourth telephone call to Ann Brown and had pinned her down to a meeting. She had sounded reluctant. There was this marriage business, quite irrelevant as far as he could see. It had cost him fourteen shillings in small silver and a short fierce argument with an overworked operator to get the story from her in its raw details. She had been a nurse, and there'd been a man, this particular man, who had thought he was dying—which in fact he was, she said—dying of shrapnel wounds. And he had wanted her to marry him, so that there'd be a pretty girl to leave his money to, because he had nobody else at all, and when she tried to head him off it he got really scared and said it was as good as telling him he was done for ("But you said he knew that, anyway," Peter told her. "Oh, he *did*, but this made it look—all right." Peter said, "Just go on from there"), because no girl wanted to marry a dying man just because——

"He was terribly kind, you see, Peter."

"Yes."

"In the end I said I'd do it. We had a parson in."

Peter had to stop a bitter-sounding laugh. She said the man recovered in three weeks and was discharged, and wrote saying he'd torn up the will because 'he must have been a bit rocky in his mind, being so ill and all that,' and he was sorry he'd given her so much trouble.

"So I suppose it saved his life, Peter. I mean he thought he must have had a chance, if I was willing to marry him. I suppose it gave him the will to fight for himself."

"You don't really believe that, do you?"

Her voice had been bleak on the long-distance telephone. "No."

And there it was. Divorce was expensive. There was undeniable desertion, of course. He said he would fix it for her, find a lawyer, but—"It's not easy, Peter. I don't know where he lives."

He had wanted to put his fist through one of the glass panels in the telephone-box. They were very inviting, these small square panels, if you wanted to let off steam. Didn't the Postmaster General realise that a lot of highly frustrating conversations must go on in these little boxes, all over the country?

"I'll fix it somehow, Ann. When I see you, we'll talk about it, and I'll fix it."

She had said yes, reluctantly, and they had arranged when and where to meet.

He stood in the drizzle, fretting. Was it just an excuse of hers to get rid of him? But she'd said she loved him. Did she mean that? Did she know what love meant? Try to see her point of view: she was a responsible woman doing a rather wonderful job, when you thought about it, and he was just a wandering third mate with no home, kicking about the globe and getting little enough pay for doing it. Not much of a catch.

Why couldn't she just drop a hint, then?

The rain crept down inside his turned-up collar. He listened to Art Starley profaning to someone. Either she loved him or she didn't, and if she did, it would be all right.

Wouldn't it?

"D'you know anything about women, Starley?"

"Yessir. They're p'ison."

The newsreel van crept on soft springs along the harbour wall. A constable kept the people back. An hour ago the horizon had come into view through the rain-haze; now it was possible to see the dark shapes, sometimes two, sometimes three; but no one could make out which ship was the *Atlantic Whipper*. From here they all looked the same.

They looked the same all over the world. Margaret Harkness was at the window of her room in the Metropole. She had been talking to the young man and his wife, the Jocelyns. He said he was a journalist but he seemed different from the others. But they were among the people who felt that a ship was something more than rivets and timber. They spoke about the *Atlantic Whipper* as if it were something unique. She would have asked to be left alone, except that they spoke, too, about Matthew Harkness. They were among the people, the strangers, whom she had sometimes met by chance and who had talked of her husband with a deep affection; and this outweighed their odd defect of the heart, this absurd devotion to rivets and timber. She had long ago ceased to ask them to explain it. Matthew had never been able to. It was as if she had asked someone to explain why they believed in God. They would have said: 'It's a thing you feel, and if you don't feel it for yourself, you'll never understand.'

She had let the Jocelyns stay with her, and no one else. How much had the young man engineered her tolerance of them? He was a journalist and had a job to do; but if he had partly persuaded her, it had been done very subtly in his bland-faced way (rather like Matthew, to look at, a young Matthew with his face as yet unlined—there were strange likenesses in the people you met, and surely it must influence your opinion of them when they reminded you of someone you liked, or didn't like).

"If I were in your place," the girl was saying, standing beside her looking like a pert child in the duffle-coat and slacks, "I'd be doing something awful now. Climbing up the curtains or blowing a trumpet or something. Just lack of poise, I suppose. I used to bite my nails, at this kind of time. Usually with my gloves still on."

She lit another cigarette. In a mild voice Alan Jocelyn said: "That was before she took up chain-smoking."

A little later, about noon, he said, "The rain's stopped."

The day took on a glare, shining across the pavements and the sea.

Down at the South Docks, Turnbull was standing in the crowd, not far from Costain and the others. They had seen him, but no one went up to him.

Bloody Matthew looked like doing it. Even if Steve had hated Matthew he would have come here to stand like this at the edge of the sea, urging him home with his ship. And he didn't hate him. Matthew was just a man he would have liked to be himself. There weren't many; but he was one.

The newsreel van was not moving any more. This seemed to be the best vantage-point. The band was a few yards away, and the platform well in focus. A lane was being kept clear by police, for the Mayor to drive through. Captain Harkness would get into the Mayor's car, after the preliminary speech of congratulation, and the newsreel van could turn and follow the procession to the Town Hall, and the boys inside take over with their cameras. It was a nice exclusive set-up, and even the rain had stopped.

A man was going through the crowd, selling postcards—actual photographs of the *Atlantic Whipper*. Where had he found them? He was a man of initiative. There was a small trade in autograph-books—your new autograph-book was a sure winner if the first name in it was Harkness.

A woman fainted and was taken out of the throng.

In a radio-van against which Starley the bosun and two seamen leaned, a short-wave set was tuned to 140 metres. People had lodged themselves near the open door at the back of it, but there'd been no signal since eleven-thirty when H.M.S. *Vixen* had passed on a message from Captain Harkness to the *Salvado*: *Slight chafing, have used last grease.* There had been no action taken: Captain Howes had decided the tow would last the trip.

That was over two hours ago, before the three ships had been sighted over the horizon. It was now possible to tell one from another by their size and position. The *Atlantic Whipper*, lying over at a steep angle, dominated the two smaller vessels. There was a shifting haze, getting a little thicker as the sea rose and the wind took spindrift from the crests. Sometimes only two of the ships were visible, but the third would reappear, relieving the nerves of the people who watched, their eyes hot and feet numbed as they stood in the puddles, hunched in chill mackintoshes and drenched overcoats. But it was going to be worth it. Nothing could make them leave here now.

A mobile canteen pulled up near the radio-van, claiming a few of the faithful. The others were too chilled to want to move, even for tea, even to find a sodden cigarette and try to light it. There was a spell on them.

It was broken by a sound that came from the sea. Some

of them didn't hear it at first, and went on talking, and were hushed by others who were listening to the sad far-away sound.

The face of Steve Turnbull had drained white.

Someone asked: "Where's it coming from?" Another said: "The sea." It was like the war, a woman said, it gave you quite a shiver.

"Ships' sirens," Tich Copley said, not wanting to breathe. He could see nothing through the flying salt haze—a dark blob or two, nothing identifiable. "Bose," he said. "Bose!"

Starley turned and pushed his way through the shoulders, trying to reach the open door of the radio-van. People moved back for him, surprised and frightened by the look of his face.

In a little while the far sound died away. Soon voices were heard from the pack of people round the radio-van. It sounded as if they were arguing, or protesting. Was someone drunk? Others pressed nearer, trying to hear what was being shouted, to see who was shouting.

It looked like a fight starting, because Art Starley had forced his way round to the open door of the van and was shouting at one of the men inside, one of the men with headphones on. The bosun reached inside and grabbed him by the collar.

"She can't have! You got it wrong! She can't have!"

The shout was full of anger. The people on the fringe of the crowd were certain it was a fight; a big man was trying to force his way into the van, and the men inside were trying to keep him out. The people swayed together, asking one another what was happening; but for a few minutes nobody seemed to know, until the news came through to them, passed as quickly as a ball tossed shoulder-high across the crowd, the few words flicked by the sudden turn of a head, and repeated, and repeated, until everyone had heard.

After they had heard, there was a strange low sound from them, flowing in a sad wave along the harbour wall. A small boy, jostled by the people about him, dropped his glossy postcard, and a shifting foot sent mud across it at the edge of a puddle, and the picture of the ship was blotted out.

An aircraft had been over the sea, flying very low and circling, probably taking the last photographs. Matthew had heard the drone of its engines above the destroyer's wash. He was not interested in the aeroplane, nor in anything at all.

He had been in the water less than ten minutes. He had jumped from the funnel, when the doors of the wheelhouse had blown out. The water had rushed in below-deck, compressing the air, and the doors had burst outwards. Then he had jumped, for a man must use his good sense at sea, though he will hold on longer than a rat.

He had floated in his life-jacket among the débris that was still dropping from the decks as the *Whipper* rolled on to her side. Water went rushing into the funnel, and the great length of her shuddered, again and again, until with his one good arm he turned his body in the water so that he need no longer look at her. She lay in the scum of flotsam and floating grain. After five days the slack water in number one hold had swelled the grain and she had been split open by its pressure. The grain floated, pale as vomit, and he denied that it could humiliate her, that a ship's death could look as ugly as a sick woman's. He began swimming away from her, driving his right arm and kicking with his legs, until a boat from the destroyer made towards him and picked him out of the sea.

When he was on board H.M.S. *Vixen*, her surgeon wanted him to go below, because with his blood-red eyes and white face he looked in great need of attention; but he asked the captain if he might stay on the bridge for a few minutes. They fetched blankets and put them round his shoulders. The sea had been winter-cold and he did not cease trembling.

From the bridge of the destroyer he watched the *Whipper* go. Her stern was still above water when he first sighted her. She was nothing of a ship now, but just a dark stump above the waves, poking up through the débris with spray breaking against it. The rudder swung from side to side, freed by a broken gear. It flapped slowly like the fin of a dying fish.

When her time came she went quickly, for her size. The dark stump drew downwards and the waves rose about it; then the water rushed white, threshing into whirlpools with the débris tossing in the foam; then she was gone.

The tug sounded her siren, and the destroyer joined her in the salute. Matthew turned away and told the surgeon that he was sorry to have kept him waiting; he would go below with him now.

At nine minutes to two, H.M.S. *Vixen* sent a signal.

The 'Atlantic Whipper' has gone down. Her captain is safely on board with me.

Then the destroyer was turned in the short white sea and her stern went down as she began steaming for the land.